TRAFFIC

A Jessie McIntyre Novel

JOSEPH CASTAGNO

10/31/23

Shelby the first of the Jessie series hope you enjoy her adventures

Joe

This is a work of fiction. Names, characters, places, and incidents either are the product of the author's imagination or are used fictitiously. Any resemblance to actual persons, living or dead, or to events, or locales is entirely coincidental.

There are a number of real places in this story the author's descriptions and use of them may or may not be accurate, you can visit them and develop your own opinions if you so choose; any particular descriptions are the opinions and observations of the author and may not represent historical facts or even current conditions.

Copyright © 2017 by Joseph Castagno

All rights reserved. No part of this book may be reproduced, scanned, or distributed in any printed or electronic form without permission.

First Edition: [June 2017]

ISBN-13: 9781521544853

Published in the United States of America

<u>Jessie McIntyre Series</u>
"TRAFFIC" – June 2017
"AZRAEL" – May 2018

<u>Jake Series</u>
"Jake" – April 2016
"Peakeville" – November 2017

www.amazon.com/author/jjcastagno

Please leave a review on Amazon if you enjoyed "TRAFFIC"

Table of Contents

- THE CABIN 6
- THE BROKER 10
- STEPDADS & MOTORCYCLES 15
- VEGAS – 72 HOURS EARLIER 20
- WARRIOR 26
- TOO QUIET 31
- THE JUNGLE 39
- AN UNEXPECTED DETOUR 44
- EVERGREEN 48
- PAPPY & PLANS 54
- PRISONER 61
- HEADING EAST 65
- THE BRIDE & THE BABY 69
- THE WINDY CITY 73
- OLD FAVORS 78
- SOKOLOV 83
- MR. A'S 88
- THE BOX 93
- FAR FROM HOME 97
- BRIGHTON BEACH 102
- TOM CASEY 108
- THE FEDS 113
- CAPTIVE 117
- PROBABILITIES 122
- TAMPA 128
- WASHINGTON DC 133
- COMING HOME TO QUEENS 138
- HARRINGTON 143
- THRUST, PARRY, & FEINT 149
- PREMONITIONS 154
- HIDING IN PLAIN SIGHT 159
- QUID PRO QUO 164
- AROUND TOWN 171
- NEO 177
- CASTING A NET 182
- TRAILER #3 187
- A FLY IN THE WEB 193
- THE THING ABOUT JACK 198
- IN CUSTODY 203
- AND THAT MAKES SIX 210
- TAMPA FEDERAL COURTHOUSE 215
- 100° CENTIGRADE 221
- UNEXPECTED PARTNERS 226
- TEA TIME 232
- CLOSING UP SHOP 238
- BATTLE PLANS 243
- COMING IN 248
- FIREFIGHT 255
- REUNION 260
- FIGHT OR FLIGHT 267
- FEDERAL PLAZA NYC 273
- SINKING SHIP 279
- ALMOST DOESN'T COUNT 284
- OUT OF REACH 291
- AN INTERESTING OFFER 298
- ODESSA 305

LANGLEY	310
REBUILDING AN EMPIRE	316
IN THE FIELD	323
COUNTDOWN	328
THE ENEMY OF MY ENEMY	334
KOVBASA	340
EPILOGUE	347
ACKNOWLEDGMENTS	349
STATISTICS & INFORMATION	350

The Cabin

Jessie McIntyre tosses and turns vainly fluffing the pillows again, but not even the coolness of the silk sheets offers any comfort tonight, her mind throttled wide open, the past seventy-two hours on loop offering no answers, reassurances, or any hope of sleep. Frustrated, she pushes the comforter onto the floor wrapping his dress shirt around her like a robe. She imagines, more than smells, the faint remnants of the Dolce, or was it Hermes cologne she had given him for Christmas, something she had picked up her last time in Milan. They had spent a much too brief Christmas weekend at the cabin where she had found the shirt in the closet; he must have overlooked it when packing up. Funny how little things like a song, or a whiff of cologne could take you back to a moment as if you were there again. *God, only a few months ago, it might as well have been forever,* she thinks. The hallway seems to stretch out in front of her as she pads towards the kitchen, each creak of the old wood floor echoes in the empty cabin magnifying the silence. The crashing of the automatic icemaker reverberates in the darkness startling her and causing TK, the old tabby, to look up sleepily from his perch on the counter. He glances at her accusingly before nodding back off. "Fucking cat," she mutters as she pulls an Evian from the fridge and sits glancing out the kitchen window. The tall firs faintly silhouetted in the inky black by the waning moon, a glistening patchwork of spring snow stretches beyond to the clearing. She had shut her SAT phone off three days earlier as she fled Vegas, but she knew it was just a matter of time before he would show up. Her father, "Big Lou", would intuitively know she would run here, *really, where else was there to go after all*? She had replayed the arguments a hundred times, but she already knew he wouldn't listen her; dad was "old school" still believing you had to face your problems head on. He lived in a world where deals were still sealed with a handshake and a "man's" word was his bond, she knew those days had long since passed away, but he was steadfast in his ways and of course she loved him for it. Her dad was the smartest man she knew and always faced problems head on but this was something she felt sure was beyond his experience.

    She had been replaying the details over and over again but none of them seemed to fit together. Fact was it just didn't make any sense and she was even a bit surprised that no one had shown up yet. Well, there was no point delaying any longer, this puzzle wasn't going to solve itself and she wasn't happy about it, but knows what she has to do. She heads back to the bedroom pulling out the backpack and opening it on the bed. Six boxes of 9MM ammunition, the stainless Kimber with three full magazines; a father's proud gift when she graduated the

Academy, the tactical knife she had earned the hard way one dark night in Panama, both passports, three sets of clothes, thin leather driving gloves, laptop and almost a hundred and sixty thousand in cash. It seems like enough, but Jessie knows to stay off the grid she is going to have to make it last. She slips into her jeans, black turtleneck, and soft leather boots, grabs the bag and heads back to kitchen and TK. He purrs as she tickles him behind the ears, reaching into the fridge she grabs the remaining bottles of water, it was time to go. The black was already fading and a thin line of blue hi-lighted the eastern horizon. Grabbing the keys to the Jeep she excoriates herself again, *how the fuck did I not see this coming*, the dark holds no answers as she softly closes the door behind her.

    The icy snow crunches underfoot and she can smell the firs in the clean cold air, God, she loved it up here. Tossing the bag in the back of the jeep she keeps the phone, pistol, magazines, and a box of ammunition with her up front. Leaning her forehead on the cold steering wheel she wonders if she should just wait, let the chips fall where they may. She knows she won't though, more than anything she doesn't want to have to explain this mess to her father and she was sure the less he knew the better, it wasn't like she had a clear picture yet herself. The Army had taught her self-reliance, how to solve problems when there didn't seem to be any solutions, how to use the information and tools at hand, it was time to fall back on her training.

In the way we sometimes find ourselves at the end of a task without a clear recollection of how we got there, Jessie is already halfway down the single lane mountain road, more of a trail really. She picks her way carefully through the ruts mostly by memory the lights are off more reflex than conscious thought. The silver trunks of the aspen groves on either side faintly glow showing the way. The highway is empty as the dawn brightens to her left it was time to make a decision. She knew nowhere was going to be safe but she needed to resupply and find a place to hole up while she worked through this. Complicating things was the fact that she wasn't sure yet who could be trusted. She only hesitates a moment before making the turn East, it was time to light her phone up if only for a few minutes, people had a habit of exposing their intentions without meaning to and her missed call log would be her first indication of who might be looking for her. It was a calculated risk, but she figured running to the cabin hadn't taken much imagination so she wasn't giving too much away. Adding a clean phone to the lengthening list of items she is going to need, she flips the lights on and accelerates into the burgeoning dawn.

The Broker

    The broker was a strikingly handsome man, six feet two, lean but not muscled, with just a touch of grey starting to show in his sandy brown hair, he had turned forty earlier that year but didn't really consider it a milestone. He smiles to himself as he walks down the marble steps into the palace's immense foyer the massive columns and gold leaf applique slightly overwhelming, having successfully wrapped up his deal with the prince moments earlier he was feeling pretty proud of himself. The nature of his business sometimes caused a twinge in his conscience but it was the rush of closing a deal that got him off and sweet Jesus, the money was unbelievable.

    The prince was an ass and several layers removed from the ruling family and it seemed everyone here was a prince of one sort or another, but even so this was a serious account for him. He pulls the black designer sunglasses from the inner pocket of the perfectly tailored grey pinstripe Armani suit simultaneously loosening the knot of the Hermes tie and unbuttoning the collar of his custom-made shirt. He anticipates the heat of the Arab sun, but has never really become accustomed to the force of it radiating off the marble as the Mercedes glides to a stop at the bottom of the steps.

He waits until the wheels are up on the Gulfstream 650 the twin Rolls Royce engines quietly launching him Northeast over the Persian Gulf before turning West to chase the sun, only then does he use the SAT phone to call in his update. "The Prince is closed, he wants three premium units on the twenty-seventh and another dozen work units as soon as we can deliver." The phones were secure, using a Russian communications conglomerate's satellite network his boss had paid dearly to have shielded from any prying eyes, but he still insisted on basic code: premium units were "unspoiled" Caucasian American or European girls age fifteen to eighteen and certified virgins, he never had figured out how you certified a virgin but that wasn't his problem. Work units could be male or female and any age up to twenty-five and were mostly used for domestic or manufacturing help. He had long since moved past the moral issues of commoditizing human beings.

"Excellent, what rate did you quote him?"

"Usual $200,000 US each for the premium units, I had to negotiate some on the others, we did the whole lot for a flat $250,000 US, so $850,000 total." He holds his breath wondering if he is going to have to explain the discount, you never could tell.

"Fine work, upload the profiles to Brighton, and I'll have our people in India arrange for the work units from there."

"Already uploaded everything sir, before I called, figured I better lock in the Prince's choices before someone else moved them."

"Ok that's good, I'll have your cut wired this afternoon, now why don't you take a few days, you earned it."

"Thanks, I was thinking about spending some time stateside..." The Broker hopes he can leave the jet in New York, he tried to avoid flying the cramped commercial cattle carriers whenever possible.

"You seeing that skirt again aren't you?" the man laughs, "why you want to trouble with that, I can give you a couple of nice girls, won't give you any grief." Laughing again, "leave the jet on Long Island, we'll use it to take the units back at the end of the week."

"Thanks, I appreciate, I'll touch base next week, I've got a possible lead on placing some 'B' units with our friends in Chicago... apparently they have a series of conventions coming in and need extras to work the hotels."

"Sounds good we have capacity in Atlanta that's not producing enough, we can move those."

He clicks off leaning back in the leather chair with a sigh. The flight attendant comes forward barely dressed. She is topless and leans into him giving him a close up of her young firm breasts. She hands him a leaded crystal glass of bourbon before kneeling and getting down to business. It isn't long before he is too distracted to calculate his commissions on the morning's deal. He drifts off as the jet settles into a gentle vibration chasing the sun West, having served her purpose the girl has retreated to the back reapplying her lipstick and slipping back into her clothes. He makes a point of never asking their names, it isn't so much that he doesn't care, but it just doesn't cross his mind they have become just another accessory no different than the leather chair he reclines in or the glass holding the amber liquid he savors.

    The jet barely beating the sunrise gently touches down in Farmingdale Long Island at Republic Airport a small private airfield used exclusively by charter companies and private jets. The jets are all housed and maintained here and their frequent landings and departures no longer garner any real attention. Grabbing his overnight bag, he scrambles down the stairway to the waiting SUV the driver drops him a quick thirty minutes later at JFK's terminal five. The TSA agents at the security check point pull his overnighter for additional inspection placing the bag on the long metal tables at the end of the screening lines. The agent paws through the bag barely bothering to look inside before swabbing it down to check for explosives residue. With a perfunctory nod, he hands the bag back to Tom sending him on his way. The hand off of the thumb drive had been so cleverly hidden in the routine that even if you had known it was happening you probably would have missed it. He had been feeding the FBI background information for close to six months but it was a dangerous game; the people he worked for would kill him without a second thought if they knew. He had made a mistake in Chicago months earlier, a little too much to drink, a little too comfortable with a potential client – the FBI had picked him up that evening and offered him a deal, better than prison he had thought at the time. Not better than dead however, so he had been feeding them low-level information wondering when they would figure out it was mostly bullshit.

A quick stop at Starbucks before he heads for Gate 22 and the 8:00AM direct to Vegas, twenty minutes later he is safely ensconced in his seat blithely unaware that he won't need his return ticket.

Agent Jackson left the TSA security checkpoint, making his way to the curb where an unmarked car was waiting to take the smart drive into Bureau headquarters in Manhattan. Neither of them had noticed the "suit" watching from the line of benches just past the security exit.

Stepdads & Motorcycles

Allison Chambers would be seventeen in two weeks and like most teenagers she was sure she was the smartest and prettiest person living in her little community. She had always been little Allie to her mom, but she had long since outgrown the nickname, not that she liked Allison any better she longed for a cool name just one more thing she planned on changing once she escaped this back water little place her mom had resigned herself to.

Her stepdad liked to call their trailer a manufactured home, but it was a trailer. They lived at lot number three in the Strawberry Fields trailer park, one of the myriad of parks – had to be a trailer if it was in a trailer park, right? - that dotted the landscape of Eastern Hillsborough County in central Florida. It wasn't that she thought her mom and little brother Jason were stupid, but she had bigger plans than this trailer could hold and they certainly weren't going to drag her down into their sad world. She was going places, maybe even modeling in New York City. She had almost won Junior Homecoming Queen that fall; it hadn't been fair, she was much prettier and had better tits than that bitch Blair Kingsman. She saw how all the guys looked at her, she had what it took, she was sure of it.

Allie had only been eight years old when her mom started bringing Billy home after her bartending shifts at Pit Stop Bar & Grill over on Travers Road, things had been different ever since. Fact was she had felt like an outsider once her mom had decided to marry him and things didn't get better when her little brother had been born a year later. Billy had been fine at first; nice to her even but that had all changed in the last couple of years, well since she had "developed" as her mom called it. He had turned into a real creeper always trying to get a look at her coming out of the shower or getting changed, a total perv and of course her mother refused to believe it, instead, just blaming her.

Her mom's favorite refrain "he's just a man, what do you expect flaunting yourself around like that…"

Flaunting really? Who even used that word anymore, it was stupid, she really couldn't wait to get out of here.

She had met Trevor online, he had been a friend of a friend and once she had "friended" him they had started exchanging private messages, the rest was history and she was in love! Trevor "got her" and it didn't hurt that he lived in Tampa with some friends; he was older than her by a few years but that just made it mysterious. Besides, he had a motorcycle, which would drive her mom crazy when she found out. In fact, he kept trying to talk her into taking off with him, they could go anywhere she wanted to he said. It was fun to fantasize about where they might go, driving off into the sunset on his motorcycle, just the two of them against the world.

As brave as Allie was the idea of running off with Trevor still scared her a little, that was until this morning when her stepdad had walked in on her getting out of the shower. Usually he made some excuse and shut door, but not today he had just stood there looking at her with this creepy smile before handing her the towel. She hadn't even been able to cover up, she would have screamed but there was no one else there so what was the point? She wasn't waiting to see what happened next though, she was pretty sure her mother wouldn't have believed her anyway. She had packed some clothes in her book bag and messaged Trevor to pick her up at school, it was time to go.

The warm Florida sun beat down on her back as the bike's vibration reverberated through her body. She clung tightly to Trevor, her cheek pressed against him as the wind whipped her hair. Trevor weaved the bike through the eight lanes of morning traffic on the Selmon Expressway it was terrifying and exhilarating all at once and she had never felt so free.

It seemed like only a few minutes since she had walked off the grounds of Newsome High School into an exciting and mysterious future, she lifts her head up, glancing around as they pull into the parking lot of a large warehouse. She doesn't know this part of town and for just a moment a kernel of doubt creeps into her mind, but she brushes it aside with the brashness of youth and slips off the back as Trevor cuts the engine and kicks out the stand. He turns and gives her a grin, "Come on Allie, I want you to meet someone..."

"Who?" she asks unable to hide the nerves she is feeling.

Trevor takes her hand, "just some friends, nothin' to worry about my sweetness... Trust me..."

She would replay this moment over and over during the next few days, but it was already too late and the part of her that knew she was in trouble couldn't do anything about it.

It was hot in the warehouse, even in springtime the Florida sun bounced off the corrugated metal of the walls to create an oven like effect. Inside was dim and stale with just enough sunlight filtering through the high windows lining the edge of the ceiling to create a shadowy gloom. Along the back is a series of chain link walls forming a room that had long ago housed parts and inventory, the shelves are gone and there is only a card table, three folding chairs and four cots on the dusty floor.

She had grabbed Trevor's arm when she saw the two men coming toward them, dressed in suits, they didn't look like they would be friends of his. He had held her tight pinning her arms to her side as they injected her with the sedative; her screams had been short lived echoing off the walls as the drug coursed through her veins. Trevor would be long gone with his five hundred in cash when she finally regained consciousness, locked in the metal cage like room, her phone and shoes gone, two bottles of water on the table and the sunlight quickly fading to darkness. The trailer she shared with her brother, mom, and stepdad didn't seem so bad all of a sudden...

Vegas – 72 Hours Earlier

Jessie cradled his head in her lap watching the reflection of her face fading from his clear blue eyes, she continued to hold him as his breath slipped away ending in a soft gurgling sigh. The red bloom on his chest had made CPR an irrelevant afterthought. She had just wanted him to know she was here with him as he joined a world she couldn't rescue him from. To her left the fallen body of the shooter laid, legs askew, two perfectly placed holes in his forehead. No look of shock or surprise on his face – that was the stuff of movies and detective novels after all. No, he was just gone, the residue of his final thoughts staining the wallpaper behind him.

The scene replays one more time, she had hit the gym for an early morning workout leaving Tom sleeping, coming back to find the door slightly ajar and hearing the soft spit of a suppressed shot, she had dropped her bag while pulling her pistol out as she pushed the door open, seeing Tom falling to the floor, the crimson puddle already forming around him. She never went anywhere without her pistol, not even the gym; this time it had probably saved her life. She had fired two rapid rounds of her own – all triggered by her training and it had happened without any hesitation.

Time to go though, two un-suppressed shots, especially on the top floor of a luxury hotel, is going to bring pretty immediate attention and an armed response shortly after that. A final look around, check the pockets of the shooter – empty of course - grab the money, passports, and her clothes, shoving everything into her backpack, a final look in Tom's direction. Nothing, not even a tear, *what the hell was wrong with her*?

No doubt Tom had loved her and she did care for him, but not even she believed her chronic protestations, *my training makes it hard for me to let anyone in.* No, it went deeper than that, much deeper. *Now is not the time for another round of psychoanalysis* she thinks, pushing through the fire door and heading down the concrete steps to the parking garage. *Methodical, no rush, just another thirty-something fitness freak using the stairs instead of the elevator – training: fit in, be calm, act like you're supposed to be here, the obvious is obvious...* a silent metronome as the lessons tick through her subconscious, she reaches the garage level.

Popping the battery on the SAT phone she starts the jeep, pulling out the side entrance and following the alley down past the service entrance onto the street. It's empty this early on a Saturday but she can hear the sirens frantically approaching from the other direction. She hadn't really thought about it, but heads for the cabin by default, hoping to stick mostly to back roads. It was probably going to take better than ten hours to make the trip from Vegas to Durango giving her plenty of time to think things through. Heading onto I15N she plugs her music thumb drive in and fires up the "80's Rock" playlist, AC/DC provides a momentary distraction. She would have preferred staying off the interstate but there wouldn't be an alternative till she crossed the Utah border, *just have to be careful,* she thinks to herself.

Damn, it's no good... she mutters turning the stereo down, this just wasn't making any sense.

Jessie was halfway to her thirty-fourth birthday, at five-ten she was slightly taller than average, probably thanks to her dad, he was six five so height ran in the family. She had her mother's blues and brunette hair but the hundred and thirty-five pounds of lean muscle was all hers she earned it in the gym every day. She had left the service eighteen months earlier; ten years had been enough for her once it became obvious there were just some barriers women were never going to overcome. She had applied to "Q" school two consecutive years hoping to be the first woman to join the Special Forces and wear the beret, but the Army had made it clear it wasn't going to happen. No question she had achieved beyond anyone's expectation and was an excellent soldier, but she finally got the message.

She had definitely stayed sharp since getting out though. Keeping a steady schedule at the range and a workout routine that would frighten most Cross Fit contenders. Of course, her position with Thompson Security had necessitated a certain level of competence. Although to be honest personal security services for celebrities and the world's super rich rarely required protecting them from anything more dangerous than themselves. But the pay was great and the opportunity to travel first class all over the world was a nice perk, even if it was overwhelmingly boring most of the time. She had been in Vegas babysitting the pop princess of the hour, a discouraging waste of her talent, the pool parties, all night drinking and giggling girlfriends had her wanting to shoot someone.

Tom had surprised her the night before, flying in unannounced. They had cleaned up at the tables clearing more than a hundred and sixty grand and scoring a complimentary suite in the process, well not her exactly Tom was the big roller and liked to play the high dollar tables. Her partner Derek had just smiled and told her to have a good time he would watch the "brat" for the night.

Shit, this doesn't make a bit of sense, she thinks. She had run thinking something or someone from her past had come looking to settle a score, *but what if she had stumbled into something else entirely*?

She had met Tom Casey in a Moscow bar on one of her first security assignments. He had been drinking bourbon, not just any bourbon, but a Pappy Van Winkle. Jessie knew her bourbon, she had searched for months and dropped fifteen hundred dollars for a bottle of "Pappy 23" giving it to her father as a gift when he had taken Paradigm Tech public six years earlier, pretty big dollars even for a Ranger Captain.

She had taken Tom's story at face value and had matched him drink for drink as he had explained the ins and outs of high-end international investing. He managed accounts for a string of clients remarkably similar to some of the people Thompson provided security for. She had done a cursory check of his background of course, mostly out of habit, being cautious didn't just fade away when you left the "service", but she hadn't really found anything noteworthy. They had met up several times since then, mostly overseas, but about six months ago she had been held over in Chicago for a few days and they had only left his condo on the water twice; the first night to grab a steak at Gibson's and the next a deep dish at Gino's. Then again at the cabin for three days over the Christmas holiday.

Fuck me dead, she mutters her favorite phrase, *I'm for sure in it now*, she had taken the shooter out and fled the scene, no amount of explaining was going to make this right, what she really needed was to understand what the hell Tom was into, or *was he just in the wrong place at the wrong time*? Of course, that would mean she was the real target... *Ok, just need to get to the cabin and think this through, focus on that the details will wait*, she tells herself. This wasn't some shadow government movie where you make a call and someone cleans up after you, never mind that she didn't even work for the government anymore.

Nope a double homicide in the trendiest Vegas casino going, her prints everywhere, pictures on who knew how many security cameras... no this was a serious cluster fuck for sure.

Warrior

Jessie had known as early as her freshman year of high school that she wanted to be a warrior, not just a soldier in "today's" new Army. No, she wanted to be a warrior. The 2019 graduating class at the Military Academy – West Point would be the first to commission women directly into front line combat units and as one of the top graduates she would have a choice billet if she wanted it. Jessie had excelled, the rigid discipline and demanding physical requirements appealed to her. Completing the Advanced Marksmanship course her freshman summer was just a refresher as she had been shooting with her father for years. It had always just been the two of them as far back as she could remember he had never even had a girlfriend, her dad had struggled to make her life as normal as possible, but they gravitated to the things they both loved, hiking, biking, hunting – she loved the outdoors as much as he did.

The real thrill that first summer had been completing Airborne School and the rush of her first series of jumps was something she would never forget. Her dad had just shaken his head, "why would you jump out of a perfectly good airplane," he always asked with a smile. She tried to explain the rush of dropping toward the earth in free-fall, but clearly her dad preferred to have his feet on the ground, she was the adventurer in the family.

She had been a top swimmer and distance runner in high school and the strength and stamina developed in the pool and on the track served her well at the Academy. But it was in the fall of her second year that she had made her mark and cemented herself as the equal of any of the male cadets in her class. Cadets compete in Military Individual Advanced Development assessment also known as MIAD to qualify for selection to the elite summer programs the following year. The assessment is considered an extreme test of physical and mental toughness combined with an evaluation of leadership and problem-solving skills. The program insures cadets are capable of completing the more difficult summer courses before they are offered slots.

What she had lacked in pure strength she more than made up for in stamina, mental toughness, and her ability to quickly solve problems. When the smoke had cleared she was the only female cadet to finish and she had qualified for her top two choices: Jungle Warfare School and the Combat Divers Qual Course. She had her eye on SFAS, the prep course for "Q School" the Special Forces qualifications school, but she would learn later there were some doors that no amount of enlightenment was going to open.

Growing up just outside of Boulder on the front range of the Colorado Rockies in the shadow of the Flatirons she had developed a fierce independent spirit fostered by her father, forged in the clean mountain air and quenched in the clear cold streams they would fish in the spring. When she had left for the Academy he had held her for a long time then kissed her forehead, no words were needed, she knew what he meant and he knew why she needed to go. True, he had asked her to consider the Air Force Academy in Colorado Springs, she would have been close to home, but that alone was reason enough not to consider it.

    Her dad had visited a few times, Parent's weekend, and the Army – Navy game, but she had immersed herself in the cadet life and he was busy running his expanding technology company, life happened. The summer after her Junior (third class) year she had qualified to take the Pre-Ranger course known as RTAC and had spent the entire spring adhering to a grueling fitness regimen in preparation. The Army had only been allowing women to participate for the last few years and the success rate was hovering around twenty percent. Jessie was not going to allow herself to be a statistic like that. She had come home for a long weekend before shipping off to Fort Benning in Georgia, it had been almost a year since her last visit and the first two days had been awkward. She knew her dad loved her, but she wasn't anyone's little girl anymore, no this test would certify her ascension to warrior status. He understood her desire and dedication it had always been part of who she was, but this was a definite crossing over. Successful completion would set her up for Ranger School upon graduation and the chance to be one of only a handful of women to actually be assigned a combat role in the 75th Ranger Regiment.

They had grilled out thick cut bone in rib eye steaks and corn on the cob that final night, making small talk till the meal was gone. With the embers of the grill burning down and the dogs gnawing on the bones they had grabbed a couple of ice cold Corona's from the cooler and lain on the patio chairs. The mountain peaks stretched for the sky in the distance and the Milky Way spread out above them. This was maybe her favorite place on earth and she didn't want to leave with an awkward silence between them.

"Daddy, I love you..." She didn't really know what else to say.

"I know baby girl, I love you too..." and in his typical way it was enough.

She told him about her spring training routine and what the next few weeks would hold. The excitement in her voice made him smile to himself, he worried about her of course, any parent would, but she had always been able to take care of herself and this would be no different. They talked about doing some hiking later in the summer, maybe hitting their favorite fly-fishing spots, it seemed like old times. He had left her there wrapped in a blanket hoping this wasn't the last iteration of what had always been an early summer ritual for them.

Of course, she had completed RTAC with flying colors and graduated the following spring with a degree in International Relations and minor in Foreign Languages, Lou had been there as proud as a father could be, she was headed to Ranger School and the warrior status she coveted.

Too Quiet

The satellite (SAT) phone chirped and buzzed on the seat next to her as it updated. She would need to be connected for at least a few minutes before disconnecting from the network. Even after that there was still some risk leaving the phone powered up that someone could "ping" her location but at least in passive mode she wouldn't be broadcasting her location to every satellite.

Glancing over she sees there are twelve digital messages, three missed voice calls, seventy-eight emails, and one video chat request. *Hmmm, that seems pretty light considering, it should have lit up like a Christmas tree...* she thinks. Well it would have to wait for the next rest area, she pops the battery again and reaches for another bottle of water. It was funny how fast the "field craft" came back under stress, she was hydrating, one of the basic survival lessons from her time in uniform.

This whole mess had to come back to Tom, didn't it? There just wasn't another rational explanation. She had been involved in a number of drug interdiction joint ops with the Columbian Army and the Panamanian Border Security forces, but this just didn't fit with how the cartels operated. Never-mind that they had pretty successfully exterminated the major South American players. Combine that with the Federal government finally capitulating and legalizing marijuana in 2024 and the demand for illegal drugs had dropped significantly. Besides, why kill Tom? it didn't fit. No, this had to be something else and that meant she was going to have to dig a bit deeper into Tom.

    Even the local roads in Colorado are dotted with scenic overlooks so she picks the next one and pulls over. She needed to review her messages and decide on a destination, time was slipping the sun was already reflecting off the higher peaks around her having just breached the Eastern horizon. Scanning the road ahead and behind she starts scrolling through her messages first. Three from her dad, she leaves them for last, six from Derek, she expected those, and three from a number she doesn't recognize.

She starts with Derek's all dated Saturday:
    12:37AM - "hope you're having fun you owe me big"
    6:17AM - "lobby cafe 0800 for debrief work for you"
    8:15AM - "0815 you coming"
    8:17AM - "WTF all hell breaking loose where are you"
    9:18AM – "jess you need to call me now"
    10:13AM – "thompson corp looking for you i cant cover you any longer call me"

She had to smile Derek believed punctuation was for snobs, pretty much what she expected though, funny that he didn't mention Tom though and nothing since that day. She had Derek's private SAT number, she would call him later and see if he knew anything more. No way she was calling into Thompson yet though, and interesting that they hadn't reached out to her directly.

She checks her dad's next all Saturday also:

11:13AM - "hey kiddo check out this prerelease new encryption app we are working on https://paradigm/encryp1286/v3.1.4 use your usual login"

1:22PM - "ARE YOU OK??? 3 calls asking for you today wont identify themselves"

3:31PM – "officially worried – contact me in the usual way when safe to talk"

She wasn't surprised her dad hadn't continued to message her. He understood better than most that she wouldn't intentionally be unresponsive. He would wait for her to reach out when she could, although the not knowing was probably killing him. She would have to call him though, her dad kept a fully scrambled SAT phone with him at all times. It was convenient for her, but a necessary precaution in his business. He had been writing satellite communication encryption programs for the military the last fifteen years and always made sure she had the latest pre-release software. It was a nice way to field test what they were working on, but it also meant they could talk without fear of someone hacking their conversation.

No longer able to avoid it she brings up the last three messages:

Saturday:

9:01AM – Call this number +380-482-763-1414

10:00AM – Call this number +380-482-763-1414

11:03AM – you not target call +380-482-763-1414

She recognized the country code as Ukraine but she would need to look up the city, but any contact from Eastern Europe wasn't going to be positive. She hadn't worked in that theater but knew people that had, and the brutality of the organized crime lords of the Baltic States was the stuff of legends. Famous for drugs, weapons, human trafficking and assassination for hire it was one of the areas of the world that seemed to resist any level of policing. How they had her phone number already should have been a bigger red flag if she had thought it through.

Her dad picked up on the third ring there was a brief series of beeps as the encryption synced. "Hey baby what's up? You ok?"

"I'm okay daddy, things just got a little mixed up in Vegas…" She had never lost the habit of calling him "daddy" when she was down or stressing out.

"You want to talk about it? Anything I can do to help?" he asked.

"No, I am okay, spent a couple days at the cabin and I'm headed out now…" the silence stretched out for a moment as she started to cry. "Daddy I love you, I'll call you later okay..." She cut the call off before he could answer.

It hit her all at once, the loss of Tom, the close-range shooting of another person – you never really got used to it – but most of all hearing her dad's voice. She let the tears come knowing it was better to let it out than try to bottle the emotions up inside, sometimes a good cry was the best way to relieve stress. She had only been laughed at once for that, after her first and what had been an especially ugly mission in Panama. She had lost three of her platoon that night, the tears had flowed after the extraction pickup, leave it to an asshole Captain to make a "girl" comment on the chopper ride back to base. They had dropped rank upon landing and she had kicked his ass and good. Nobody had much to say about a few tears after that. To his credit he had taken it like a "man" and had put her in for a commendation for saving the rest of her two squads including carrying one of the wounded out through six miles of jungle to the extraction point.

The memory brought a small smile, she still had the combat knife he had given her after apologizing. Drying her eyes, she thinks about what to do next. Calling Derek was the most obvious choice she thinks, dialing his number.

"Yo Jess, where the hell are you?" he shouts before she can even get a word out.

"Derek, I can't tell you that, bring me up to speed on what happened Saturday..." she let it hang not wanting to give away anything.

"You never showed up, that's what the fuck happened."

"Come on Derek..."

He pauses for a second, "Ok, Ok, well, I sent you a text hoping to hand off the 'princess' around eight so I could catch some sleep before we had to leave, but you never answered or showed for that matter. Anyway, couldn't have been ten or fifteen minutes later all hell breaks loose, I was in the cafe downstairs by the lobby, you know the one..." He pauses waiting for an answer, nothing, "anyway had to be a dozen cop cars show up and they're piling in all armored up, sealed everything up tight."

"Ok, what else? Were you able to find out what was going on?" she asks.

"Seriously Jess, you're the bad ass ex-military that just disappeared, why don't you tell me what the fuck is going on..."

"Ok, Ok, I guess I deserve that, just finish telling me what happened and I'll fill in the blanks if I can."

"Well nothing else happened, about two minutes later a dozen suits show up, probably Homeland Security or maybe FBI, I don't know, serious looking dudes though, they went up in the elevators and that was it, they locked down the upper floors and told everyone everything was under control. I couldn't get a word out of anyone not even the locals, next thing I know Thompson central is calling me wanting to know where the fuck you are, so where the fuck are you?"

"I can't tell you that... I know that's shitty but I just can't."

He explodes on her, "that's fucked up Jess, you left me in the shit here, holding the bag and no backup, least you can do is tell me why... hell we're supposed to be partners."

She pauses for a second contemplating how much she can tell him, "look Derek, cool it, I'll tell you as much as I can, alright?"

"Sure, Jess I'm just worried about you..."

"Ok listen, I know this is going to be a little tough to believe but let me get it out. Saturday probably a little before eight I was coming back up from the gym and walked in on a shooter."

"What the fuck, a shooter? What are you talking about...?"

"Yes, a shooter, he had just put two rounds in the center ring on Tom, I got off two rounds took him down, packed my shit and got out of there, I don't know, maybe I should have stayed but I didn't want to chance there being another one..."

"Got two off? Who the fuck are you, Jason Bourne?" He lets out a sigh, "this is pretty fucked up, listen I don't know what's the right thing but if I can help I will..." A pause, "shit, sorry about Tom too..."

"Thanks Derek, seriously, I'm not sure what I am doing yet, but I appreciate it... let me work through this and I'll try to give you a call in a few days... in the meantime probably best not to mention this call." She cuts the line before he can respond, she already knows she won't be calling him back.

She drops the Jeep in gear and pulls back onto the road, she hadn't been ready to call the third number just yet. Without any real answers, there was no reason to engage whoever it was. She needed information and that started with Tom and that meant she was going to Chicago.

The Jungle

Jessie had made 1st lieutenant in just less than twenty months only a few shy of the minimum time in service requirements. She had been assigned Platoon leader of 2nd Platoon Bravo Company, 1st Battalion, 75th Ranger Regiment. She only had her platoon two weeks before Bravo Company was deploying to Panama, they were supposed to suppress an uprising of the Columbian guerrilla group FARC in the Darien Gap.

The group had resurrected itself with a vengeance after almost petering out ten years earlier. Intel claimed they were ferrying Middle Eastern terror groups as a way to raise cash for further insurgent operations. Satellite intel seemed to confirm that the group was moving North on the Atrato River through the swamps to Travesia before cutting through the Gap to El Real in Panama where they had established a regular schedule of single and double engine planes using the airstrip there. The satellite guys claimed they were moving in groups of twenty or less using the motorized long canoes common to that portion of the river.

The plan was to deploy the rifle teams from the 1st Battalion in coordination with the Panama Border Security known as SENAFRONT in the Darien Gap about ten miles Southwest of the drop zone in Paya Panama in an attempt to strangle any infiltration into Panama. Situated between the two opposing mountain ranges it offered a natural choke point. The Gap is a hundred miles long but only thirty-one miles wide and the unforgiving terrain includes everything from mountainous rainforest to tropical jungle with no permanent roads. It is considered some of the most unforgiving terrain in the world, but just the environment the Rangers were trained to operate in and a perfect place to trap the insurgents.

This would be Jessie' first real test under fire and she couldn't wait to hit the field. 2nd Platoon was deployed along the Eastern most vector of a three-pronged approach from the East while the SENAFRONT troops were using a similar approach from the West. Thirty-six hours later she would be holding what was left of the two fire teams from 1st Squad together while her 2nd and 3rd squads leap frogged back and forth allowing them to make it to the extraction point. It had been a cluster from the first contact, they had been told to expect a force of a hundred, maybe a hundred and fifty FARC guerillas with no heavy weaponry. What they ran into was three hundred plus well-equipped guerillas nearly twenty-fours earlier than expected. 1st Squad had been leading them in and came under heavy fire losing three men immediately before regrouping. They had two more wounded and radioed a heads up to the platoons North and West of them, but the chatter of AKs told them all they needed to know everyone was already engaged. What ensued was a cat and mouse game all the way back to the pickup. She had kept her men together using a classic advance and leapfrog approach with the wounded and casualties always in the middle.

Although she hadn't lost anyone else, these first casualties under fire would stay with her long after she had left the Army. They had given better than they got on the way back out, nobody stopped to count but later during her debrief they would estimate her platoon's kills at thirty-eight.

It had been on the chopper ride back that she had finally let her emotions get the better of her. Her dad always told her to just let it out, bleed the frustration and anxiety off there was no shame in crying, man or woman, it made no difference, but never give into the fear or hopelessness use it as a tool and move on. Of course, the Company Commander, a Captain Chambers had seen it as just another reason why women shouldn't be in his Rangers modern day enlightenment apparently didn't extend this far no matter what the modern media claimed... and his quip about crying like a girl hadn't sat well with her and didn't elicit the reaction he was looking for from her men either. She would never be openly insubordinate, but this Captain was begging for it. She looked right at him and toggled her mic... "You and me sir, no rank, when we land first to tap out, then we'll see who cries like a girl..." She let it hang there, it was definitely crossing the line, but with three of her men dead and two more wounded she just wasn't in the fucking mood for it. He was stuck and she knew

41

it, he had broken protocol with the "girl" comment and now she had called him on it.

"OK Lieutenant you want it that way, we'll settle it old school, no report, no payback, just you and me no spectators. Once this is done, it's done though... neither one mentions it again, got it?"

"Yes sir, I got it five by five," she said with a grin the adrenaline from their earlier run through the jungle still coursing through her.

He was stronger and taller but she was just too quick for him. Maybe he had hesitated, maybe not but she had hit him with a quick jab and roundhouse kick that knocked the wind out of him bringing him to his knees. Fifteen seconds later he was tapping out from an arm-bar he never saw coming.

"Jesus Fucking Christ Lieutenant!" he splutters.

"I'm sorry sir, but you asked for it..." Jessie says trying not to smile.

"Alright, alright I am sorry that was a bullshit move on my part... and look you did good bringing your men out of there without losing any more than you did. We got cut up pretty fucking bad on this one," he said brushing himself off and massaging his shoulder and wincing. "Remind me not to run my mouth again, Jesus..." They had shaken hands, he had given her his personal SOG Seal Pup Elite tactical knife, "to the victor go the spoils," he said.

She had rejoined her platoon, and hadn't thought any more of it, until she was notified that the Captain had recommended her for a Silver Star. Neither she or any of her peers had any previous combat experience; the Rangers had not been significantly deployed since being pulled out of Iraq and Afghanistan back when most of them were just starting at the Academy. The After Action Review (AAR) conducted by the Battalion staff had singled her out as the platoon leader that had properly relied on her training, acting quickly enough to minimize the platoon's casualties and extracting her troops safely even while under continuous fire.

Jessie hadn't been looking for attention, medals, or anything more than a chance to do her job and show that she was the equal of any other officer. Fortunately, or unfortunately as one of the few women to make it into the Rangers she was going to be the focus of a great deal of attention moving forward. It wasn't the only factor, but this singling out would ultimately be part of her decision to not go career and leave the Army after just ten years.

An Unexpected Detour

She had thought it through and was pretty sure the answers she needed were going to come from Tom and his past, the only question remaining was whether to take the slow and careful route to Chicago or go with speed and hit the interstate for a visible but much quicker trip. She was going to have to make the decision pretty quickly as she was coming up on the Rte. 160 / Rte. 285 split, she opted for speed taking the left onto Rte. 285 toward Denver where she would pick up Interstate 76 East. Maybe she would sidetrack over to Boulder for a quick stop at her dad's, she wasn't ready to share anything with him, but she could definitely resupply there. It was a calculated risk, she didn't want to bring him into this if she could avoid it; on the other hand, her dad seemed more than able to handle himself. She hadn't realized it when she was younger but as an adult the signs were much more obvious, her dad was a serious dude in his own right, maybe not exactly on this type of stuff but still maybe she had underestimated him.

The sun was up over the front range and the warm spring air felt good on her face as she pulled the Jeep into the Feelin' Good Coffee House in South Fork. She and her dad had made a habit of stopping here for breakfast on the trips home from the cabin, she always ordered the French toast and a black coffee, extra butter and real maple syrup made it complete. She sat in the back eating quickly while scanning the door looking for anyone that seemed out of place. South Fork was a small town and even though it had its share of tourist traffic you could tell who belonged and who didn't. She settled up with cash and took a large coffee to go as she headed north. She should have noticed the navy Crown Vic parked two blocks down, but Jessie still felt relatively safe, and why not, it had been three days and no one had tracked her down yet, or so it seemed.

    Six hours later she pulls into the Whole Foods parking lot just outside of Boulder and circles around the back parking between the recycling dumpsters and the Power Yoga studio. Facing out with the dumpsters behind her she has a good view of the only entrance into the lot. This close to home she isn't feeling nearly as secure as she had been. Earlier in the day she had felt more than seen someone following her and a navy Crown Vic had popped up in her rear view at least three times, maybe nothing but her paranoia was beginning to kick in. Granted, she hadn't seen the car again in the past three hours and was pretty sure her round about detour through Denver would have thrown all but the best tail off. No sense in taking any chances though, she pulls out the encrypted SAT phone and dials her dad's number.

    Three rings, four rings, she is about to hang up, "Don't say anything, just text me your GPS coordinates," her dad says quietly and hangs up.

She has a moment of panic, does this mean her dad's in trouble, has someone been ahead of her this whole time? She takes a deep breath and sets the phone down next to her, *what to do, what to do*? Finally lifting the phone, she sends the GPS coordinates, her first inclination had been to just start running, but her dad would not have asked if he didn't need to see her. Getting out of the Jeep she checks to make sure there's a round chambered in the Kimber and slips the extra magazines into her pocket. It's just approaching twilight and she wants to take a quick look around before it starts to get dark. She has the pistol in her right jacket pocket and the magazines in her left as she casually strolls along the back of the store looking for any movement and in particular the navy Crown Vic, she is pretty sure now it wasn't just a coincidence.

She is just getting in the Jeep when her dad's black fully restored 1973 Bronco pulls around the corner, she has to smile, he loves that beast and has refused a dozen or more offers to buy it. He doesn't even slow down just waves her to follow him and circles back out into the parking lot turning right on 27th Street. He picks up speed making the left on Broadway and heading south back out of town. Their home was on the northwest side of town so he must be taking her somewhere else, a quick left on Baseline and soon they are beginning to head further out, Baseline turns into Flagstaff Road where it begins a series of cut-backs climbing rapidly. It's at this point her dad pulls into an almost hidden drive, parks the Bronco and motions for her to follow him. The sky still has streaks of rose and turquoise but the stars are already starting to prick through, its dark up here there are no streetlights and glow of the town below is a distant twinkling of lights. She follows him to the door where he gives two quick knocks and opens it ushering her into the foyer.

"This her, Big Lou?" He must be early sixties she thinks, older than her dad by a couple of years but it was hard to tell. He was medium everything, non-descript, the type of person you would never remember seeing, it was his eyes though that were the give-away, grey blue, cold, hard in spite of the smile he was working at, this guy was a very serious operator...

"Jess, meet a very old friend of mine, Jack Hardy... Jack this is my daughter Jess..."

"Pleased to meet you sir," she extends her hand giving him a firm grip like her dad had taught her; he returns it just as firmly. Jack looks over at Big Lou and just nods.

Without any preamble Jack says, "okay young lady, lets pour a couple of bourbons and you can tell me and your dad what the hell is going on..."

Evergreen

It was the summer of 1996; Lou McIntyre had been a field officer for the Central Intelligence Agency for almost four years. He had graduated early from CalTech finishing in three years with a degree in electrical engineering and had signed up the day after graduation. Entering the Agency had seemed like a huge mistake to his parents and most folks that knew him. He could have joined any engineering or tech firm and profited handsomely, but he yearned for a place to apply his knowledge and skill in a real way, with tangible and immediate visible results, not just stuck in a lab for some huge faceless multinational company. The Agency had offered an opportunity to work with the latest hi-tech equipment available and like-minded people. They had tried to put him in a lab working deep inside the bowels of the Agency, but had insisted on being in the field. Of course, he hadn't necessarily envisioned himself stuck in the small neighborhood of Masagana in central Manila with Jack, maybe the scariest stone-cold operative he had ever met but a good friend nonetheless. It didn't help that the heat was oppressive and the two Americans could only leave the small two-room apartment at night for fear of being noticed. They had been holed up for the last six days surviving on cardboard containers of food from the hole in the wall kitchen/cafe downstairs, plus cigarettes and bottled water.

By the fourth day it had seemed like a month. Unfortunately, you had to go where the intel led you and they had tracked the Al-Quaeda operative to this shithole of an apartment. Al-Quaeda was popping up on a regular basis these days, they were fervent sons-a-bitches and their hate for America burned bright.

The radio crackled in his ear, "Eagle is moving – lobby in three..."

Lou fiddled with the intercept gear trying desperately to filter out the white noise and zero in on the frequency Jack had just given him, he was still young by CIA standards, but he was the best electronics and communications expert the Agency had. The challenge with picking up hand-held radio signals was proximity, even with the best equipment and this was better than most since he had personally re-engineered it, it was still a crapshoot that they would hear anything. Turning to Jack, "did he give you a trigger word or a location?"

Jack shakes his head, "nope, just kept saying: 'delivered the wedding cake'."

Lou purses his lips, "Fuck me dead, these bastards have been leaving explosives all over town! This is the third one." He turns back to his headphones and tries to sift through the noise again. "Any chance we get anything else from this one..." he nods in the direction of the back room.

Jack's expression never changes, "Nope, he's done, but the bastard won't be baking any more fucking 'cakes', that's for sure."

The earpiece crackles again, "Eagle enroute heading south on Quezon five minutes out..."

Lou holds up his hand, mostly reflex, even though it's just the two of them in the rundown room.

"Kaeikat zifaf - jisr Quezon," the phrase repeated three times and then nothing... Lou could speak Arabic like a native, "Wedding Cake – Quezon Bridge!" it was all he needed.

There was no hesitation as he keyed the mic on his headset... "ABORT ABORT ABORT" and then "QUEZON BRIDGE, QUEZON BRIDGE, ABORT CONFIRM ABORT..."

"Copy Evergreen aborting..." a few seconds later... "Evergreen confirm Quezon Bridge..." Lou had taken the moniker "Evergreen" in reference to his beloved Colorado.

He can't believe it, "are you fucking kidding me?" he keys the mic again, "well, there is a big fucking bomb on that bridge so do what you think is best..."

"Copy Evergreen... Mother Goose out - diverting now..."

He turns to Jack, who is grinning at him... "Fucking Secret Service assholes... Mother Goose? Surprised he didn't just go with Maverick, asshole." He starts to pack up the gear, "let's get the fuck out of here..."

Jack pats him on the back laughing, "don't let them get to you buddy, you just saved the President's life..." He helps Lou stow the gear in their duffel bags, shame they were just going to drop it in the nearest river but you couldn't very well check CIA issued radio intercept sets as baggage. Neither one mentioned the body in the back room, clean-up wasn't their problem, and the CIA didn't mind leaving a message behind every now and again.

Jack looks over at his partner as they make their way down the back stairs, "Lou why are you still doing this? Seriously, you're too smart for this man and you got a beautiful lady at home, I don't get it?"

Lou smiles ruefully, "same reason you do, world travel, five star hotels, gourmet food, hot women, adventure..."

Jack gives him that look, "you know you have a serious problem right?"

They both laugh breaking the tension, "see you back in DC in a couple of weeks, I am going to catch a little down time with Maggie, before the debrief."

Jack nods, "sounds good, give Mags my best... you know Lou, you really should think about getting out..."

It would take Lou a little over eighteen hours to get home, a quick flight to Tokyo and then the long haul across the Pacific into newly opened Denver International. Grabbing his Jeep from long-term parking he takes Pena Avenue over to I70 before heading through town on Rte. 36 to Boulder and his waiting darling Maggie.

    Maggie worked as programmer for one of the many startup tech companies benefitting from the new dot.com frenzy. They had been introduced by mutual friends during one of Lou's long weekends home and had been inseparable ever since. He had fallen at first sight, her long dark hair, her piercing blues, and just a hint of freckles, was irresistible. Maggie hadn't been far behind falling for his incredible smarts and it didn't hurt that he was a tall good-looking guy either. Her down to earth nature and sharp mind appealed to him and of course her love of hiking and outdoors didn't hurt either but it was so much more than that. Of course, Lou was a brilliant international man of mystery with a job he couldn't talk about, what wasn't to love there?

    Lou hadn't told anyone, not his parents or even Jack, but he planned on asking Maggie to marry him this weekend. He had some downtime for stateside training scheduled in December and hoped they could get married while he was home. Always the planner, he still felt serious butterflies just thinking about it. What if she didn't like the ring, what if she said no or I am not ready, he didn't think he could survive it. He felt the small black velvet box in his pocket, he been traveling for twenty hours straight and nothing was going to ruin this night for him, not even his own silly nerves.

Charlie's in the center of town was a rustic style steak house with hand-hewn beams, rough-cut stone and two giant fireplaces. They were famous for their dry aged steaks and during the summer months you could dine on their huge deck overlooking Boulder Creek. It was a favorite of Lou and Maggie's but usually only for special occasions. The steaks had been perfect and the bottle of wine much more expensive than he usually indulged in. They were down to dessert and Lou was a bundle of nerves as he played around with his crème brulee a soft breeze made the gas lamps flutter in their sconces and the creek serenaded them softly; Maggie could tell he was struggling with something but she was wise enough not to press him.

Finally, unable to stand it any longer he grabs her hand, "Mags I don't how to say this right and I know it's a lot to ask of a person, but well..."

She puts a finger to his lips... "Lou you are the best thing that ever happened to me and if you are trying to ask me to marry you, well then the answer is yes a hundred times yes..."

They both have tears in their eyes as he slips the ring on her finger, neither is ready for the sickening ride that is coming, but tonight at least life is perfect.

Pappy & Plans

Jack ushers them into the den, double glass doors open onto an expansive deck looking out over the city. Jessie turns as she hears the clink of glasses, Jack is pouring three glasses of Pappy Van Winkle for them, no ice of course. She smiles, remembering the trouble she had gone through to find a bottle for her dad a few years earlier. She takes in the rest of the room, it's obvious this is a "man's" house, there isn't a feminine touch anywhere and the walls are adorned with art from all over the world. It's an eclectic mix of paintings, rugs, and sculpture. She sits on the edge of the leather crouch cradling the drink in her hands, her dad is next to her while Jack is in what she is sure is his favorite recliner across from her. She hadn't wanted to involve her dad in this and she wasn't quite sure what to make of this "friend" of his, but her dad had some explaining to do when this was over. She also knew she wasn't getting out of here without some kind of explanation since both of them seemed to know she was in trouble.

She looks at both of them deciding where to start, "listen, no disrespect dad, but why don't you tell me what you know and I'll fill in the gaps."

Jack gives a hearty laugh, "Oh Lou, she is good, just as smart as you said," turning to Jessie, "well played young lady, see what we know and only share what you absolutely have to, well played indeed." Shaking his head and then in a much more serious tone, "but listen Jessie, we can't help you if you don't give us the full picture so start at the beginning, believe me nothing will surprise us and no one in this room is going to judge you..."

Her dad cuts in, "Jess honey, we don't know much, I was able to reverse trace the unidentified calls back to Ukraine, but don't really have any more than that. But I also had a visit from two very senior FBI agents this afternoon asking if I had heard from you, of course they wouldn't tell me anything, just said it was important they talk to you as soon as possible..." holding his hands out, "and that's about it."

Jess pauses and glances over at Jack, "what's your background sir? Special Forces, NSA?... Agency?"

Jack looks over at Lou who just gives him a small nod... "Jessie, I spent thirty plus years in the Agency as a field operative mostly in the Middle East, Eastern Europe and Asia. Your dad and I worked together for almost five years when we were both getting our feet wet and well, he's been one of my closest friends ever since..." The silence envelopes the room as Jessie nods to herself.

She doesn't say anything, just takes a sip of the warm whiskey, letting it rest in her mouth and absorbing the taste before swallowing it. Turning to her dad, "It appears we have some things to talk about dad…"

"Listen honey let me…"

She cuts him off sharply, "not now dad, I can't deal with that and this other mess at the same time, when this is over though you owe me a conversation…"

"Fair enough," he says, "now tell us what's going on."

Jessie spends the next two hours recounting the last few days beginning with her arrival in Vegas. The two men don't ask any questions, allowing her to sort through the memories on her own without interruption. She is a little surprised how clinical her recitation is, *God, I can be a cold fish when needed*, she thinks. She finishes up with the trip up to Boulder and the navy Crown Vic that seemed to be shadowing her most of the day, they all agree probably FBI and it explains the visit Lou had received. Obviously, the Feds had figured where she was headed and had jumped ahead to see if her dad would give anything up.

Jack gives her a smile, "nice debrief young lady, no assumptions… your dad tells me you gave up being a Ranger and got out after your last tour, you were a Major right? I'm just curious about why, seems like you were on the fast track?"

She holds his gaze for a moment the color rising in her cheeks, "well sir, the bastards wouldn't let me go Special Forces, after my second rejection they made it crystal clear it wasn't going to happen so I decided not to re-up."

Jack studies her for a moment, "no shame in being a Ranger you know..."

She bristles even though she knows he is poking her, "that had nothing to do with it, I just don't like being told I can't do something because I'm a woman..."

Jack holds his hands up with a smile and turns to Lou, "well buddy, I think she is going to be just fine..." Looking back to Jessie, "just remember to keep those emotions in check, it's fine to let your guard down here, but out there," he motions towards the glass doors lining the living room wall, "calm, cool, collected, period, no exceptions, got it?"

"Yes sir, I understand," and with a smile, "so how are you two ancient spies going to help me? Is the Agency issuing walkers these days?"

"All right smart-ass!" her dad laughs. "First how were you planning to proceed from here?"

"Honestly dad, I'm open to some suggestions here, but I had planned on heading to Chicago quickest way possible. Like I was saying I thought this might have been someone coming for me, but the more I think about it Tom had to be the target. I don't know what he was mixed up in, but I figured I would start with his condo in Chicago and see what I could dig up."

Her dad is silent for a moment... "What about this Ukrainian connection? You have any idea what he might have been hooked into there?"

Jess just shrugs, "no, not really, he never mentioned anything specific and I don't recall him even talking about any part of the Baltic." She hesitates, "probably no connection but the first time I met him was in Moscow at one of those clubs where the super-rich hang out and act like Russia has joined the rest of the world."

Jack looks up from his phone, "he mention what he was doing there?"

"No, I figured he had clients there, should have triggered a red flag I guess, the Russians are always trying to legitimize their money," and mostly to herself, "I can't believe I let that asshole sweet talk me..."

Her dad puts his arm around her shoulders, "Don't be so hard on yourself, no way you could have seen this coming... let's just focus on where we go from here, besides we don't know whether he was actually involved or just in the wrong place at the wrong time." Jessie and Jack give him a look like he has lost his mind.

"You're not serious are you Lou?" Jack asks, "who gets whacked in a swanky hotel room with a suppressed pistol cause they were in the wrong place?"

"Okay, okay, wishful thinking I guess, we'll need to figure out who he was doing business with, maybe this is a money deal gone bad, some of those Russians don't take too kindly to their money disappearing, doesn't matter whose fault it is."

The rest of the evening was spent developing an initial plan, Jess was going to head to Chicago in the morning and see if she could gain access to the condo and do some digging there. Her dad and Jack would call in some favors and see if they could uncover anything on the Ukrainian connection. It was decided Jess would use the guest room at Jack's just in case the FBI had her dad's place under surveillance and they would regroup in the morning with any updates. Strangely enough, although they didn't talk about it, going to the police or the FBI didn't surface as an option.

Jess walks her dad to the door where he turns and gives her a hug, "I'm sorry honey, I should have told you, but I just never found the right time... Listen, when this is over I'll tell you everything... whatever you want to know, ok?"

She leans into him holding on to the hug, "I know daddy, it's okay, I love you..."

Lou kisses her forehead, "I love you too honey, I've got some new gear I'll bring up in the morning, okay? And don't worry, we'll figure this thing out together."

She doesn't want to but lets him go and turns back into the house, Jack is in the kitchen putting on a pot of coffee, "how about some bacon and eggs? I always think better over breakfast... doesn't matter what time it is," he asks.

Jess gives him a nod, "sounds great, I'm starving, I'm going to grab my bag out of the Jeep, where do you want me?"

He points down the hall, "Take the room on the left."

Twenty minutes later after washing up she heads back out to the kitchen, Jack is sliding two perfectly formed goat cheese and bell pepper omelets on the plates, the bacon is already on the table. He points to the cabinet above the coffee pot. "Cups right up there, cream in the fridge if you use it, let me finish buttering the toast and we are good to go."

Jess pours two cups and heads back to the table, "better drink up, going to be a long night you telling me about my dad..."

Jack gives her a wan smile, "not my story to tell, but I'll give you this much... your dad was an amazing officer, truly brilliant. Not going to ruin the surprise, but make sure he tells you about how he saved the President in Manila back in '96. And Jess... don't go too hard on him, he got out because he loved your mother more than anything... he never looked back, never regretted leaving, and I think that's what I appreciate the most about him."

Prisoner

Everything seemed foggy as Allie came to, her head was pounding, and a wave of nausea swept over her as she tried to sit up. She fell back on the cot struggling to sort out where she was and what had happened, but she was having trouble piecing it together. A pair of strong hands lifted her into a sitting position and handed her a bottle of water forcing two pills into her mouth. She swallowed them too confused to put up any resistance. He forced her to drink the rest of the bottle before letting her lay back down. She could hear men's voices but none of the words seemed to make any sense as she fell back into a dreamless sleep.

She didn't know how long she had been out when she woke again but it seemed to be late afternoon from the way the light was filtering into the warehouse, having learned her lesson the first time she is careful not to get up too quickly as she looks around the caged room. To her right another girl seems to be sleeping on one of the other cots, she starts to jump up but thinks better of it as another wave of nausea sweeps over her. Bits and pieces of things were coming back to her and even in her drugged state a growing surge of fear threatens to plunge her into a state of hysteria. Gulping in quick gasps of air she tries to calm herself long enough to take another look around. She can't tell if the other girl is sleeping or not, so swinging her legs over the edge of the cot she gingerly pushes herself up on unsteady legs and wobbles over to the other cot. Kneeling down next to her she shakes her hard but the girl doesn't wake up and her shallow rasping breaths seem to echo through the warehouse. Looking around there doesn't seem to be any way out, the walls remind her of the chain link fence surrounding her school, it seems like forever ago she had walked out behind the gym and jumped on Trevor's bike. She briefly wonders what happened to Trevor before the memory of him pinning her arms to her side overwhelms her, the hot tears streaming down her cheeks taste salty as she licks her dry lips.

  The door has a padlock on the outside and there doesn't seem to be any way to get out. The chain link is attached to a metal beam in the floor and stretches into the gloom above her. Allie hears the scrape of a door opening on the far side of the building and hurriedly lies down on her cot hoping maybe it's someone coming to rescue her, but not wanting to risk it being the man that had pushed the needle into her arm. She wasn't even sure how long she had been here, but surely her mom had reported her missing by now. She can't help the hot tears starting again accompanied by a full-blown snuffling she can't seem to control. Burying her head in the crook of her arm she lies face down on the cot, the deep sobs uncontrollable and the ache in her chest sharp enough to make her catch her breath. Allie is no longer the brash know it all teenager that smugly dreamed of leaving her mother's trailer behind for the big city, but a scared little girl, truly just a child, living a nightmare she can't wake up from.

The two men unlock the door, closing it behind them. The bigger of the two stands at the door as if to guard the girls from trying to escape. Allie holds her breath praying the will just let her be, but there is no God coming to her rescue as the man leans over her, the bright needle glinting in the low light. She whimpers as the sharp steel penetrates her arm and she can feel the warmth flooding through her before she fades out completely.

They kept her drugged and in the cell for four days. The few times she wakes up they feed her a steady diet of water and pop tarts interspersed with a regimen of U-47700 known on the street as "pink". It was eight times more powerful than heroin and the perfect low-cost solution to managing the girls and creating an overnight dependence - one of the key components of long term control. With the exception of twice a day bathroom breaks the girls spend most of the time in a drugged haze lying on their cots.

The local Sheriff's department had coordinated quickly with the Missing Endangered Persons Information Clearinghouse (MEPIC) which had issued the AMBER alert within the first twenty-four hours, Allie's mother had plastered the neighborhood with flyers asking for information, the school had asked anyone who had seen anything to contact the Sheriff's office, and of course all of her friends talked about it online... unfortunately all to no avail and it was as if she had simply disappeared into thin air. They tracked down "Trevor's" online profile and of course all the messages but he was as much a mystery as her whereabouts. It seemed he had simply vanished a virtual creation in an online world that the authorities couldn't penetrate. Allie had become a statistic, another lost child in the epidemic of human trafficking. The statistics were overwhelming and law enforcement did not have the resources to begin keeping up with the problem. The latest figures claimed that close to half a million young people were either being actively sexually exploited or were at risk the vast majority being under eighteen and woman. Teenage runaway girls were in the greatest danger of being forced into prostitution and pornography while in essence being held captive. Allie fit the demographic perfectly and like many in this group she had simply disappeared without a trace.

Heading East

It was still dark when Jessie woke; she dressed quickly, repacked the backpack and headed down the hall to the kitchen. She had hoped to have a few minutes alone with a cup of coffee to assimilate last night but it wasn't to be, her dad and Jack were already talking quietly at the kitchen table. She helps herself to a cup and pulls a still warm sesame bagel out of the Einstein's bag. She sits next to her dad slathering her bagel with enough veggie cream cheese to the point where you can't see much else. Lou just smiles. It hadn't been so long ago when she would hand him the bagel and tub of cream cheese wanting him to spread it for her... he didn't remember exactly when that had stopped but it was a sweet memory.

Jack laughs, "having a little bagel with your cream cheese I see..."

For a moment, she grins and was a kid again, "Yup, best way to eat them..."

"Never was able to cure her of that habit..." Lou says. "Listen Jess, I have a few things for you... here, let me show you," he opens the box sitting on the chair next to him. "Ok, first things first, new SAT phone – got our newest encryption algorithm – nobody has this yet. I haven't even released it into beta testing yet, Jack one for you too." Next, he pulls out what looks like a

USB stick with a black metallic card about the size of an average credit card attached.

Jess reaches for it, "What is this thing?"

"That's a master card key with an RFID reader / writer, it'll read any lock ID that requires an RF card to unlock it. It also scrambles the ID when you press that button rendering the lock inoperable by anyone but you." Reaching back into the box he brings out what looks like a small tablet, "okay, this works similar to a radar or ultrasound – it'll penetrate most anything short of a lead lined wall, that includes people by the way. The image appears here on the screen and you control the depth of penetration with this slider on the side." Her dad hands Jess the tablet, "go ahead and try it..."

Jessie gives him a sideways look, "Do I even want to ask where you came up with this stuff, I thought you were out of the spy game?" she laughs.

He gives her a classic dad look, "Never you mind where I got them, but seriously Jess you can't let anyone take these from you, if you think you might be... be uh compromised you have to destroy them ok?"

She can tell he is trying not to choke up, she pats his hand, "I got it daddy, don't worry, I know the drill... I'm all about avoiding trouble, quick in and out, it's a small condo, shouldn't take long to check it out."

Jack breaks in, "we figured you could use this stuff once you got there, should make it easier to get into the condo without detection and find anything even if it's pretty well hidden." Lou gets up to get another cup of coffee and pull himself together. Jack continues, "while you're up there we'll see if we can't break some intel out of the FBI and the Agency, I still know some folks over there..." Jack stands up, "give me a second..." he heads down the hall, "...be right back" he says over his shoulder.

Jessie puts the new items in her backpack, zipping it up she stands, ready to go but now hesitant to leave her dad. He seems to sense her dismay and wraps her up in his trademark hug kissing her forehead. "Jess, just be careful okay, I know you can handle yourself, but until we know who we're dealing with... well just promise you'll be careful."

She gives him a squeeze, "I will daddy, promise... I'm really sorry about all this... I really never meant to get you in the middle of it."

He gives her another squeeze, "listen it's you and me kiddo so no worries, I am always here for you no matter what..."

She grabs the bag up as Jack comes back down the hall carrying a black leather case slightly smaller than a briefcase. Setting it down on the counter he unzips it.

"Okay Jess, I want you to take this... a fully suppressed Colt 45 with three extra magazines and four boxes of Hornady

Critical Defense rounds, only round I ever use..." The full impact of that statement isn't lost on her.

"Sir, I can't take your personal weapon..."

"Young lady take it, you can't go running around Chicago with an un-suppressed pistol, I'm not going to need it and well, if everything goes right you won't either, but just in case I'd feel better if you had it." Jack glances Lou's way for support.

"Take it Jess," her dad says, "no reason not to, better safe than sorry..." Laughing he says, "Besides Jack has an unhealthy obsession with it, some time away will do him good..."

"Shut up Lou, I just want her to be safe..."

Lou puts his hands up in surrender, "I know just kidding buddy, but seriously Jess, take the pistol."

"Ok, you two, I got it, but I need to go if I leave now I can make it there before the last train downtown, don't want to park any closer than necessary."

She shakes Jack's hand and thanks him again as her dad is loading her backpack and the leather case into the Jeep for her. They share a final embrace and she backs out of the drive heading back toward Boulder, the Interstate and what she hopes are some answers. The two men watch her go, standing there even after she has disappeared around the bend, neither wanting to say anything. One is worried about his little girl and the other worried about his oldest friend.

The Bride & the Baby

That summer of 1996 Lou had already made up his mind to leave the Agency, now that he was engaged to Maggie he couldn't bear the thought of being away from her. He spent a week in DC being debriefed on the Manila operation, receiving a commendation he couldn't tell anyone about, a promotion he wouldn't be using, and turning in his resignation. Although it wasn't quite that simple, the paperwork necessary to leave the agency was staggering, the consequences of disclosing information clearly laid out in agonizing detail, but Lou was steadfast in his decision and in the end, they grudgingly let him go, leaving the door open for his return if he so wished. He knew he wasn't coming back because he was never leaving Maggie again. He planned on spending the rest of his life making sure she was the happiest girl in the world.

Now that he was out, there was no reason to wait till December. He called her that night with the good news that he was coming home. Lou wanted to move the wedding up and get married right away, they loved each other so why wait, he argued passionately. Maggie laughed and said a girl had to have some time to plan, in the end he won her over and they decided to move the wedding up. They were married two weeks later in a simple ceremony with a few friends and no fanfare, it wasn't about anything more than two people perfectly matched and in love, having the good fortune of finding each other in spite of the world's chaos. Lou started Paradigm Tech less than a month later and was taking orders for his encryption technology from the CIA, if they couldn't have him they would at least leverage his technology and they believed, control him that way. It was a win-win, though Paradigm was flush with cash and contracts and the United States government was able to lock up one of the brightest minds and his cutting-edge technology. While the CIA controlled access to the most advanced algorithms, Paradigm was already starting to sell a watered-down version to the larger international communications market.

Lou had purchased a little more than twenty-five acres northwest of downtown a few years earlier, he had planned on just building a simple cabin for himself, the foothills offering a great view of the peaks to the north and west. The back line was bordered by a trout stream and dotted with the towering firs and aspens he loved. This was going to be his getaway cabin, but now he was intent on building Maggie the home of her dreams. In the end, they had expanded on his original plan, building a beautiful log home with a large back deck looking out over the stream and the mountains in the distance. The house was only about a third of the way done in early March when Maggie broke the good news she was pregnant. Lou had thought he was already the happiest man in the world, but the thought of being a dad was all time high for him! They had celebrated with take-out Chinese in what would one day be the kitchen of their new home. With cartons spread out on a stack of sheetrock lit by a lantern, they talked about the future, their dreams, what it would be like to have a baby, they both felt like life couldn't get better than this. They laughed, planned, kissed and dreamed of the days to come long into the evening. Maggie wanted a son, a boy to carry on Lou's name, he claimed not to care just as long as it was healthy... but deep inside he hoped for a baby girl, someone to call him daddy and curl up in his lap by the fire, he would dedicate himself to taking care of his "girls".

Winter turned to spring and then summer; they moved into their home the first week of July, throwing a party for friends and the few employees at Paradigm, Lou had recruited the best and brightest and treated them like family. Maggie glowed with that special light reserved for mothers to be, Lou wouldn't leave her side, the ultrasound the week earlier had confirmed their little "girl" was right on track and healthy. He hadn't stopped smiling like a silly goose since and carried a copy of the picture with him everywhere.

Summer waned and the aspens turned to gold as autumn brought a chill to the air, Maggie had developed a craving for Brussels sprouts of all things, which had resulted in more than a few harried trips to the farmers market and some late nights in the kitchen for Lou. As fall began to run away and with early winter around the corner they had taken to walking down to the stream after dinner or cuddling under a blanket on the porch, gazing at the stars as the flames from the fire pit flickered over them. They talked of the future and the little one that would soon be there.

November 2nd fell on a Sunday and Lou was up early putting on a pot of coffee while whipping together eggs, heavy cream, a dash cinnamon and a splash of vanilla for his special French toast. He had just started slicing the fresh Brioche loaf when Maggie screamed from the bedroom. He wouldn't be able to recall later exactly what she had screamed, but there was scared urgency in her voice that had him running for the bedroom.

His whole world had been torn asunder and rebuilt in the space of a couple of hours that cold November morning, he now held his entire future in a small pink and blue baby blanket while the rest of his life seemed to be crashing down around him, his tears christening the baby girl in his arms.

Maggie had never made it out of the delivery room, the physicians had been unable to stop the hemorrhaging while the beginning and end of life's journey had passed within a breath of each other.

The Windy City

Jessie parked in one of the smaller commuter train stations on the northwest side of Chicago, Arlington Heights a quiet semi-suburban enclave of upper middle-class neighborhoods, coffee shops and grocery stores. She caught the 12:44AM NW Yellow line downtown to the Chicago Ogilve Station, it was the last train down and thankfully empty of the normal bustle of commuters.

It was half past one in the morning as she stepped out into the chilly night on Washington Street, she headed East it was a little more than a mile to Tom's condo and she wanted a chance to clear her head and stretch her legs out a bit. She took the short cuts through Millennium and Grant Park, not considering whether it was safe or not, she had transferred her "tools" and "gadgets" to the backpack and the 45 felt comfortable in the shoulder holster hidden under her jacket. At 2:17AM Jessie lets herself in through the service entrance, luckily devoid of any security cameras and takes the service elevator up to the 51st floor. Tom's condo was on the 50th floor but she didn't want any surprises exiting the elevator, better to be safe and use the stairs. Making her way down the stairs she pauses at the door to his floor, three deep breaths focuses her energy as she listens for any out of place noise before she pushes through entering the quiet hallway. Tom's studio unit #5017 was on the southeast corner of the building and had spectacular views of downtown and Lake Michigan, not that she was there for the sights. Jessie stops in front of the door, listening again for anything out of the ordinary. It's quiet, almost too quiet, no TV noise, no music, she can barely hear the normal sounds of the city below her, while she pushes a gloved hand on the door, gently exerting pressure – nothing. She slips the key card reader out of the backpack and slides it into the slot waiting for the light to flash green, she presses the button initiating the scrambler insuring no one can open the door after she is in. The door clicks behind her as she stands in the entry, the beating of her heart reverberating in her ears. The sounds of traffic and an occasional siren float up from the streets below, the apartment is bathed in the soft ambient golden glow of Chicago's skyline.

  Jessie stands still, as her eyes adjust to the dim light before she slowly walks forward. She remembers it's a simple layout, bathroom immediately to the right; coat closet to the left and a walk-in closet follows beyond the bathroom. The hallway opens into the living space and bedroom combination. Immediately to the left is the small kitchen – nowhere to hide and nowhere to really hide anything – Spartan but tasteful and what a view she thinks again as she heads to the floor to ceiling windows. When Tom had first brought her here she had just stood in the window staring, you could see the whole city spread out against the shore of Lake Michigan, it was beautiful.

The condo has that pent up feeling to it as if no one has been there in a quite a while. *Is it possible she was able to get here before anyone else,* she wonders, closing the drapes?

With the shades drawn she clicks on the table lamp and does a quick but thorough search, nothing of any note, a few suits in the closet, empty fridge and freezer, a couple of boxes of pasta and a jar of sauce in the cabinets, but not a clue as to what Tom may have been mixed up in. In fact, it was unnaturally clean, she sits on the couch, backpack next to her reviewing the long weekend she had spent here. She can't recall a moment they weren't together, they had even showered together. A small smile escapes her, she had changed in the bedroom and Tom had been whining about how tired he was from the closet... She had teased him about his stamina, but she picks up the tablet device and heads back to the closet; has to be here she thinks, starting with the interior wall. Pay dirt! The common wall with the bathroom shows a ghostly green image of what looks like a thin box tucked behind the shower water pipes, but there is no obvious way to get to it. There must be a hidden panel or something but she isn't interested in searching for it, not knowing how much time it will take. She grabs her backpack off the couch and extracts the tactical knife from its sheath, it makes quick work of the wallboard and soon she has a hole large enough to reach the metal box. Unfortunately, if anyone else shows up there isn't going to be any way to hide this she thinks. A quick glance at her watch, it's nearing four in the morning, she has already been here longer than she should have. The box is about the size of a legal pad and only a couple of inches thick, but she manages to stuff it in the backpack. Now in a hurry and not wanting to waste any more time in the condo she moves toward the door. The sharp click of a keycard freezes her halfway down the hallway, another click as it's swiped again. Jessie sets the pack against the wall and slowly draws the 45, barely breathing, watching the door in front of her.

    Her training kicking in she brings the pistol up, hoping whoever is trying to unlock the door will give up, but she knows that isn't going to happen. She can hear garbled conversation - clearly not English, indicating at least two people are outside, at the same time the metal lock plate begins to bubble. *Shit* she thinks, *they must have one of the handheld CO2 laser units* she has heard about, *damn things look like a mini light saber and can silently cut through a lock in under a minute*. She retreats further down the short hall, the inky black of the apartment her best protection now. When the door opened whoever was there would be silhouetted in the hall light for at least a few moments while their eyes adjusted to the darkness, it wasn't much but she didn't need much. Time slows down as the door pops, she is in the classical military pistol fighting stance; legs shoulder width apart, firing side slightly back, knees bent. The four quick coughs of the suppressed 45 are almost simultaneous as the two men crumple in the doorway. *Please don't let them be wearing body armor* she thinks, moving forward to check, gun at the ready as the smell of spent gunpowder fills the hall. She considers dragging them inside but with the door lock disabled there isn't going to be any hiding this, so checking the hallway she grabs her bag and heads for the stairs, hoping some early rising do-gooder doesn't sound the alarm before she is clear of the area. No point in second guessing things now, but messy is not her style and things have been nothing but messy since Vegas.

Old Favors

Lou had headed into his office at Paradigm having to take care of some issues there, while Jack opted to make some calls from home. They had agreed to reach out to anyone they thought might be helpful and regroup that evening for dinner to share anything that might have turned up.

Lou and Jack were already working their connections at the Agency and FBI before Jessie had cleared Colorado, with the East Coast two hours ahead, the folks they needed were already in their offices. Their peers had left the fieldwork to a generation of younger agents and were now in positions of leadership with much better access to the information they would need. It was just a matter of finding someone that one wouldn't mind sharing a bit, they both knew better than to expect any real clarity as old friendships could only take you so far and the government, particularly the Agency, was notoriously close-mouthed about intel and ongoing operations.

Their first real break came early and from an unexpected direction, Lou on a whim had reached out to Jimmy Pascalerio at the FBI, Jimmy had been working with him on an encryption cracking project with Homeland Security that would let them passively monitor the newest generation of SAT phones being used by the Jihadist groups in the Middle East. Lou had asked him to nose around and see if there were any open investigations on a "Tom Casey".

Forty minutes later Lou's phone had started ringing, "Lou I have a flash dispatch on a Tom Casey, I'm sending the packet now..." agent Pascalerio said, "it's not much but it's the best I can do under the circumstances, hope it helps... and you did not get this from me."

Lou didn't even have a chance to thank the agent on the other end as his phone began vibrating indicating the data packet's arrival. He hadn't really expected to turn anything up this quick. Suppressing his desire to open it up right away, he punches in Jack's number listening absently as the random series of clicks indicate the syncing of the encryption algorithms, he knows a hit on Tom Casey this quickly isn't going to be a positive no matter what's in the dispatch.

"Hey Jack, got a hit from a buddy at the FBI, I'm heading over now so we can look at it together, thinking about grabbing some 'cue at KT's, you want?"

"Sounds good, no luck on my end yet, get some brisket and slaw, oh, and a tea, will you?" Jack had a sweet tea habit he couldn't seem to break and KT's had the best in town.

"No problem my friend, see you in a bit..."

They had killed the deeply smoked meat and sweet slaw, the foam containers now pushed to the side of the table, Jack was sipping his tea trying to make it last. Lou had transferred the data packet containing the flash dispatch to his laptop and "unpacked" it. There were two folders labeled: "Tom Casey" and "Associates". Jack looks at Lou for a second then motions to the "Tom Casey" folder, "well, might as well have a look see I guess..."

Lou double clicks on the icon bringing up a series of twenty-three documents, the first one is labeled "profile", the others are just dates. "Here we go..." he says as he double clicks on the profile file. The first two pages are a series of black and white obviously surveillance photos, but there is no question, it's Jessie's Tom but they don't recognize any of the others, but they look pretty unsavory. They read the rest of the report together, it's broken into three sections: Demographics – Background – Operations. The demographics covers family history, aliases, education, known addresses and employment history.

Jack lets out a low whistle... "Motherfucker, this guy's a real piece of shit Lou..."

"Not anymore Jack, not anymore," Lou shakes his head thinking about Jessie and wondering how she is going to handle this. The short version is that Tom was a key US operative for one of the largest international human trafficking cartels the FBI had ever uncovered. According to the notes he had been "burned" about six months earlier in Chicago trying to move some girls to a strip club owner the FBI had turned. Hoping to save his ass he had been feeding the FBI a steady diet of intel ever since, but it didn't make him any less a piece shit, but it probably explained the hit in Vegas.

Lou clicks on the "Associates" folder, "Okay, let's see if we know any of these low-life bastards..." the anger is simmering just below the surface and Jack can see clearly enough the pain in his old friend's eyes. Together they scroll through the profile pages all formatted the same with a picture and brief bio, a veritable roster of Eastern European ex-military even so they don't recognize any of the "soldiers", the second to last one labeled simply "Sampson" only had a few long-range photos but the man's long braid was visible in all of them. His bio was short but emphasized his propensity for dispensing death with his bare hands. "Jesus..." Lou exclaims, "This guy is a regular angel of death..."

As they reach the last page they both simultaneously exclaim, "no shit!" It's a name they recognize from the past, Alexi Sokolov, probably the most violent and brutal Ukrainian mobster of them all. They had run into Alexi in the nineties when he was just beginning to consolidate his power base in Odessa, he had been funneling Soviet era weapons to anyone willing to pay cash for them.

"Should have killed that son of a bitch when I had the chance," Jack exclaims. "Christ, I can't believe nobody's gotten to him..." he stands up stretching, they had been reading for a few hours and the day had stretched to late afternoon, "I need a scotch, want one?"

Lou still staring at the screen a bit distracted, "yeah I guess, you know Jack…"

"Yeah buddy I know, nothing good going to come out of this…"

Sokolov

Port Odessa - 1994 3:37AM - the cargo ship Singkao, lights blazing, the huge diesels humming deep in the hull, prepares to get underway. The docks are empty by design as three tractor-trailers pull up. The cranes are already moving as the air brakes hiss and the truck drivers jump down from the cabs. The containers are loaded and secured in less than thirty minutes as the hum of ship's diesels increase in pitch and the trucks disappear the way they arrived.

Alexi Sokolov, his black eyes blazing, passes the envelope of rubber banded cash to the captain, the few men he trusts wait on the dock, weapons at the ready if anyone should unexpectedly show up as he and the captain, his cousin Nikolai, exchange a final embrace. Alexi turns without a second look and bounds down the gangplank heading for the long black BMW waiting for him. The containers are packed with pirated Soviet Red Army weapons: AK 47s, AGS-17 grenade launchers, and a full container of rounds bound for the genocidal wars of Central Africa. This deal, the first of many, will launch Alexi's march to the top of the Eastern European crime syndicates and ultimately enable him to become one of the most powerful crime lords in modern history. Tonight however, he is a bundle of nerves, adrenaline, and ambition and won't sleep until his cousin confirms delivery.

The motor drive on the camera quietly whirs as Lou reels off another twenty shots of Sokolov working his way down the gangplank. He was planted in one of the towering crane cabs one berth over from the Singkao praying he couldn't be seen from the dock while his partner Jack was hidden among the containers stacked on the dock waiting for the next cargo ship to arrive.

The Agency had been tracking chatter on upcoming weapon shipments into the Mid-East and Africa for the past six months, but no one had been able to give them any hard intel until now. The Russian Army officer that had sold Sokolov the weapons was also a double agent for the Agency and didn't have any qualms about taking money from both sides. He had tipped his local contact that a shipment was leaving that night. Lou and Jack were the closest team and had only arrived a couple hours earlier hoping they would have time to find a place to hole up and wait. It had been Jack's idea for Lou to climb into the cab while he kept watch down below. If Lou had more time to think it through he probably wouldn't have agreed but here he was snapping pics of what was an obvious unscheduled delivery of some kind.

Unfortunately, no one had heard of Alexi Sokolov yet and the agency had opted to continue to watch and track the shipment rather than take any action. Arming warring tribes in

Africa, although clearly a violation of international law and a number of United Nations statutes, didn't warrant any overt action from the United States, for now public displays of political outrage would be more than enough to appease an apathetic American public.

The Sokolov kingdom was being built on Soviet weapons and extreme violence: Alexi played no favorites, his clients ranged from Middle Eastern terror cells, South American narco-terrorists, Mexican drug cartels, as well as anyone else with a taste for blood and enough cash to pay. It wasn't just the weapons though, cross Alexi and his men would publicly and grotesquely make an example of you, as a certain Russian Army Officer would later learn. His appetite for money, power, woman, and blood seemed insatiable, but tonight he was small time player and had not drawn the full attention of those that should have been watching more closely.

As the ship lumbered away from the dock churning the black waters behind it, Lou clambers down the steel ladder where Jack is waiting pistol still out. "I can't believe I let you talk me into climbing up there..."

Jack laughs, "yeah, well, I had your back, no worries my friend..."

They make their way carefully through the stacks of containers to the break in the fencing they had cut earlier. Jack doesn't relax until they are out the gates and making their way through the dark streets of Odessa to an Agency safe house. Jack turns to Lou, "I hate this watching shit, they should let us take this scum out..."

Lou smiles in the dark, his partner is singular in his solutions to most every problem, "doesn't work like that partner, you know that... we watch, report, watch some more, and somebody smart enough not to be out here decides what we can do..."

"Smarter my ass, mark my words that dude is bad news! You saw him, he had that hyped up crusader look about him, that fucker is going to be a problem sooner or later and my bet is sooner." Neither had any idea how truly prophetic those words would turn out to be.

Lou just nodded, this was a running conversation with Jack, and if you were on the other side a permanent solution was the only prescription he agreed with. They were so different Lou thought, but he trusted Jack implicitly and wouldn't have wanted anyone else as a partner, they were opposites but it worked for them.

Alexi and his men had already made their way back to the "Twenty-One" club, one of the high-end strip clubs that had been popping up in Odessa – the girls imported from small Russian towns were pretty enough even if they wore painted on masks of false emotions in an attempt at self-preservation. Alexi had made this club his un-official headquarters and it wouldn't be long before he owned the building and managed his growing empire from the floors directly above. But tonight, he drank his vodka, a young girl on each side and dreamed a future of bloody conquests.

Mr. A's

Jessie takes the steps two at a time, in a hurry to clear the building and gain the anonymity of a morning commuter train. She gains the ground floor, sensing the shadow at the last second but it's moving too quickly for her to get out of the way. She hits the double doors as he knocks her down from behind, she doesn't even have time to pull the 45 as the concrete rises up to greet her. Most of the impact is broken by the backpack and she can hear the laptop and scan device cracking as her shoulder goes numb. Things are moving too fast at this point and she doesn't stop but continues to roll trying to stay out from under him, but he is as fast as he is huge, she tumbles off the loading dock finally pulling the pistol free and bringing it up in front of her.

Todd Gildon and Trevor Johnson had been running Truck Nine for Floyd Brothers Waste Management for the past eight years and both liked to get an early start on the day as there wasn't too many things worse than navigating Chicago traffic with a menagerie of putrid smells permeating the cab – there were just some things no amount of Vicks rub under the nose would fix. North Harbor Tower was always the first stop, Todd swings the big truck around the back heading for the double dumpsters at the rear entrance, the sharp hiss of the air brakes brings the truck up short throwing Trevor into the dash and dumping both cups of Dunkin' coffee on the floor. The headlights illuminate the dock as the young woman in black, still on her back; fires two shots into the chest of a linebacker looking suit as he is jumping off the loading dock just a few feet in front of her. The men look at each other for a moment – neither can quite believe what had just gone down in front of them... She is already up and running before either can react, the gun pointed square at them, her eyes daring them to move, neither of the men do, each silently praying as she makes the hedge along the drive and disappears. Todd puts the truck in reverse without a word and starts to back out of the drive.

Trevor looks over at him, "Dude, what the fuck?"

Todd doesn't answer for a moment, "listen man, we can go back if you want, but I don't need any shit like this in my life... I did my time and believe me what we don't know is way better for both of us..."

Trevor nods, "okay buddy your call, just hope nobody saw us..." he hesitates, "I didn't even hear no shots, did you?"

"I didn't hear nuthin' and I didn't see nuthin' and neither did you – period, end of story – got it?"

"Yeah, yeah, I got it, but..."

"Listen Trev... no buts man, better to stay clear of whatever the fuck that was all about..."

Fact was, Todd was scared, and not just a little scared, he knew a professional kill when he saw it, and no way that chic had missed their faces or the huge FLOYD on the side of the green garbage truck. Last thing he wanted was waking up to some psycho bitch killer pointing a gun at his head. Trevor had never been "inside" but Todd had done enough time to know there were some seriously bad folks out there and it was always best to just steer clear – wasn't none of us his business, but he wasn't going to forget looking down the barrel of that 45 in her hand steady as you please any time soon either.

Jessie made the jog to Ogilve station in under ten minutes, her shoulder settling into a steady throb, she didn't think it was dislocated but it was definitely stiffening up and hurt like a bitch, luckily the backpack had broken most of the impact. The trip out to Arlington Heights takes a little over an hour, she sits in the last car watching folks come and go, the jacket pulled tight around her, praying she can make it to the Jeep without anything else going wrong. She replays it all in her ahead for the umpteenth time, once again her training kicks in and she examines it all with a clinical objectiveness. She had made a critical error in judgment, should have expected the exits to be covered – *fuck, that was an amateur mistake*, she thinks. Fact was, she had been lucky; the garbage truck had distracted him just long enough for her to get two rounds off, but three bodies in one night, this was getting out of control. If that wasn't enough she still had no real answers as to what the hell this was all about. She had taken four of these guys down, if she wasn't a target before she sure as hell would be now.

She made it back without further incident, threw the backpack in the passenger seat and drove away from the station without a second look. Less than a mile later Jessie starts to shake, the adrenaline finally bleeding off, she pulls into a small strip of single story businesses. In the middle is Mr. Allison's Restaurant, 'Mr. A's' to the neighborhood locals that frequent the breakfast spot. She grabs the backpack and heads inside where the fifty something waitress greets her with a cackle, "grab a seat honey... anywhere is good!"

"Thanks..." Jessie mumbles and takes a seat in the booth all the way in the back. She sits with her back to the wall facing the floor to ceiling windows across the front, trying not to draw any attention to herself, a most unlikely undertaking.

"Okay sweetie, need a menu?" the waitress asks as she sets down a water and silver ware.

"Uhh yeah, I guess, thanks..." she tries to smile, "oh, and a coffee please, with some cream..."

"Sure honey, I'm Shirley, you just look that over and I'll be right back with that coffee."

Jessie orders the ham and cheese omelet with rye toast and home fries. Shirley had just smiled at her shaking her head. Jessie didn't get it until the platter showed up with a huge pile of thick cut ham draped by a paper-thin covering of eggs, enough potatoes for two people and two slices of seeded rye toasted golden brown, with huge pats of butter melting between them. It was a feast and just what Jessie needed to settle herself and recharge after the insanity of the past eight hours. Shirley had just whistled claiming she had construction workers that couldn't finish that off. Jessie had grinned sheepishly and gladly accepted a to-go coffee for the road.

    She had headed out with a wave and picked up one of the many county roads north, her plan was to find an out-of-the-way place somewhere just across the border in Wisconsin where she could grab some shut eye and examine the box in that order. First things first though, she needed to call her dad and let him know she was okay.

The Box

The call to her father had been brief, he had updated her on what they had found leaving out most of the details but using a broad brush to paint a picture of Tom as an FBI informant for an organized crime syndicate in the Ukraine. She hadn't seemed too surprised and he figured the details would wait. She told him about the box and left out most of the details on the "trouble" she had run into. Both knew the other was holding back but it would wait till they were together again. Her plan was to take Route 14 west into Wisconsin picking up I90 on the Minnesota border. She wanted to take a roundabout route back to Colorado and there were a thousand small towns in Wisconsin where she could lay up and catch some sleep, and examine the box. Lou wanted her home but didn't argue the point, she wasn't an amateur and he trusted her judgment.

She found a roadside motel just south of Madison, the faded green and yellow paint peeling and the gravel parking lot devoid of any other vehicles. The sign simply stated, 'Roadside Motel' as if any other name would speak to a pomposity unnecessary here in heart of Wisconsin farm country. The vacancy light flashed through the grimy windows in the small office set off to the left of the six cabin-like rooms. She paid the forty dollars in cash, the old fella handing her the keys to number four without a word and she just nodded on her way out the door. There was no hiding her vehicle, but she backed into the slot in front of number six hoping if she had been followed it would give her a few moments head start.

The room smelled stale and had the faint odor of bug spray, she wasn't sure if that was a good thing or not. She dropped the backpack on the bed and extracted the thin metal box she had killed three men earlier in the day for. She pushes the button on the side and the soft click echoes in the quiet room as she looks around once more before pushing open the top. Not much to see, two passports, five stacks of hundreds with the "$10,000" bands still intact and two thumb drives. She sets the cash on the bed and opens the first passport, it had been issued in the Ukraine to Vitaliy Borodkin but the picture was Tom. She opened the other, a Canadian passport issued to Dennis Mason; clearly Tom had any number of names, she briefly wondered if Tom was even his actual name. She stuffed the cash in the backpack with the passports and the thumb drives, leaving the metal box on the bed. With the laptop smashed in the fall the drives would have to wait till she got back to Colorado.

The sun was low in the western sky peaking around the edges of the dirty grey curtains and spreading long shadows in the small room. Jessie stretches, pulling herself up from behind the bed where she has been sleeping fitfully, dark dreams of the past twenty-four hours plaguing her. She pops four Motrin hoping to dim the throbbing pain in her shoulder. *What a fucking mess*, she thinks again. The two garbage guys worried her a bit, but no way she could have lived with taking them out, it would be what it would be. She hoped they would just mind their own business... wishful thinking probably but not much she could do about it now.

With the backpack on her shoulder she looks out on the parking lot, careful not to touch the curtains, knowing even the slightest movement would draw attention, giving away her position. The place is empty, she can see the sputtering vacancy sign behind the grimy office windows, a lone fluorescent light shines through the slats of the blinds. She leaves the key on the bed, not bothering to lock the door as the sun fades and twilight sets in.

Jessie picks up a couple of burgers and a chocolate shake at a Culvers just outside of Madison before heading down Route 151 towards Iowa City, her plan was to stay off the main roads that far, then pick up I80 and head straight West. The freshly planted farmland of southern Wisconsin and Iowa stretched for miles on either side of the road before giving way to the seemingly endless plains of Nebraska, as the minutes turned into hours she attempts to keep her thoughts from wandering. However, things were just not adding up, Tom or whatever his name was had been mixed up in something much more serious than she had originally thought. These guys were either relentless or she had run into an epic string of bad luck. With four dead behind her she knew the body count was going to be an issue, you couldn't just take out four people, even if they were thugs, and expect no one to notice. There are plenty of questions, but no answers in the dark as the white lines run together and the sky begins to brighten behind her.

    Early that morning she made the turn on to I76 at the Colorado border. She had gassed up, grabbed a large black coffee and two breakfast taquitos in their paper wrapping at the Flying J Travel Plaza outside of Big Springs thirty minutes earlier. She preferred the big truck stops, there was a subculture that looked out for each other but also knew when to mind its own business. It didn't hurt that you could buy just about anything you needed, including a hot shower if you desired.

    That many of the truck stops were cash generators earned on the backs of young prostitutes exploited by people like Sokolov and his ilk didn't occur to her, nor would it have had the significance another four hours was going to create. She was almost home and soon she would be able to let her breath out and relax, even if just a little, popping another four Motrin and washing them down with the tepid black coffee, she scans the highway for the trouble she knows is there lurking just beyond her view.

Far from Home

The girls had been zip tied and blindfolded for the duration of the eighteen-hour trip, there were three of them now, and the last had been brought to the warehouse late the previous night. The only stops had been for fuel and a couple of out of the way bathroom breaks. The restraints were an unnecessary precaution as the drugs had rendered them unable to function and their glassy eyed stares confirmed their inability to offer any resistance. The van was a standard white work van with no windows it was so cliché no one noticed it. "24 Hour PC Repair" was stenciled on the side along with an eight hundred number that rang a pre-recorded message monitored by a computer in a non-descript building in Brighton Beach New York. Sokolov's group had been running this particular delivery corridor for almost ten years, every stop was a pre-planned location controlled by Sokolov. There had never been an incident and this time would be no different.

Jessie had just been pulling into the Flying J as the van, eight states east of her, pulled through the gates of the Republic Airport in Farmingdale, NY and up to the private hangar. The G650 jet was already fueled and warmed up waiting to take them on the final leg of their journey and a future none of the three girls could have imagined only days earlier.

The flight would take just under twelve hours during which the girls would undergo a complete makeover. Sokolov always delivered quality products in top condition, it was part of what let him charge so much. The jet had specially configured for just this type of transport with an onboard shower and all the accessories of a mainstream salon. The prep team had followed the same routine for hundreds of girls, with a quick shot of Narcan to counteract the pink and wake them up. The girls would be stripped, washed, shaved, manicured, receive haircuts, and dressed in designer club wear before the jet touched down. The operation operated with immaculate precision, Sokolov didn't tolerate mistakes or subpar work, no one on any of his teams wanted a visit from Sampson, or God forbid, Sokolov himself.

Pump Station Three was fifty miles east of Riyadh, one in a string of massive pumps moving oil from the fields in the East to the ports in the West. Every pump station had an airstrip built adjacent to the control buildings and equipment, the strip was long enough to handle even a midsize commercial jet as they were used to ferry engineers, technicians and the occasional oil executive from station to station. The strip was owned by ARAMCO, but like everything else in the country it was simply the business face of the Saudi Royal Family. In the case of Pump Three's airfield, it served double duty with a certain "prince's" periodic deliveries so the touchdown of the G650 didn't raise any red flags. They had even cleared Saudi airspace after identifying themselves to the Saudi Air Command out of Prince Sultan Air Base. Palms having been greased well in advance of every delivery so they had never had an issue.

The routine was the same with every set of girls that that were brought in a blacked-out Mercedes which would be waiting when the jet touched down. The girls would be hustled into the vehicle and the jet would be wheels up after refueling in less than thirty minutes.

The Middle East and the Saudis in particular were a perfect market for Sokolov, the large royal family had members on both ends of the extreme spectrum; there were the corrupt worshippers of western women, drugs, liquor, and Italian sports cars and those with the fervent fires of radical Islamic fundamentalism burning bright. All supported by a ruling middle faction that accepted the dalliances of its brethren without so much as a second thought. Sokolov didn't care how they wanted to fuck Americans... in the bedroom or screaming Allah Akbar with an AK and C4 vest as long as they paid his price it mattered not to him. He was happy to supply any and all of their particular needs.

The Mercedes sped away from the airfield heading west back toward Riyadh and one of the mini palaces inhabited by a "prince". With fifteen thousand members in the royal family "prince" didn't really carry the weight one might think but it was enough. There were substantial benefits even if you were only a third cousin to the Crown Prince, one of which was access to the airstrip at Pump Station Three and the ability to afford and indulge a taste for young American girls on a regular basis.

The ride to the palatial estate would take little more than forty minutes with the girls completely disoriented and still trying to recover from the drugs and the jet lag, wouldn't remember it.

The prince's residence, offices, and the family common areas are arranged over two stories on the right side of the complex. The left side houses the kitchens, laundries, the hired help's quarters and a very plush guest suite. Suite doesn't begin to describe the six bedrooms, four bathrooms, two fully equipped offices, gym, entertainment room, and common area. The fleet of working vehicles was also housed on this side of the complex. The prince had a private garage on the right side where his sports cars were kept. Directly out the back the Olympic size swimming pool and four tennis courts could be accessed from either wing. The prince didn't play tennis but it was another symbol of his status and wealth.

The Mercedes pulls into the garage on the left side of the complex and the three girls are ushered into the guest suite, it doubles as the prince's "pleasure parlor" when the urge strikes him.

Allie looks around, not sure what to think. She still isn't clear what has happened to her, but thinks that this is a significant upgrade from the warehouse they were held prisoner in two days ago, or was it three, time had begun to slip away from her. She attempts to talk to the other girls, but they have curled up on two of the three beds and are unresponsive, leaving them there she explores the suite looking for a phone or if possible a way out, God she wishes she was home.

Brighton Beach

Sokolov, through one of his many shell corporations had purchased the penthouse overlooking the Atlantic in the Oceana Condo complex for nine million dollars in 2019 and after a year of renovations, mostly security focused, he had set up his US operations there. It was his home away from home, the neighborhood allowed him and his soldiers to indulge their ethnic tastes and the mostly Russian community knew through long experience with his kind to look the other way and steer clear. Sokolov got what Sokolov wanted period end of discussion. The U.S. market for trafficking had been fragmented split between the Latin gangs and the Italian families, neither having the power or organizational infrastructure Sokolov did. He had rolled up the strip clubs, prostitution, and pornography operations in less than eighteen months. Sure, it had been bloody and expensive but once things had settled down the gangs and families had lined up behind him and the profits started rolling in, he knew then it had all been worth it.

Alexi sits behind the oversize hand carved mahogany desk charcoal pinstripe suit perfectly pressed the lavender tie slightly askew, he could have been a corporate CEO in any boardroom in America, except for the twin stainless 9MM pistols on the desk and the two topless girls in thongs and garters lounging on the couch to the left. Alexi was no longer a young man, but he still liked his women, quiet, undressed, and subservient.

It's only mid-morning but his frustration is already peaking. There are two of his bodyguards standing by the double doors trying to appear disinterested while the red-haired giant known only as Sampson sits across the desk from Alexi. Sampson is Alexi's right hand, he had grown up an orphan on the streets of Odessa his Jewish great grandparents and their two young children had escaped Warsaw in the months leading up to German occupation in World War II fleeing as far as Odessa before the coming war had overtaken them. The rest of his story was murky at best and no one really knew if any of it was true, but he had met Alexi when he had been just a teenager, the young crime lord was already consolidating his power and had taken him under his wing and they had been inseparable ever since. Like the Jewish legend he wore his hair long in a single braid down past his shoulders and the number of men he had killed with just his hands was a matter of legend.

"Did we get that shipment out to that ass the Prince?"

Sampson nods, "they went out on the jet this morning," looking at his watch, "should be there in about eight hours. The client will take delivery at the airfield... our people will refuel and head home same as always."

"Okay, that's fine, I don't want us on the ground there any longer than necessary. His money is good but this shit with

Tom and the fucking FBI I'm beginning to think it's no longer worth the risk." Motioning Sampson in closer and lowering his voice he asks, "what did they find in Chicago...?" his fingers absently drumming the desk.

"No word yet," Sampson answers "should be calling in any time now, they were going in last night."

"What's the story on this girl? You think she's the one that took Tomifev out in Vegas?"

"I don't know Alexi, she's ex US Army Ranger... so military trained..." Sampson trails off, he isn't accustomed to not having answers.

"Well, where the fuck is she now?" Alexi is obviously angry as he stands and moves toward the windows looking out at the bay and the Atlantic beyond that. "Sampson, I can't have someone taking down our people... especially not some fucking woman!" his voice rising as he turns. "So, send someone that knows how to handle it and bring the bitch back here..." sitting back down, "I want her alive, is that clear, I want to deal with her myself."

Sampson just nods, they have been together long enough that a response isn't required. He motions to the two by the door to follow him as the brunette is already kneeling in front of Sokolov as the door quietly closes.

Sampson doesn't bother to call the men he sent to Chicago, if they were still alive they would have already checked in, nobody deviated in Sokolov's world, it was the quickest way to wake up dead. His phone was untraceable, but he would replace it anyway the Sokolov operation was as high-tech and as careful as it was brutal. Sampson walks briskly through the condo courtyards toward 12th Street, he stops at La Brioche for a cardboard cup of coffee and a sweet roll before heading around the corner to the electronics store that serves as a front for the organization's tech center. He doesn't bother to use the entrance in the alley nor does he acknowledge the young man serving as today's clerk as he passes into the back room, pausing at the steel door he submits to the retinal scan, waiting for the telltale click as the locks release before pushing into the back room.

The room is cool, almost cold, along the left side is a bank of computers with high definition screens. Six women with headsets are busy taking calls and typing into their computers, it could pass for any high volume online ordering center. The right side of the room is lined with workbenches where technicians are busy with phones, computers, and a myriad of other electronic devices. Sampson walks silently through the center aisle ignoring all of it and pushes into the glass lined room at the back. It is the nerve center of Sokolov's US operations, it's here the organization processes surveillance footage, initiates system hacks, maintains its thousands of websites and manages the profiles of all the "assets" in its portfolio. Sokolov still dabbled in weapons but the real money was now made in online pornography and human trafficking.

They called it trafficking but it was slavery, simply as it had always been throughout human history. It didn't bother him though the money was good and his people had been slaves more times than most. The forced servitude and sexual exploitation of woman and in most cases, underage girls - prostitution, sexual slavery, and pornography had surpassed black market arms and drawn even with illegal drugs in late 2016. The traffic as it was called had reached well over fifty billion dollars a year and Sokolov was enjoying the biggest slice. They controlled everything from the twenty-dollar trailer hookers in communities all over the U.S. to the high priced underage girls demanded by their obscenely wealthy clients and of course everything in between. If you could dream it you could buy it and Sokolov was more than willing to sell it to you.

Sampson looks around at the young men manning the computers, they could have been in any Silicon Valley startup's command center he thinks, but these men all owed Alexi something and were well paid for their loyalty. "The Spider", few people knew his real name, managed the "web" of technology for Alexi. Looking up he sees Sampson and motions for him to come over.

"Sampson!" he shakes the big man's hand, "what brings you to my little shop of horrors?"

With a grunt, "I need a new phone... and Alexi wants you to help track down this girl." Sampson hands over a picture of Jessie, her name; social security number and phone number are printed on the back.

"Is she one of ours...?" The Spider asks spinning his chair back to the keyboard and screen behind him.

"No, no just someone he wants found... and keep it quiet, when you have something call nobody but me..."

"Will do, uh, what she do?" He asks raising an eyebrow.

"It doesn't matter, and see if you can pull her military record also, she was US Army, Rangers, I need everything you can find on her."

"Ahhh, this should be interesting... take any one of those phones over there." He points to a table, "they're all clean."

"Thanks..." Sampson mutters, "and no one but me got it?"

"Yeah, yeah, I got it, now get out of here, you make my boys nervous, and Sampson, you and your men really should use the back door."

Tom Casey

They had decided to meet at the Paradigm offices, which were as secure as any military facility in the country, a byproduct of the government contracts and the need to protect access to the technology they were developing. The gates were manned twenty-four hours a day and were constructed to withstand almost any attempt at forced entry. A series of infrared and high definition cameras covered the grounds and fed into both the security command center as well as an offsite monitoring facility. Big Lou wasn't leaving anything to chance from a security standpoint. Once inside employees and guests would have to present a keycard and submit to a voice recognition scan to enter beyond the lobby of the building. Of course, Jesse had full access to the executive suites, but even she would have needed a security clearance to enter the development labs.

Her dad and Jack had been waiting for her in his office when she had finally pulled in late that morning. Lou had sandwiches, chips, and tea sent up from the onsite cafe used by the employees. It was as much a convenience as a continuation of the secure environment he had created, it didn't hurt that the food was excellent and fresh, created by a classically trained chef. Two tuna salad sandwiches on fresh baked whole wheat and a bag of jalapeno chips later Jesse was sucking on her tea straw and feeling much better. Jack just shook his head, "your girl can put some food away Lou..."

Lou just smiles, "cost me a fortune growing up!"

"Hmmph, I work harder than you two old men... leave me alone..."

"The brashness of youth..." Jack says, "Now tell us what happened in Chicago, your dad says you retrieved some things and ran into a bit of trouble?"

She hesitates for a moment before relating the details of her trip to the condo, she doesn't leave anything out knowing her dad and Jack can only help her if they know everything. "So, the shoulder hurts like a bitch to say the least..."

Jack lets out a low whistle, "well, I'm glad I gave you the 45." Shaking his head, "not quite sure I agree with letting the two sanitation guys go, but I see your point on that, no reason they should pay the price for these assholes."

Lou just hangs his head, "Jess, I'm sorry honey, this is getting too dangerous, we really need to figure this out." He holds out his hand, "let's see this thumb drive then we can show you what the Bureau sent over..." her dad says, reaching for the backpack. "Then you are going over to Dr. Simpson so he can look at that shoulder..."

Simpson owned High Country Orthopedics, had been a family friend for years and could be counted on for not only his expertise, but he understood all about the need for discretion as

109

well. Of course, it didn't hurt that he had his own MRI in house and could perform just about any diagnostic test you could think of.

"It's alright dad, just a bruise, I'll be fine..." Jesse says rubbing the shoulder and trying to pretend like it's not on fire.

Her dad gives her that look... then I know you're full of shit look... "Uh, I don't think so... we are getting it checked out anyway." His tone makes it clear there won't be any argument about it as he pops the thumb drive into his laptop.

"Listen Dad, I don't like this anymore than you do, but I am not ready to pack it in and pretend something isn't going on here." She bites her lip, "I'm certainly not happy about having to shoot those people, but it was them or me, I'm not going to lose any sleep over it." She knows this comes out harsher than she intended but the more she thought about it the angrier it made her. People were trying to kill her, what was she supposed to do, let them?

Jack looks over at Lou, "you know she's right my friend..."

"Dammit, I know Jack, I just don't like it..." he trails off. He has hooked the laptop display to the fifty-inch high definition screen mounted on the wall next to the small conference table to the left of his desk. "Let's take a look at this then we can talk about what to do next."

Both Jack and Jessie let it go as he begins tapping a few keys and brings up the drive's file listing organizing it by type and title. Surprisingly, it's not encrypted, not even a password, Tom was either not concerned with security or knew if someone had the drive it no longer mattered. There are two folders, the first is labeled "TRANSACTIONS" and the second "REPORTS". Lou chooses the first one; it opens up to twenty-four individual documents using a simple date naming convention. The oldest one is dated three years earlier and fills the screen as Lou clicks on it.

"Dad? What the fuck is this?" Jesse exclaims, looking at the screen in disbelief.

"I'm sorry honey, no easy way to say this but Tom was brokering... well... it's human trafficking Jess..." the phrase hangs in the air as Lou and Jack give each other a glance, neither wanting to say anything more.

"That son of a bitch... I should have killed him myself..." she half says to herself. She turns back to the screen looking at the black and white photo of the young girl. The transaction details listed below the picture include her age, measurements, location, and price, but no name and maybe more importantly it didn't include the buyer either. "Jesus, open another one..." she demands.

"Jess, are you sure you want to do this, isn't one enough?" her dad asks.

"Just do it dad..." her hands clenched into fists, "that motherfucker..."

The second file opens showing three teenage girls and the transaction information for each of them.

Jessie slumps in her chair, tears in her eyes, "I just can't believe this... they're just, just little girls?"

Lou slides his chair next to her, "I know honey, I know..." There really isn't anything else to say as they all sit quietly, the three faces on the screen seem to be waiting for something more. Jesse wasn't naive to the inherent evil in the world or even the enslavement of human beings, but to have them staring back at her from the screen made it personal, made it somehow different. It didn't help that she had been sleeping with the perpetrator of this evil, a wave of nausea sweeps over her just thinking about it.

"Jess, you okay?" Jack asks softly.

Her dad had moved to the window, he turns back toward the table grim faced. "We need to get all this to the FBI, maybe they can track down some of these kids."

"Ok, fine, but it's not enough Dad..." she says, turning to look at the two men. "It's not fucking enough..."

"I understand you're upset Jess but..." he doesn't get a chance to finish.

"Upset?" she points to the screen, "that bastard did four deals while I was with him... I can't, I won't let that stand." She is shaking with rage now, "I should have known, Dad I should have known..."

The Feds

They had looked through the rest of the files on Tom's drive. The sheer horror of men selling these young women was overwhelming but they felt compelled to review them all. Almost as if they needed to acknowledge the full evil of the crimes perpetrated on these girls, so that by bearing witness they were in some way honoring the memory of each one.

"Alright Jimmy, I'll let you know if we come up with anything else... no, no, really can't disclose the source on this... sure keep in touch." Lou hangs the phone up and looks across the desk at his daughter and Jack knowing full well the FBI agent hadn't believed much if any of his explanation. He felt bad not being able to be more open with the agent, he had operated in good faith sending the Lou the file to start with, but the safety and wellbeing of his daughter trumped any fair play with the FBI. "Well, you heard, he didn't press me, but he wasn't buying my story either," he says shaking his head. "We have better data than they do and it's only a matter of time before they decide they have to know where we got it."

"Should I just turn myself in dad?" Jessie asks softly. "They may not have connected Chicago yet, but that won't last, especially if they were already working Tom." She turns to Jack, "this won't come back on you because of your pistol, will it?"

"First off young lady if the FBI wanted you in custody it would have happened already, and don't worry, that pistol isn't going to show up on any record anywhere," Jack assures her. "Now that you mention it though not sure why they are holding off, but someone pretty high up must have made the call... hmmm, I wonder," he says mostly to himself.

"Jack?"

"What?" He looks up at Lou's questioning tone, "Oh well, this isn't going to sound right, and sorry for that, but I wonder if they've left Jess on the outside trying to draw Sokolov and his boys out? I mean, think about it, we've seen the file on Tom, it's pretty thin in my opinion, certainly not enough to build an ironclad case against Sokolov."

"Well, that's a pretty big gamble to be playing with someone's life..." Lou says angrily.

"Sure, I agree and certainly not by the book, but Lou she has taken four of them out already, they have to know that Sokolov isn't going to sit still for that," Jack says with just a hint of pride in his voice. Lou just gives him a look, Jack may be retired, but he is still a stone-cold operator and Lou isn't quite sure how he feels about Jessie starting to display a comparable skill set.

"Other than the Vegas shooting we aren't even sure if the FBI has connected Jessie to any of this, and that was clearly a self-defense shooting..." Lou trails off knowing it won't take very long for the Feds to put it all together, if they haven't already.

"Well, that plays both ways then...," Jessie says. "What I mean is if they are going to leave me out here, then I am not going to sit still and be a target for anyone. Let's roll these bastards up." She is angry again and isn't bothering to hide it.

"Jess you can't just go around..." Lou hesitates thinking about where this is going. It's a little late for recriminations he realizes, and he knows his daughter well enough to know she didn't take a life easily or needlessly. "Listen, we have been lucky so far, don't get worked up Jess. I am not questioning your skills but seriously these aren't a bunch of amateurs... Jack, tell her!" Lou says, turning to his old friend, not sure there is any real support there.

Jack shrugs and holding his hands out, "Lou I don't know what's the right answer here, I wouldn't put her in danger any more than you would, but they are coming and you know it, not much we can do about it. I don't know, maybe we turn it around on them, either way I don't like sitting still waiting to see what happens."

Jessie stands up looking at the two men seeing the anguish on her dad's face, "look, you two aren't part of this, there's no reason to give them three targets..." She hesitates for a second not quite sure how to say what she means, "what I mean is, I'm the one they want... Dad, you can't risk everything by getting involved in this."

He just looks at her, "Jessie, there is nothing here that means anything to me compared to you, don't you know that by now? I lost the one thing I loved more than life the day you were born and by some miracle I was given you in its place, honestly it's probably the only thing that saved me..." there are tears in his eyes now, "Jessie, without you there is none of this... so we are doing this together."

"I am in too Jess, your dad is the only friend I've ever had and well, this is the only thing I've ever been any good at anyway," Jack says with a wan smile.

She smiles ruefully and wipes her eyes, "well, you two old men better not expect me to carry you..." There are guarded smiles all around, but they all know this is a path there is probably no coming back from.

Captive

Allie could hear the other two girls crying softly in the dark, she hadn't been able to get them to speak to her. Even though the three beds were only separated by a thin curtain, they had ignored her whispers. The suite was more luxurious than anything she had ever seen before, the marble floors covered in Persian rugs, silk tapestries hung on the walls, the bathroom had gleaming gold fixtures and a tub so huge all three girls could have fit in it, but for all the glamour and glitz it was still a prison cell. The locked doors and windows a reminder that their lives were not their own anymore. She had beat on the door when they had first arrived only to have it open quickly followed by a vicious blow to the stomach knocking her to the ground, leaving her gasping for breath and gagging; she hadn't made that mistake again.

The first thirty-six hours had been worse than any nightmare they could have imagined, the man seemed to have an insatiable appetite for the young girls, raping each of them repeatedly, seeming to take as much pleasure in their frightened and painful pleading as the sex itself. As the hours passed it had become more about degradation and domination than satisfying his sexual needs. The girls battered and bruised absorbed his seemingly endless supply of anger and aggression, their young bodies serving as the temporary salve for his affliction. That first night Allie had spent an hour in the shower trying to wash the feeling of him off of her. No amount of soap or hot water seemed to help though and she had finally fallen asleep nursing a swollen lip and the feeling that her insides were on fire.

The prince was the very definition of what psychologists define as a vindictive rapist. They're angry and their actions are about power, domination, and retribution – rape is the weapon of choice but it's not about the sex itself. This prince fit the profile perfectly, he had grown up being abused by his older cousins, raped repeatedly himself, his mother and had turned a blind eye, not wanting to anger her older brother. His self-loathing and shame mixed with his unresolved anger at his mother created a violent cocktail of emotions that he was indulging on a more and more frequent basis. Unfortunately, each episode was proving less and less effective; and although he could afford to import his victims, satisfying his need to punish and his desire for young girls in one macabre transaction, a time was coming when even this would not be enough.

It was usually about a week before he tired of the sleepless nights, the pounding headaches, a side effect of the cocaine driven intermissions, and maybe most of the all the pathetic whining of the girls. He would pay Sokolov to dispose of them, his demons sated for a short time until the anger and shame overwhelmed his self-control again.

It was a perfect system for Sokolov; the girls would be shuttled into one of his low-end Ukrainian whorehouses to service his less prestigious clientele. Most would only last a few years before overdosing or falling prey to a particularly violent client, it didn't matter to Sokolov though he had more than made his investment back and there seemed to be an endless supply of "product".

Of course, none of this mattered or changed the current nightmare for Allie, her existence had been distilled down to pain, fear, and an uncontrollable flee reflex. When she was lucky enough to not be chosen her time in the room was punctuated with fitful naps and a continuous exploration in search of some way out. Her basic survival instincts had taken over and as terrible as it seemed she was relieved every time one of the other girls was led out of the room. She knew the other two girls were broken, their waking hours spent whimpering on their beds, unable to speak or move, but Allie had found a strength that was as exciting as it was unexpected and as she was going to find out quite infuriating to her captor.

He had come for her that next evening, his rage bubbling just under the surface, grabbing her by the hair he ripped the thin nightgown off of her before throwing her to the floor. Her head was on fire where he had pulled a handful of her blond hair out, she knew by now what was coming, his routine was mind numbingly consistent. He would force her to take him in her mouth like he was trying to choke her with it before turning her over and brutally raping her from behind. The pain was almost unbearable and she had become numb to the constant slaps and punches, sometimes wondering if it wouldn't be better to just die.

Something deep inside her wouldn't let her give up though and she had decided she would rather fight back and suffer the consequences than continue to let him abuse her. Maybe it was instinct, or desperation, or just an unwillingness to continue being a victim but she bit down as hard as she could, tasting the coppery blood in her mouth. Immediately her head exploded, his fist breaking her nose with the first blow. His screams of pain mixed with an animal anger rang throughout the marble columns bringing his men running. Blood was running out her nose and a gash had opened above her eye blinding her as she tried to crawl away from the blows and kicks raining down on her. She only made it a few feet her blood streaking the marble floor as everything faded to black and her body succumbed to the incessant beating. He didn't stop his assault until the side of her young face was a pulpy mess; his breath came in ragged gasps as his men pulled him off of her.

They buried her body in the shifting desert sands east of Riyadh, the crystalline particles running into the shallow hole sticking to the still wet blood oozing out of the plastic they had wrapped her ruined body. The two men shoveled silently, neither willing to say anything. The sad story of Allie Chambers had ended in a bloody but brief courageously defiant act half a world away from the fluttering "missing flyers" her mother had tacked to the mailbox posts of a non-descript trailer park in Florida, it was all a sad testament to the brevity of life.

Probabilities

Jessie headed out to Dr. Simpson's as her dad and Jack went into planning mode. She was still trying to wrap her head around him being a CIA operative, but in strange way it explained some things about him that had always been there but never really made sense. The government connections, the strings he always seemed able to pull, never mind the ridiculous world geography knowledge – he was simply impossible to beat at any type of trivia game and although she was an impressive marksman with a pistol he was just as good. No, it all fit, she just couldn't believe she had never put it all together before. Still, it didn't change the fact that he should have told her, even if he had thought he was protecting her.

She knocked on the back entrance of the office. Dr. Simpson himself opened it up giving her a smile, "I can't wait to see what you've done this time young lady!"

"Really not a big deal sir, but you know how my dad is, wants to make sure everything is alright, but I'm okay."

"Well, I'll be the judge of that... let's take a look." He leads her into one of the empty exam rooms where he examines the shoulder which is an impressive collage of colors ranging from purple to green, he didn't bother asking what had happened knowing the answer would be some fantastical story with absolutely no link to reality. "Okay, well you've done quite a number on it, I think we should do a quick MRI just to make sure you didn't tear anything."

"Do we really need to?" Jessie asks as she rotates her arm, "I can move it fine..." but her grimace gives her away.

"Let's do it just to be sure, plus I know your dad's going to ask me if I did one so let's just be sure."

The MRI surprisingly didn't show any permanent damage but the bruising was deep and it was going to take a while to fully heal. "Well, definitely a deep bruise, but you were lucky this time, it's going to be sore for probably a few weeks at least."

"Thank you sir, definitely going to take it easy for a bit..."

He gave her the classic sideways bullshit look, "I am sure you are..." he said, laughing; "now get out here and tell your dad I said hello."

She left with a prescription for painkillers she wouldn't be filling, an admonishment to rest, which she wouldn't be doing either and some stretching exercises, which had a significantly better chance than the others of actually happening.

Paradigm's development group had recently branched out from its core encryption business working on an AI based analytics engine that could consume data from disparate sources including photographs and identify underlying patterns. Then through an examination of historical events and unrelated data sources "teach" itself to provide predictive outcomes of future

123

events. Tech companies, the government and particularly political campaigns had been analyzing big data for years to determine everything from behavioral trends, healthcare trends, and voting tendencies. Focused marketing campaigns had been relying on big data since the late nineties, but no one had made the jump forward yet to focus on predictive outcomes of potential future events. It was ambitious but Lou and his group believed there existed enough underlying consistency and predictability in human behavior combined with the now vast amount of data available via the web to make the project viable. With extensive funding and access to most of the government databases they had been in development for the last eighteen months and were rapidly approaching readiness to launch an alpha version of the system for testing. One of the unexpected outcomes of their development was a tool that evaluated what appeared to be unrelated data and created what the programming group was calling a "probability matrix"; in its simplest terms a ranked list of potential intersects between what was seemingly unrelated data points – the team in true geek fashion had nicknamed it NEO.

    Lou had sent down all the documents, pictures, reports and information from Tom's thumb drives and what the FBI had shared with the development group and asked them to load it into the new system. It wasn't precisely what they had designed it for, but they needed a break and this would make for an interesting test of the system's capabilities.

They were just getting the first set of results in when Jessie returned to the office. "Find anything..." she asked, pushing through the office door.

"Not really sure, actually," her dad replies, "had the team run everything through NEO – here is the initial list," he says, spinning the monitor around so she and Jack can take a look.

The output was a matrix listing with a probability score to the right. The first three items: Sokolov, Tom Casey, and Ukraine all had scores of 100%, no surprise of course, but the rest of the list was an interesting mix of information:

Sokolov – 100%

Tom Casey – 100%

Ukraine – 100%

Tampa – 67%

Brighton Beach – 58%

Republic Airport NY – 36%

24-Hour PC Repair – 21%

AMRAMCON Pump Station 3 – 17%

Baltimore – 16%

NH376 – 12%

Pole Cats – 2%

Honey Pot – 1.7%

Pink Pony – 1.4%

Sugar Babies – 1.2%

Followed by a long list of what appeared to be Eastern European cities all ranking at less than 1%.

"Dad, what does this all mean?" Jessie asks.

"Well," turning the screen back towards him, "we fed all the data points we had, including photos, into NEO which cross references all of it looking for underlying connections and then bounces that off a general web search looking for data points that have enough matching intersects so the analytics engine can extrapolate a probabilities matrix… short answer though - this is a list of potential leads…"

"Okay, I think I get it, but what are the percentages?" Jessie asks.

"Simple really - they represent the degree each item intersects the original data parameters – these are our best bet for follow up." He turns the screen back towards Jessie and Jack, "the really cool part is if you click on any of these it will give you the data point detail that's behind each probability score." He clicks on the Brighton Beach entry and the screen shows a series of web articles on Brighton Beach followed by series of entries that expands each of the data points that NEO used to formulate the probability score. "See, here we have the basic data on Brighton Beach but also a break down showing property tied at least three companies Sokolov is tied to, including this condo unit on the beach and an electronics store a couple blocks over." Lou excitedly clicks on one of the entries expanding it further, "We can take this down a number of levels including geo-pics of the buildings, maps of the area, traffic patterns, and because we have access to Homeland Security databases any surveillance that has been tagged to these locations also shows up." Lou's geek side is showing through, "It's pretty damn amazing if I do say so myself..."

Jessie and Jack are both grinning at him.

"What?" he asks defensively.

"Nothing dad, just fun seeing you so excited, knew you were just a big geek under all that tough guy stuff..." she says laughing. "Seriously though, that's pretty amazing but now what?" she asks.

"Now we go hunting..." Jack says quietly.

Tampa

Lou had wanted to keep the three of them together, but Jessie and Jack had successfully argued that more ground would be covered by splitting up and the quicker they figured this out the better. Besides, how easy would it be to spot the three of them together? Jessie had taken fifty thousand of the cash, knowing her plastic was being tracked made it risky to use anything else. Lou and Jack figured they were okay on cards, but each took twenty thousand in cash as well, informants, street folks, and most of the people they would be dealing with didn't take credit cards.

She was scrunched against the window in 6A on the Southwest flight to Tampa, she knew her dad just wanted to be able to keep an eye on her, but Jack had won the day pointing out that she was more capable of taking care of herself than they were, they all knew that wasn't exactly true but she had insisted and her dad had finally conceded the point. She was headed to Tampa, not even sure where to start or what she was looking for, but Lou having lost the bigger battle had held the line on this. He had probably figured it was the safest of the three places they had picked. He was heading to DC to meet with the FBI, hoping to break something loose or at least understand why they had left Jessie out of it for now. He would also dig into Baltimore while he was there. Jack had drawn the most dangerous assignment of the three he was headed to Brighton Beach, the most likely place to find Sokolov or some of his people. His argument had been simple; he knew the streets and how to operate without being seen, there was no disagreeing with that.

Jessie had caught the 10AM direct to Tampa having left a few hours earlier than her dad and Jack. It was 3:15PM in Tampa when she touched down, grabbing her backpack from under the seat in front her she headed up the jet way to catch the trolley to the main terminal. Tampa was an easy airport to navigate and she was hailing a cab just a few minutes later outside the red baggage claim area. She had found online a "buy here pay here" car lot on Florida Avenue and directed the cabbie to drop her there. First order of business was a vehicle, second stop was an "acquaintance" of Jack's who could set her up with whatever weapons she wanted. Thirty minutes later she was driving off the lot, the twelve-year-old white Ford Fusion had a hundred and thirteen thousand miles on it and "ice cold air", she would be testing that soon enough not believing how hot and humid it was already this early in the year. It reminded her of the time she had spent in the jungles of South America. The dealer had been more than happy to do a cash deal and it had only set her back twenty-five hundred, another five hundred had answered any questions about the registration.

The old cigar shop was located in the Latin section of old Tampa, the local signs all in Spanish. The place smelled of stale smoke and cheap tobacco, but the old man had just nodded when she asked for Salazar Hernandez and led her to the back room. The exchange and had been quick and to the point she used another five thousand of her cash on two suppressed Berretta 92FS 9MMs - the military standard for decades, four magazines, ten boxes of Federal Premium personal defense rounds, a tactical knife, and a carbon fiber vest, the latest in moldable bullet proof technology. The vest was a last-minute decision; she wasn't taking any more risks than necessary. She knew the price was high, but you paid for anonymity and it wasn't like she had an alternative source.

She turned just as she was leaving, "quick question... who do I call if I want a young girl?" she asks.

The old man didn't even hesitate, "how young?"

Jessie hesitates for an instant not sure if this is such a good idea, "say around sixteen..." it hangs in the air.

The old man seems to be thinking... "Why you want a girl like that?"

"That's my business..." she tries to keep the nerves out of her voice, it doesn't work.

"Humph," he gives a guttural laugh, "it's my business if you want the number chica."

"How much old man?"

He gives a chuckle, "two grand, and you never come back here," he says writing a number on a slip of paper.

"Thanks..." she hands him the cash and takes the slip.

"Don't thank me chica, you probably won't live long enough for it to matter, now go, you been here too long already."

Jessie hadn't been in Tampa for twelve hours and she had already had her life threatened or at least it seemed that way, so much for being the safer bet. She needed to find a place to stay, it was getting late and she had promised to check in with her dad and Jack. She points the Ford toward St. Pete Beach where there are still a number of small motels that don't ask too many questions and where she can blend in as another late season tourist. She picks the Beachcomber Motel, its run down but not quite seedy, she asks for a first-floor room on the gulf side, paying cash for the week.

She had backed into a space as close to her room as possible and walked around the entire property getting a feel for it. She had learned her lesson in Chicago and wasn't going to be caught by surprise again; lady luck wasn't likely to help her out twice. She settles into the room unpacking her bag and laying out the afternoon's purchases. The guns have had their numbers filed off, but are in excellent shape, would be nice to fire a couple of rounds off to get the feel of them, but there was no chance of that happening. In fact, she truly hoped she wouldn't have to fire them at all. She loads up all four magazines, each holds fifteen rounds, and chambers a round in each pistol. Things would have to go seriously awry for this not to be enough firepower. Of course, things had been going sideways since Vegas so the real possibility existed she wasn't quite done defending herself yet.

Washington DC

Lou had made a couple of calls setting up meetings with his contacts at Homeland Security and the FBI, ostensibly to review the latest updates from Paradigm before boarding his flight to DC, it was thin but probably enough to cover the real reason for his trip. He spent a fair bit of time in DC anyway so although put together on the fly he hoped it wouldn't set off too many red flags.

What worried him the most wasn't whether the FBI knew what he was up to but how deep Sokolov's group had managed to infiltrate the Bureau. Add to that the degree they had seemed able to penetrate Jessie's identity even down to her SAT phone number and maybe even by extension his identity. There was no way to determine this, they were operating under a worst-case scenario just to be safe. He had no illusions about the sophistication of today's criminal enterprises, he made a living trying to stay one-step ahead of them. Unfortunately, they had the money to buy some of the best tech talent out there and not everybody's moral compass was well tuned enough to worry about where the cash came from.

The Frontier flight landed on time at Reagan National, Lou collected his bags at carousel twelve and caught the shuttle to the Crystal City DoubleTree, it was close to the Pentagon and he had been staying there for years, no reason to deviate from his normal patterns now.

"Your usual room, Mr. McIntyre?" the clerk asked.

"That would be great, thank you," he replied, accepting the card key from the young man. Lou always stayed on the tenth floor in a king suite at the end of the hall by the stairs. It was quieter and far enough up from the street to minimize the traffic noise, but truth was old habits die hard and he liked having an alternative exit close at hand.

He had decided to stay in for dinner. Dialing up room service he ordered the Chicken Caesar Salad, two bottles of Pellegrino and a couple of the DoubleTree chocolate chip cookies... they were always warm no matter when you ordered them. He fired up his laptop sending two emails confirming his meetings the next morning and scanning through the two hundred or so that had populated his inbox since leaving the office that morning. He wished he had thought to invent a program to sort through them all and answer the ones that just required an electronic nod of the head. No one had solved the email issue, the bane of many a tech CEO, reply all and copying him was just too easy and it didn't seem to matter how many memos he put out pleading with his management staff to minimize it as best they could. He had a better chance of curing the common cold, well actually someone had done that already, but email management was proving to be a more difficult task.

With a sigh, he logs off and brings up a "shadow" browser session, Paradigm had created this tool years ago to mask their activity from hackers and competitors, it simply made it impossible to track his browsing history or even identify that he was on web. He started with some simple searches looking for missing children statistics in Maryland, he was surprised to find that the state routinely had more than a thousand missing teenagers go unrecovered every year with a very large percentage of these being teenage girls. The number was staggering, how could you lose a thousand teens every year and it not be nightly news? Lou got lost in the statistics not wanting to believe what he was reading; the government estimated there to be over a hundred thousand open missing person cases at any one time. The number was hard to grasp, in fact it was almost the population of Boulder, wouldn't someone notice if a whole town that size went missing? The buzz of his SAT phone interrupted his musing, it was a little after nine and well past the time Jessie was to have called him.

"Hey dad, sorry I'm late, took a little longer to get dinner than I thought," Jessie explained.

"No problem sweetheart, let me guess, drive thru burgers, supersize fries and a chocolate shake!" he laughed.

"You know I never eat that! Actually, they've got some great seafood down here, found a place on the beach, almost seemed normal for a moment," she said wistfully.

He promised himself he wouldn't get emotional with her, "I know Jess, I wish things were different but we'll get this figured out."

"Have you heard from Jack yet?" she asked.

"Nope, but his flight didn't get in until around eight so I expect he is still getting settled in, but you never know with Jack, I learned a long time ago sometimes the less questions you ask him the better."

"He really is one of 'those guys', isn't he?"

"You have no idea honey, but there isn't anyone else I would want to cover my back..."

They talked for another forty minutes reviewing their next steps and comparing notes. Jessie didn't mention the number the old man had given her. No reason to worry her dad any more than needed if it turned something up she would update him on their next call.

"Love you dad..."

"Love you too baby girl, talk to you tomorrow."

It never ceased to amaze him how grown up his little girl was, sometimes he still thought of her as that cute six-year-old tugging on his arm with an insatiable list of questions. God, he had missed Maggie in those days, truth was he missed her all the time, he had never even considered another woman, she had been his one and only. Jessie had given him a reason to go to keep living, but she was also a constant reminder of her mother, he never resented her for it, not even once, in fact those little reminders made their bond even stronger. He would do whatever was necessary to protect her; he already knew there wasn't a sacrifice he wouldn't make.

Coming Home to Queens

Jack had taken United flight #406 out of Denver to LaGuardia in New York; he preferred the non-stops where possible. LaGuardia put him on the northern edge of Queens near Flushing where he had grown up, a mix of Italian and Irish heritage, he had mirrored the melting pot these neighborhoods represented. He had been a serious kid who always seemed to have his head in a book, but being smart wasn't enough, these streets forced you to be tough if you wanted to survive. Jack had joined the Marines at seventeen and the Agency after serving a four-year stint. He was too bright to be a foot soldier and truth-be-told he was a little too comfortable with the personal combat side of the job for his superior officers. He had found a home and calling if you will at the Agency and had never looked back.

Jack packed light, toting only a backpack with a couple changes of clothes he cabbed over to the old neighborhood. Dropping a couple of twenties over the seat he gets out and walks the two blocks to the back door of Danny's Caribbean Cafe, he knocks twice and waits until a young Asian peers through the screen door apparently the melting pot had expanded over the years. "What you want old man?" he asks.

"Looking for Salazar Hernandez, used to work here, he still around?" Jack asks.

The young man doesn't bother answering, he just pushes open the door and points down the hallway, "last door on the left, knock or the old fool might shoot you."

Jack nods and heads down the hall, he was pretty sure Salazar had never shot anyone but he knocks just the same, maybe things had changed and there was no need to be out of the game before he even got started. The grizzled old man looks up from the bench where he is cleaning an old Colt revolver, "son of a bitch, little Jack Spignelli!"

Jack smiles, "Jack Hardy now, nobody knows or even remembers Spignelli, and let's keep it that way."

"I haven't seen you since you joined the Marines son, you coming home to the neighborhood?"

Hernandez must be pressing eighty plus by now Jack thinks, he wonders if the old man would think it flattering that he had used his name at every drop he had setup around the globe? "No sir, but if you still keep some hardware I could use a setup..."

"Well not like the old days son, but tell me what you need and let's see what we can do."

"Okay, if you have them I could use two suppressed 9MMs, two extra magazines each, shoulder rig, and if you have eight boxes Hornady Critical Defense rounds or something comparable, that should get me started?"

"Madre de Dios... son, what kind of trouble are you in?"

"No trouble old friend, just a precaution..."

The old man gives a deep laugh, "okay, keep your own counsel, I've got everything but the rounds, can have them in the morning if you really think you need them."

Jack draws out the wad of hundreds, "what do I owe you?"

"The pistols are on me, call it a favor for the old time's sake and you're going to love these babies, rounds are going to cost though, figure hundred a box, should be enough..."

Jack peels off a grand and hands it to him, "let's hope so, there's an extra four hundred for your trouble."

Hernandez rummages in the trunk behind him, "ahh, here we go," as he hands Jack two CZ 75s – Czech made 9MM pistols, looking new except for the bulbous suppressor on each one, a holster and extra magazines follow. "These babies hold eighteen rounds and the recoil is less than anything you can imagine, never mind that feel how light it is... polymer!" the old man bubbles as he hands them to Jack.

"Here are a couple boxes of regular rounds just in case, come back around in the morning and I'll have the rest." Salazar loads up the magazines for him before handing everything over.

Jack shrugs into the shoulder rig and holsters the pistols placing the boxes of rounds in his backpack. Clasping the old man's hand, "thank you my old friend, and listen, safer for both of us if you don't mention me to anyone."

Backpack slung over his shoulder and jacket zipped far enough to conceal the holster he heads three blocks over to grab take out from Hunan House, their spicy garlic chicken and scallion pancakes were a fond memory of days long ago. Food in tow he heads another couple of blocks over to the Flushing Motel on Linden, a seedy hourly joint where payment in cash was preferred and there was enough traffic no one would notice him. If he was honest there was a certain nostalgia associated with being back in the field. The cheap motels with their paper-thin walls, moaning whores, and tripping addicts, eating steaming spicy food out of cardboard containers; it wasn't healthy but it felt like home. He had been out of the field for a while, but the adjustment to civilized life hadn't come easy and as if he had never left, he felt himself slipping back into the comfortable cadence of the street.

It was after midnight when he headed out the back entrance to call Lou, paper-thin walls worked both ways and he didn't want to risk anyone listening in. The apartment building across the street had a couple of benches shadowed by the tall buildings and a few struggling trees. Camping out on the furthest one he dials the SAT phone, waiting for the telltale beeps of the synchronization. Lou answers on the first ring.

"Hey, wasn't sure if I was going to hear from you tonight... everything ok?"

"Yes, all is well," Jack hesitates not sure what he wants to say... "Lou..."

"Yeah buddy... you sure you're okay?"

"Yeah, I'm okay, it's just that... this is going to sound crazy, but I've missed this, the shit hotel rooms, eating food out of a container, the whores, pimps, addicts, street people and... I guess even knowing someone is probably going to have to die before this is done... it doesn't bother me... in fact..."

Lou cut him off there, "listen Jack, I can't say I understand I wasn't out there like you were, but I think I get it, we weren't made to sit comfortably in our living rooms watching cable, drinking good whiskey and waiting to die. I gave all that up for Maggie and well Jessie too, but my friend, don't think I haven't felt the tug over the years." Lou hesitates, "and Jack, don't go making this some blaze of glory end of it all, I need you my friend, I got nobody else to share this with, so be careful out there."

"Thanks Lou I will, knew you would understand, talk to you tomorrow night." Jack hangs up; sitting in the dark and thinking about all the assignments over the years, he knew none were more important than this one though. He might have promised Lou but he knew deep down that he wouldn't hesitate to sacrifice everything for the two of them.

Harrington

Special Agent in Charge Timothy Harrington had the classic looks of an Irishman most comfortable in a pub as anywhere else, but hiding a sharp intellect and searing wit. He had been with the bureau for twenty-three years, a serious man he had risen through the ranks quickly and had led the Boston Field Office for four years before finally managing to get transferred to Washington DC. Not that there had been anything wrong with being in Boston, God knows there was plenty of action in his home town and a prime slot like that would have been a career worthy goal for most agents, but DC was the fastest way to the director level slots. His organized crime experience in Boston had been one of the primary reasons he had been tapped to take on the Sokolov investigation and a successful conclusion would be his golden ticket.

He looked around the room, his task force had grown to twenty-four agents, including a team of two senior agents affectionately known as "Laurel & Hardy"; Oliver "Ollie" Feather and Samuel "Sammie" Jefferson, in spite of their comedic moniker, were two of the most experienced investigators in the DC office. In contrast with his namesake Ollie was a pencil thin, Ivy League educated blue blood from Massachusetts and Sammie was anything but thin, a boisterous son of a Mississippi preacher that had played tackle at Ohio State. They were as different as night and day but had become fast friends and inseparable since coming through the Academy together.

Ollie and Sammie passed out the last of the briefing folders as Harrington moved to the lectern, they had arrived in Chicago that morning and were bringing the local agents up to speed on the Sokolov case.

Harrington motioned to bring the lights down and flipped his first slide up, his style was unconventional but it worked for him. He liked to start with a series of photos, not so much for shock value, but he had found that visuals were immediately sobering and tended to focus a group quicker than any opening statement ever had. It was a trick he had learned during the Boston Marathon bombing back in 2013. His boss had started the briefing with a series of photos showing the victims followed by the Tsarnaev brothers; it had made an impression and he had been using the technique ever since.

The first shot was the evidence photo of the two Sokolov soldiers Jessie had shot in the condo doorway, followed by the third soldier in his tailored suit framed by the loading dock and the dumpsters, it made for a disturbing contrast. Of course, the pool of blood left by two expanding 45 caliber slugs couldn't be ignored either. Interestingly enough, neither the local cops or FBI had interviewed Todd and Trevor from Floyd Brothers. Next up were photos of Tom Casey and the original shooter from Vegas.

Harrington finished up with a side by side of Jessie in uniform and a file photo of Sokolov. "Bring the lights up please," he requests, taking the laser pointer and moving back to the lectern.

"All right folks, have I got everyone's attention?" There was no answer and no need for one, it had been phrased rhetorically and he clearly had their attention. "Let's start with these two – on the right Alexi Sokolov Ukrainian crime boss made his start in black market weapons, drugs, murder for hire, but in 2019 he shifted his focus to human trafficking and set up his operations here in the states." Harrington glances around the room, they are all focused a few making notes in the margins of their briefing folders. "Sokolov took about eighteen months to roll-up the operations of the traditional families and the Latin gangs, when he was done he owned the bulk of the prostitution – pornography – strip clubs and most importantly the international trafficking here in the states. He is ruthless, smart, extremely well financed and has no qualms when it comes to killing." Harrington takes a long sip from the bottle of water sitting on the lectern. "Okay, on the left is Major Jessie McIntyre, retired from the Army Rangers as a Major almost two years ago. Until about a week ago she was providing VIP security services with Thompson Security." He uses her rank purposely wanting to impress upon the agents her military background, but also that he respects her service and expects them to as well. He flips the screen back to Tom and the dead assassin, "Major McIntyre was dating this Tom Casey, the one on the left - he is an FBI informant that's been, well, was, feeding us information on Sokolov for the past six months. We don't have an identity on the other one, but by putting together the ballistics and hotel video footage we are positive this was a Sokolov hit on Tom Casey. The video shows Major McIntyre leaving the elevators down the hall and entering the room and then shortly after taking the stairs at the other end of the hall." He pauses briefly, "we have no direct physical evidence linking her to the second shooting but the timing and precision – she holds the highest military marksmanship rating by the way – make it pretty clear what probably happened. We believe she entered the room shortly after Tom Casey was killed and fired in self-defense, it appears she grabbed some belongings and left." Looking around the room he says, "I want to make it clear... obviously we want to talk to Major McIntyre but we do not consider her a threat and she is not the target of this task force. Having said that however, we are pretty certain the three dead in Chicago are her work as well." A hand goes up in the back, "yes, you have a question?"

"Yes sir, with all due respect, if Major McIntyre has taken out four of these presumed Sokolov gang members, why isn't she under investigation?"

Harrington rubs his temples, "a good question, but under the circumstances both situations appear to be self-defense, and we have no physical evidence in Chicago linking her to the site, although there is a high probability it was her... we are, at least for now, leaving her disposition to local authorities." He pauses for a moment, "Major McIntyre is definitely a person of interest, but I want to emphasize again she is not the target and is most likely herself in real danger. Would I prefer she had turned herself in, of course, but I do not want her to distract us from our main focus – Sokolov. If we can bring her in safely we will." Motioning to Ollie and Sammie, "now let's review the briefing handouts, I want everything we can uncover on this Tom Casey, particularly anything he may have been working here in Chicago." Turning to his two assistants, "Ollie, you stay here and keep this group focused, I want you to revisit anyone or anything we may have missed here including a complete rehash of the crime scene itself, it would be nice if we could find someone that saw something." Turning to Sammie, "Take the next flight to New York, pull together all the data this Casey had been feeding them and debrief Agent Jackson from the LaGuardia drop. I've got to head back to DC but I'll be in New York tomorrow evening so see what you can put together before I get there. Anything breaks for either of you I expect an immediate call. We need to move this along, too many bodies starting to pile up."

    He shakes hands with the two agents before taking a last look around the room, this was moving fast and he understood the seriousness of it, but he loved the energy, the hunt, the pursuit of justice was a real living breathing mission for Harrington.

Thrust, Parry, & Feint

Lou had brought the latest version of the encryption cracking software and a handful of test results, but even his well-rehearsed presentation of the information wasn't dispelling the awkward mood in the room. Simply put, there was no reason for him to be here, the workgroup had met three weeks earlier and he wasn't scheduled to provide an update for another three weeks. Fifteen minutes in and only on his second slide Lou grinds to a halt.

"Listen Jimmy I need some help…"

Jimmy looks over a pained expression on his face, "Lou I understand I really do, I took a serious risk sending you that data on Casey, but listen, I can't help you with this, I just can't" Jimmy says as he reaches for the phone. "Jimmy Pascalerio sir, should I bring him up…"

Lou stands up gathering his papers and opening the leather briefcase, "listen Jimmy, I appreciate everything, I'll give you a call to schedule our next meeting in a few weeks."

"Lou, I can't stop you from leaving, but I'm asking you to meet with Special Agent in Charge Harrington if anyone can help you he can."

"Help me, really?" Lou sighs.

"Come on Lou, this thing is bigger than you know, they've got a task force of thirty plus agents working this case, do you and your daughter a favor and talk to Harrington."

Lou hesitates for a moment, "alright Jimmy, lead the way, I'll take all the help I can get at this point."

Jimmy holds the door for him and the two of them take the elevator to the eighth floor. The FBI was still housed in the Hoover building in DC, but after eight years and several delays they hoped to finally move to their new campus in Landover Maryland. For now, though, they continued to occupy what had become a seriously dilapidated and outdated monstrosity in the center of the city.

Jimmy opens the conference room door, motioning for Lou to go ahead in. There are three agents seated around the table reviewing a series of photographs and reports. Harrington rises first offering his hand, "Tim Harrington, you must be Lou McIntyre?"

Lou takes his hand just nodding, not quite sure where this is going yet he decides to let it play before offering anything up.

"These are agents Murphy and Templeton," Harrington says pointing to the other two. After perfunctory handshakes, Harrington motions to the chair next to his "Have a seat Mr. McIntyre… Jimmy, thanks for bringing him up, I'll take it from here." He turns to Lou, "May I call you Lou?"

Lou settles back in his chair, okay so he is going to play the nice guy card he thinks to himself, "sure, that's fine Tim," he responds. The familiarity is just to let Harrington know he isn't intimidated and that two can play this game. Lou may have been out of the Agency for a long time but you didn't run a billion-dollar high tech company by being a push-over either.

Harrington starts right in, "Lou, I've got a big problem..." he hesitates waiting to see if Lou will bite, nothing. "Okay, here is the situation I've got four, no five bodies, in the last week or so, I've lost my best, well only informant on the biggest human trafficker we've ever had a shot at, and your daughter is in the middle of at least one of these shootings. Then out of nowhere you send in more data than we've collected in six months..." He looks at Lou and smiles, "so help me out here Lou..."

Lou gives him a shrug, "listen, you want to talk that's fine, but just you and me, no recordings, nothing on the record period or I walk out of here now..." He had played it strong, now it was just a question of whether it would work or not. He didn't think Harrington could hold him and he certainly couldn't make him talk, but this was a gamble none-the-less.

Harrington nods, "Okay, we'll play it your way," motioning to the two agents, "give us the room fellas, I'll call you when we're finished." This more than anything reaffirmed for Lou how serious this case must be for them.

The two had thrust, parried, and feinted back and forth like a pair of expert fencers for nearly twenty minutes, neither willing to concede a point or give ground to the other. "All right, all right Harrington, this is going nowhere, let me be as plain as I can," Lou's frustration has reached a breaking point. "I'm not trying to get in the way of your operation, God knows I want nothing to do with these people, but my daughter is clearly a target of this psychopath Sokolov and you seem quite willing to leave her hanging out there like bait..." he hesitates searching for the right words to make his point. "So, I need you to tell me why I should help you, and for that matter why I shouldn't be pissed off to the point of raising hell all over town, now I hope that doesn't put too fine a point on it for you, but Jesus man, this is my daughter's life you're playing with."

Harrington holds up his hands defensively, "now look Lou, nobody wants anything to happen to your daughter, and I don't think it's fair to say we are using her as bait..." he falters knowing the speciousness of his answer isn't going to hold water. "Okay, you're right, we had hoped she would draw him out, maybe force him to make a mistake..." He pauses for a moment, "Was that her work in Chicago? Did she retrieve the data you sent us from Casey's apartment? Our guys figure there was something stashed in the wall because someone cut a pretty damn big hole to get to it... and you have to admit the timing is pretty suspect... so?"

Lou stands up, moving over to the window, there really wasn't any way around this, he was going to have to trust Harrington… "Listen Tim, none of this comes back on my girl okay? I'll tell you everything I know, but you have to guarantee you won't come after her." Lou knew it was a big ask and probably not something Harrington could technically agree to, but it would have to do.

"Alright Lou, and I'll do what I can with the locals in Vegas and Chicago, but you've got to come clean with it all, that's the deal."

"Ok, but you left her out there and from my seat that makes the three in Chicago on your watch, so it's a deal Tim, but you're in this as deep as we are, so call your boys back in, I'd rather only do this once."

Premonitions

Sampson had dispatched two of his men to Chicago to see if they could dig up anything new and confirm what he already knew. The team he had sent to Casey's condo was dead, but Sokolov would insist on proof and it was easier to send them than argue with him. The Spider had managed to pull the 911 call transcripts placed by a frantic neighbor of Casey's who had stumbled on the two bodies as she was leaving to walk her poodle. Apparently, the dog had pushed the door open and the poor old lady had barely been able to pull him off the bodies but if it hadn't been two of his men the call would have been pretty damn funny. They had also reviewed all the local media coverage, which combined with the 911 call had been enough for Sampson. In many respects, he had more faith in the Spider's team of techs than the foot soldiers Alexi still relied on. Alexi still stuck to old ways, always wanting someone to personally verify everything, even though the operation had gone hi-tech and rivaled the cyber agencies of most modern countries. Alexi still had a lingering distrust of technology though preferring to rely on men and guns for most things, of course that didn't preclude him from leveraging that same technology skill set to generate enormous amounts of cash. It was an interesting dichotomy Sampson mused to himself, but it didn't help him this morning.

The vibrating of the phone broke his thoughts, "yeah, what you have?" he asked the Spider.

"The girl you were asking about... we just picked up a hit on a Southwest flight out of Denver to Tampa landed yesterday afternoon."

"Why am I just finding out now?" Sampson demanded.

"Look Sampson, we just managed to access these systems in the past few weeks, you're lucky we caught it all..." The Spider had been around a long time, almost as long as Sampson, but it was still risky standing up to the big man.

"Ok, Ok thanks, can you have your group arrange transportation and have the condo ready, I'll fly out tonight."

"You're going yourself?" the Spider asked surprised. Things must be significantly worse than he had heard Sampson rarely handled things directly anymore.

"Yes, I'm going, why?" Sampson asks the irritation bleeding through.

"No reason, I'll let the crew down there know you're coming in, someone will be waiting at the jetport for you, let me know if you need anything else."

"Thanks Spider, if you get any more hits on her call me immediately, and good job..." Sampson wasn't generous with his compliments but it wasn't Spider's fault things had blown up. He hung up and headed down the hallway to Alexi's office, not really looking forward to a drawn-out conversation, but knowing he was going to have to explain Chicago and why he was personally heading to Tampa.

He gives two quick taps on the door before opening it, he was probably the only one that could just knock and walk in on Alexi. Sokolov is on the phone but waves him to a chair in front of the desk. Sampson takes a quick look around, strangely none of the girls are anywhere to be seen nor is the usual guard at the door. As Sokolov hangs up Sampson asks, "Where is everyone?"

"I needed some quiet, something is going on my old friend, I can feel it..." Alexi drums his fingers on the desk; "you remember when Potrosky came at us back in Odessa?"

"Yeah, I remember, I also remember you were ready for him, cut his throat while his wife and kid watched." There is no emotion in Sampson voice, it's a simple recitation of facts. "That was twenty years ago though, what could that have to do with anything today?"

Alexi waves his hand at him, "you're missing the point, I knew he was coming, don't know how... just had a feeling, we had our ear to the street Sampson, we knew what was happening even before it happened, don't you remember?"

"Alexi, there is no one left to challenge you like the old days... the world is, well it's different now."

"Sampson, we didn't last this long by thinking we were untouchable! There might not be a Potrosky out there but that doesn't mean we let our guard down, doesn't mean we go all soft in the head." Tapping his head Alexi gets up and looks out the window at the waves breaking over the beach. Almost to himself, "I don't like this Tom thing with the FBI, I don't like this girl killing our people, I particularly don't like this prick of a prince..." Still looking out over the ocean, "I just got a call from Saranosky in Odessa, did you know this fucking sand nigger beat one of the girls we just sent over there to death?" Sampson starts to answer, "it doesn't matter, I don't give a shit about her, but seems we got a lot of problems at one time and that makes me think we aren't paying enough attention."

Sampson doesn't argue the point, "Yes sir, I'm headed to Tampa tonight, the McIntyre girl is down there..."

Alexi turns away from the window, "you going yourself?" it's more of a statement than question, Sampson just nods. "Good, any idea what the fuck she is doing down there? Tom never worked Tampa."

Sampson pauses, they have been together a long time but rarely does Alexi solicit anyone's opinion even his, "the three girls for Tom's last deal came out of our Tampa group, my guess is she somehow figured it out..."

"Jesus fucking Christ... see this is what I am talking about!" Alexi explodes, "how the hell could she know that? How do you know she is there anyway?"

Sampson smiles, "The Spider finally hacked TSA, we can track flight manifests now..."

Alexi just shakes his head, "Fuckin' computers, unbelievable…"

Sampson just nods, "After Chicago I don't want anyone else taking care of this so I am going."

Neither of the men knew as much as they thought, and Jessie knew less than they believed, but their courses had been set and a collision was on the horizon.

Hiding in Plain Sight

Jack had perfected operating in plain sight, the ability to blend into any environment, look as if you not only belonged, but had also been there all along. It was trademark Agency field craft, but no one had ever been better at it than Jack Hardy, he had occasionally agreed to speak to new Agency recruiting classes giving pointers and answering questions. He maintained the most important thing to remember was not how you looked but how you acted. It meant understanding the culture, routines, personalities of the area you were infiltrating. People saw what they expected and wanted to see; variations in daily habits, inconsistencies in routine, and attitudes would give you away long before your clothing or appearance did. Jack hadn't expected to need those skills again, but here he was back in the thick of it.

Jack had stopped by Hernandez's place earlier that morning and was now walking the streets of Brighton Beach in an old wool sweater, sipping on his coffee, feeding the pigeons from one of the many benches, haggling with a sidewalk produce vendor, the perfect cranky old man. He was just another Ukrainian didus - "grandfather" wandering the neighborhood; seen but not noticed, he was hiding in plain sight.

As the morning wore on Jack was developing a grudging respect for Sokolov, he was hiding in plain sight as well. The condo's location had been in the report Agent Pascalerio had shared with Lou, Jack had started there, sitting on one of the courtyard benches drinking coffee and sharing the crumbs from his bag of khrustyky, the sweet crunchy fried dough pastry so beloved by Ukrainians. He had picked it up from the bakery down the block making sure he was seen. Maybe it was just the neighborhood or that Sokolov had been able to act with impunity for so long, but in any case, his operation had become complacent. Their obsessive focus on cyber security, satellite phones, and silence through intimidation hadn't extended to the simple daily habits of his men and these were the details that Jack was absorbing.

It was always the simplest things that were the obvious give away; bulky guys in poor fitting suits were a cliché from too many movies. However well-dressed men in their mid-thirties with overtly military mannerisms were just as easy to spot in real life. He only needed to watch a few of them enter the decrepit electronics store emerging empty handed minutes later to understand it was a front for something else, the patterns were always hiding right in front of you if you took the time to notice.

Jack shuffled from the courtyard to the boardwalk stretching along the Atlantic, in search of a hotdog cart, a taste of his long-forgotten youth. Finding one, it's blue and yellow umbrella dancing in the breeze, he orders a dog with spicy mustard and kraut. Lunch in hand he perches on the steps down to the sand munching the soft slightly squishy bun, the spicy mustard and kraut competing with each other in every bite. Washing it down with a swig of lukewarm cola he looks down the beach toward Coney Island, the rusting hulks of the Parachute Jump and the Wonder Wheel still puncture the hazy skyline but the rest of the amusement park has long since conceded its struggle to remain solvent and relevant. Youth had finally managed to erase the nostalgia of the twentieth century, opting for their virtual gaming consoles and consigning the screams and laughter that accompanied the creaks and groans of the distant giants to the memories of a fading population. Jack takes a long last swig and turns back to the moment at hand, he finds these momentary remembrances of days gone by too melancholy to dwell on.

With a sigh, Jack pushes himself up and strolls back down the boardwalk, never breaking character he meanders slowly into the courtyard between the condo and the street the electronics store is on. Taking up his perch on one of the benches he buries his nose in the Russian language newspaper he had picked up that morning at the bakery. It takes real skill to actually read the paper and still notice things around you. Too often the paper is an obvious ploy that more often gives surveillance away rather than masking it. Not for Jack though, he long ago learned you have to actually read. He watches as Sampson walks out of the condo and down the courtyard in his direction, phone in one hand and duffel in the other. A less experienced man might have given himself away, but Jack always the cool one folds the newspaper and shakes out a cigarette patting his pockets as if searching for a light. "Izvinite, no u vas yest' svet," excuse me, do you have a light, he asks in Russian. Sampson turns, seeming to notice him for the first time. Setting his bag on the bench he brings forth a classic Zippo lighter, snapping it open and holding it out. Jack leans in and lights the cigarette leaning back he takes a long drag and nods a thank you. Sampson hesitates for a moment before taking the lighter back, "what's your name old man?" he asks in English. It's an obvious ploy, but Jack had known it was coming and responds in Russian that he doesn't speak English. "I Vanya Tokorov," then switching back to Russian he explains he is visiting his granddaughter for the first time, but unfortunately, she works during the day so he is forced to wait here beside the ocean feeding the pigeons, smoking weak American cigarettes, and enjoying the beautiful weather. It's early spring in New York and not nearly that warm, but for a Russian it would seem mild, Jack plays his part never breaking character, every detail in perfect order.

    Sampson cuts him short this time in Russian, "Do svidaniya starik," and brusquely walks away.

Jack smiles to himself, *old man my ass, we will meet again my friend.* He hadn't had a cigarette in twenty years – hide in plain sight.

Quid Pro Quo

Even with Harrington's commitment to help, Lou wasn't entirely comfortable providing full transparency on the events of the last ten days, sure, they had Jessie tied to the Vegas shooting but they really didn't have any hard evidence in Chicago. Now they wanted full disclosure and that would mean detailing out the trip to Chicago and retrieval of the data Tom Casey had hidden in the condo. Of course, there was no denying Chicago since he had already sent them the data Jessie had retrieved. He was struggling with how to best handle this when agents Templeton and Murphy came back in.

Time had run out he was going to have to trust them but there would have to be some guarantees, he turns to Harrington, "Tim, we need to formalize the waiving of evidentiary rights on all this data… a grant of immunity from prosecution and a non-disclosure on the technology we're going to discuss." Looking at the two younger agents, "I know all of you fellas have Top Secret clearance but this is tech we are developing for Homeland Security and I would just be more comfortable with a non-disclosure in place."

Harrington gives him an exasperated look, seems to think better of it, and picks up the phone dialing quickly. "Albert? Yeah, any chance you can shuttle over here, no now, I am working on the Sokolov case I briefed you on last week. I've got a major break but need some paperwork drawn up." He pauses listening, "No, nothing like that, I need an Evidentiary Release, two Grants of Immunity..." Lou holds up three fingers. "Uhh, make that three grants and a couple of blank non-disclosures." Lou can't hear the other side of the conversation but it's obviously animated. Harrington finally breaks in, "Albert I understand, but I need this now and it has to be at your level, I will give you the details when you get here." Harrington hangs up the phone and turns to Lou, "Alberto Jimenez, Deputy Attorney General..." Pursing his lips, "McIntyre, this better be good, I just burned a ton of chits for you, and what's up with needing three grants?"

Lou doesn't answer him right away; "just being careful I need to make sure everyone on my side is covered." Lou sits down extracting his tablet from his bag, "going to have to access your AV network, that going to be a problem?"

Tim smiles, "your clearance is probably better than mine, hold on..." he picks up a small phone size tablet and pushes a button on the side. The device generates a randomly selected combination of letters, numbers, and symbols that act as network password. The system regenerates with every unique use and is only active for sixty seconds before expiring. "Okay ready password is: FBI#1"

Lou just looks at him, "are you fucking serious?" he asks incredulously.

"Nope, lighten up, use this..." he hands the tablet over to Lou laughing.

Lou just gives him a look, "you're not right... you know that..." but the tension in the room has dropped noticeably, another lesson learned in Boston.

Several minutes later Alberto Jimenez, Albert to everyone who knows him, comes banging through the door, briefcase held tightly to his chest, noticeably out of breath, "Harrington, you son of a bitch this better be worth it..." he splutters. Albert was known for his colorful language, a habit developed as a teenager on the mean streets of Albuquerque's South Valley, something polite society had never fully cured him of.

A third generation Mexican American, Alberto had been a "dreamer" back in the day, he had graduated New Mexico State before heading east to the University of Virginia Law School. He had planned on heading home after taking the bar, but had never made it landing in Denver where he had taken a position as a Junior DA. He was a gifted prosecutor and everyone was sure he would make the next administration's short list for Federal Judge and who knew, after that maybe the Supreme Court. Almost as round as he was tall, Albert always seemed to be out of breath and running just a little late. Of course, this had worked to his advantage in Denver where he had been chronically underestimated. The outcome, a resume glittering with high profile wins over the nation's top defense attorneys.

Lou attempts to suppress a grin as the attorney flops into one of the leather chairs grabbing a bottle of water from the center of the table and swallowing half of it before opening his briefcase and extracting a number of folders. He points to Lou, turning to Tim and says, "So is this the asshole that I owe this shit-storm to?" Tim just shakes his head with a grin and introduces everyone.

Tim starts right in, "come on Albert, give it a rest, this is important, let me run you through where we are, ok? He doesn't wait for answer, diving right in to the story and bringing Albert up to speed on where things stand.

Albert breaks in about half way through, "So let me get this straight," he turns to Lou, "your daughter, an ex-Army Ranger, is mixed up in this mess with the Sokolov gang and she has, to quote Tim here, 'taken four of them out'?" Albert is shaking his head, "well, I guess that explains the immunity part of this..." Lou starts to interject, but Albert holds his hand up, "look McIntyre, I have no problem with scum like this getting what they deserve, I just prefer to do it in a courtroom, but it is what it is, I get it."

Tim clears his throat, "alright, well let me finish this brief if you don't mind and then Lou is going to bring us up to speed on what he has." Lou starts to interject again, "I know Lou, not before we sign these forms for you, now let me get on with it or we'll never get out of here, and Albert just sit tight for me, okay?"

The attorney is fidgeting with his briefcase, "fine Tim, go ahead, but honestly if you say this is what you need let's just get it done."

"No Albert, I really want you to hear everything, another pair of ears and eyes can only help, and besides, this will probably be your case so the more you know the better."

Albert concedes the point impatiently allowing Tim to continue. When the agent is finished he opens the three folders extracting the various documents, "where do you want to start?" he asks looking at Lou.

"Well let's do the non-disclosures for agents Murphy and Templeton first, those will be easy. The evidentiary release should be straightforward as well. I want to make sure the immunity agreements cover anything that has or may happen directly related to the investigation or apprehension of Alexi Sokolov or any of his known or unknown associates." Lou looks around the table making sure everyone understands what he is asking for.

Albert sighs, "Mr. McIntyre, what you are asking for is a free pass and not just any free pass but one with a fucking hunting license." Clasping his hands in front of him, "you have to know we just don't go around writing blank checks like that."

Lou nods, "Yes I know, but in this case, you are going to have to," looking at Harrington, "the FBI has used my daughter as bait and I believe intentionally allowed her to be in harm's way. We didn't start this mess but we are here now and you can be Goddamn sure we will protect ourselves. So, I don't think I'm asking too much here," Lou is up now and visibly angry.

Albert shoots a look in Harrington's way, the agent gives him a brief nod, "Well, isn't this a beautiful shit sundae, okay you have your immunity, but let me tell you if this goes sideways this paper won't be worth wiping your ass with and it sure as shit isn't going to be enough to protect any of us."

"If this goes sideways it probably won't matter anyway," Lou says softly.

There is a brief silence while that sinks in... Albert speaks first, "Okay, who is getting these get out of jail free cards?"

"Myself, Jessie McIntyre and Jack Hardy..."

"Who the fuck is Jack Hardy?" Harrington asks.

"Jack is a close friend, spent thirty plus years as a field officer over at the Agency, we were partners back in the nineties before I got out," Lou answers him.

"Jesus Christ, this is going to be a fucking bloodbath, two ex-CIA and an angry Army Ranger, un-fucking-believable," Albert exclaims.

"Where is he right now?" Harrington demands.

"New York, can't tell you more than that..." Lou replies. "Jack's a professional, you don't have to worry about him..."

"It's not him I'm worried about," Harrington exclaims.

"Look you can be upset all you want, but we are not going to sit around like a bunch of deer waiting for hunting season to open... we just aren't going to do that, if these fuckers think they can just come gunning for my daughter well that's their mistake," he is worked up again.

"Alright Lou, we all get it, I get it, I understand... why don't you show us what you have and bring us up to speed on where your daughter is and whatever this Jack fella is doing..." letting out a long breath. "Then we can build a game plan from there, ok?"

"Yeah fine, okay," Lou says sitting down and pulling his laptop up, "here we go, hold on..."

Around Town

Sipping the pulpy orange juice and watching the gulf gently lap on the sugary white sand seemed an awful lot like a vacation to Jessie. She was pretty sure this had been her father's intention when he had suggested she take off for Tampa, it made sense for him to be in DC and of course there was no question about Jack going to New York, but it didn't feel right sitting here basking in the sun while sipping her juice and savoring a perfectly constructed eggs benedict.

She had thought about calling the number Hernandez had given her, but she had no idea what to ask and it honestly didn't make sense for a woman to be making a cold inquiry like that. Her dad had told her he would be in the FBI offices most of the day so calling him was out. In fact, they had decided to catch up later that evening so maybe she should just wait.

What would Jack do she wonders, he would hide in plain sight of course, she smiled to herself. The stories he had told her that first evening were colorful to say the least, but more than anything she had been taken with the finesse, discipline, and patience required to survive all those years in the field. Not that there hadn't been precision in the Army, especially in the Rangers, but that had still been the precise application of massive force and firepower. What Jack did was almost always solo or at most two operatives, the risks were amazing, but the impact was what really interested her. The need to eliminate people along the way didn't really bother her either. Being in the Army you understood that sometimes casualties are part of the deal, she knew that aspect of things concerned her dad, but it was just another thing they would need to sit down and talk about when this was over.

Pulling a couple of twenties out of her bag and leaving them on the table she grabs the backpack and heads out to the Fusion. Time to do some scouting, a couple of hours on the net the night before had given her an overview of the major sections of the Tampa Bay area. She had been surprised how big it was with close to nine million people living in the area. She had narrowed her search to areas she felt were most likely to yield information she could use and had downloaded those to her SAT phone. The Fusion was old enough so it didn't have the new integrated NAV systems she was used to.

Before leaving Boulder, they had pulled all the police reports on any missing person cases involving teen girls in the local area during the last six months. Strictly speaking they probably should have notified the locals, but Homeland Security had access to all local law enforcement systems and by extension so did Paradigm. They had been surprised to find seven cases of young women that had simply vanished, three had been found, unfortunate victims of rape and then murdered, one had run away and returned days later, and three were still missing, the most recent one just a couple of weeks ago. The police didn't seem to have any obvious leads or answers. The numbers seemed high to her, but she really didn't have any context with which to compare.

Her first order of business was just to drive these areas and get a feel for each one before taking any additional steps. Starting with the Port of Tampa she planned to work her way up to Ybor City and then over to the area between the port and the suburb of Brandon that was filled with strip clubs, novelty stores, and "jack shacks", commonly advertised as massage parlors. Phase two would be heading over to the university section where the University of South Florida was, before heading down Nebraska Avenue. Her review of police statistics had shown a concentration of prostitution and drug arrests in this area. She would finish up with the stadium and airport area. She figured it would take at least two days to do it right. She planned to stop along the way at the three missing girl's homes hoping to get someone to talk to her about what had happened. She was going to pose as a reporter doing a piece on kidnapping and human trafficking. It didn't occur to her that this probably wasn't the most delicate way to approach a worried and distraught family.

By mid-afternoon she had worked her way through the port area mapping out multiple ways in and out and driving them to make sure she had it memorized properly. Ybor City had been interesting but was confined to three parallel streets spanning about eight to ten blocks. The historic section was a collection of nightclubs, tattoo parlors and cafes. She had stopped for a late lunch, a slice of pizza and a diet cola while watching the odd collection of people strolling the streets. The young people barely clothed their ink on display in stark contrast with the sweater and visor wearing senior tourists in their diabetic shoes shuffling along the sidewalks, camera phones clicking away. There was a certain symbiotic symmetry to it, she thought. She came to the conclusion that as interesting as the area was it probably wasn't a good target area. The police presence with its obvious video and drone surveillance was substantial and even late in the afternoon, the sidewalks were already crowded. The surveillance should have been a red flag, but Jessie couldn't possibly have known the level of infiltration Sokolov had into the local police cyber systems.

She tried to call Jack as she walked back to the car parked a couple blocks over in a public lot, the phone rang a dozen times before finally clicking over to voice mail. She didn't bother leaving a message, nobody had these numbers but the three of them. If Jack couldn't talk he would call her back when he was free. She started the car, waiting for the air to kick in, it might be spring but the temperature was already in the high eighties in Tampa. She decided to head out toward the strip clubs near Brandon, figuring she could end her day with a quick side trip to the family of one of the missing girls. She had downloaded the missing persons poster and police bulletin to her phone and pulled it up again. The girl was two weeks shy of her seventeenth birthday and cute in an everyday sort of way, blonde with all the curves girls her age seem to have these days: Allison Chambers had disappeared from her high school almost two weeks earlier – no leads, no ransom, no nothing.

Route 60 ran from downtown Tampa out through rural Hillsborough County almost all the way to the East coast of Florida. The short six or so mile stretch between Tampa and Brandon was as advertised an industrial mix of warehouses, small businesses, strip clubs, massage parlors, and adult stores. Most of the clubs had neon signs advertising nude dancers and couples welcome. Not really the romantic night out she would have thought of for a date. There was only a sprinkling of vehicles in the parking lots, apparently there wasn't much of a crowd till later in the evening. She pulls up the map program and dials in the address she had for the missing girl's family figuring to hit the clubs on the way back when they were bound to be more crowded.

Lithia was a mix of immaculately manicured gated communities and aging mobile home parks with their sandy yards and patchy grass. These were juxtaposed in an awkward tapestry illustrating the economic dichotomy Florida represented. Jessie pulls into the Strawberry Fields Mobile Home Park, not really a park, just a circular sandy drive hosting thirty-six aging single-wide trailers. A row of mailboxes is planted right inside the entrance, flyers for Allie Chambers are stapled haphazardly to the posts. Jessie studies them, wondering if this girl could really have been a victim of Tom and the people she was now hunting, a deep sadness overwhelms her for a moment. Shaking it off she heads down the right side looking for trailer number three, pulling up in front of a non-descript white single-wide, the baby blue trim fading and the splotches of grey green mildew so prevalent in this climate, begging for a pressure washing. Three wooden steps lead up to a small landing, the weathered railing anchors three forlorn yellow balloons that have surrendered their struggle to break free, a brass number, one screw missing, lopsidedly signals this as the right manufactured home. The sun is already sinking low in the sky casting long shadows and now that she is here she hesitates, maybe she should just leave, she doesn't really have any answers, only questions that are going to cause more pain and distress for this family. Jessie doesn't have a chance to change her mind as a beat-up Toyota Corolla pulls in next to her the silver paint long since dimmed by the unrelenting sun and several dents beginning to rust. A young boy in the passenger seat presses his face up against the glass staring at her, she stares back and the sadness envelopes her again.

NEO

Lou had started his brief with an overview of the predictive analytics engine Paradigm was developing, explaining how they had unexpectedly stumbled upon the probabilities generator. He had to backtrack half a dozen times and explain the underlying technology and "big data" concepts to Albert, but Harrington seemed to be keeping up pretty well; the two junior agents didn't utter a word, just listened intently, either bored or mesmerized, it was hard to tell.

Harrington leans back in his seat, hands clasped behind his head, "Jesus Christ Lou, this is unbelievable, and it really works?"

Lou hesitates, "yeah, it works, I mean this is an alpha test version and to be perfectly honest this is the first live case test of data we have done... so I guess we are going to find out together how well it works. Let me show you the data sets we fed into this and the probabilities matrix it created and you can tell me what you think..." He walks them through the data Pascalerio had provided. It was mostly written reports from Tom Casey combined with some basic background information the New York office had developed. They had been collecting surveillance photos of the Sokolov's men once Tom had identified the location of the condo. It hadn't been too difficult to run the identities through the international law enforcement databases and come up with profiles on each person. In the years since 9/11 and ISIS the scanning and recognition technology had significantly improved and law enforcement worldwide had long ago broken through the barriers inhibiting the sharing of data. Lou explains, "your files and Tom's report were our first data pass, we added what we were able to retrieve from the condo as a second pass." The data from the condo is now displaying on the main screen as he flips through the transaction profiles. "Obviously there is some duplication between the two, but you expect that..." he haltingly stops realizing this may be the first time they have had context to the data he had sent over two days ago.

Harrington doesn't say anything, but Lou can see the pain in his face, there is no way not to be affected by this. Albert, seeing it for the first time lets out a low whistle, "These motherfuckers... they are just children... Tim these fuckers have to go down..." his roots getting the better of him again.

Tim nods, "I know Albert, I know..." Turning to Lou, "Ok show us what this all means and how it's going to help us."

Lou taps a few keys and brings up the probability matrix and begins explaining how the system integrates the two baseline data passes with known data intersects and then builds a general web search program looking for secondary, tertiary, quaternary and so on intersects of data, photos, basically

seline. He pauses
ain; "one of the
d probably elevated
bility to begin
ital media and using
t me show you an
example..." he pulls up ~ , f Sokolov's jets. "This picture was in one of the surveillance files your group sent over to us and was included in the first pass of data, you see the tail number 'NH376' there in the upper right corner?" The group nods, "Well, that's a data point, we ran into it again a number of times in the FAA systems and the Saudi Air Defense computers, which is how the program tied in this Pump Station #3 outside Riyadh."

Agent Murphy pipes up, "how did you access the FAA and the Saudis? That can't be legal..."

Lou just smiles, "that's open to interpretation actually, we have access to all US system in accordance with our working agreements with Homeland Security... and as for the Saudis... there is a great deal of data out there that belongs to foreign governments, most of it accessible if you know where to look... and well, we know where to look." He tries not to sound too smug, but didn't this guy understand nobody's data was safe anymore. "So, getting back to the probabilities matrix... the system has used the two baseline data sets plus all available intersecting data points, public or private..." Lou says, giving agent Murphy a small smile... "The derivative is the matrix, thus the name NEO by the way... I know, corny, but what do you expect from a bunch of programmers?"

Harrington is studying the list on the screen, "so, based on what you fed into the system plus all this other data this list represents what exactly?"

Lou sighs, "If this works the way we believe it does these data points are proportionally related, by the percentage listed, to the original data we entered. So, I guess the real question is what does that mean..." He lets it hang for a moment, "it means this is our leads list... people and places that are by the degrees indicated related to Sokolov's outfit since that was our baseline profile."

"Hmmm, so this is why that Hardy fella is in New York and your daughter is in Tampa..." Harrington waits for a reaction.

"I don't believe I said she was in Tampa..." Lou responds.

"Lou, you aren't the only one with resources you know..."

Albert breaks the silence, "alright, if you two are finished measuring... what do we do with this?"

Tim looks at Lou, "Well, I think the first step is, Lou tells us what he and his folks are already doing..." He turns the two younger agents, "fellas, give us a few minutes, I'll call you when I'm ready to pack up and head to New York." Turning back to Albert and Lou, "I have a full team on the ground in Chicago reviewing everything there to see if there is anything worth following up on, and the team in New York is being put together now. In fact, I'm supposed to be flying up there this evening to brief them." Harrington gets up and stretches before turning to Lou, "would you be willing to come to New York with me and brief my team there?"

Lou hesitates, "sure Tim, I can do that, need to grab my stuff over at the DoubleTree but that won't take but a minute."

"Can you get in touch with this Jack fella, might be helpful to have him join us."

Lou looks dubious, "I'll give it a shot, but once Jack is in the field he isn't always easy to get to, and I'm going to need copies of all the documents before we go anywhere."

Albert looks at both of them shaking his head, "Ok, it's settled then, we're going to New York..."

Lou and Tim simultaneously, "We???"

"Yeah, you both are crazy if you think you're leaving me out of this, besides who else is going to make sure you don't make a mess out of my case?"

Casting a Net

Sampson's jet touches down at the Tampa Executive Jet Port and taxis to a stop in front of the black Chevy Tahoe waiting for him.

He grabs his bag and walks over to the SUV getting into the passenger seat, he motions for the driver to head out. Sampson preferred to sit in the front, he didn't like the feeling of being driven around, that was for Alexi, besides, he had a better view of potential threats from the front. Tampa was Sokolov's distribution center covering the Southeast for girls, guns and drugs, they even moved a fair number of agricultural workers out of Mexico and Central America, but they didn't keep a large contingent of men here, no need to draw unneeded attention. The more efficient they were at quickly moving product, including girls, to their other operations the better. Sampson had access to eight men, add another three if the van drivers were in town, they weren't.

Tim Borodkin, "Little Timmy", the six three two-hundred-and-eighty-pound senior Sokolov man in Tampa updated him as they drove down Kennedy Boulevard toward the Channelside district; Sokolov owned a three-bedroom condo on the twenty-fifth floor of the Channelside Towers, it was a unit he had never visited. Nevertheless, he kept at least one in every major city he had operations in and Sampson had stayed in most of them at one time or another.

They didn't have a match on Jessie, the hack into TSA had tracked her coming into Tampa, but she had disappeared before showing up again around noon today in the Tampa Police facial recognition system deployed in Ybor City. Sokolov's men could place her there but there wasn't much more information than that at the moment, not what Sampson had wanted to hear and his displeasure was clear. He placed a call to the Spider to see if there were any updates, there was nothing new but Sampson asked him to canvas all available systems to see if he could develop anything specific in the greater Tampa Bay area. With only a few men at his disposal Sampson had called them before boarding the jet in New York and directed them to spread as much cash around as it took to get a hit on her, they had extensive contacts in the area and someone had to know or have seen something. He knew she was good but everyone left a trail of some kind, you just had to be persistent. It was several hours later while he was still in the air that they broke the first lead on her.

Terry Skinner was just a young man, a runner for the Sokolov gang in Tampa, not even officially part of the group, but he had grown up on these streets and knew everyone running a con or game in the area. They hadn't given him any of the cash but he knew better than most where to look. He figured if this girl was going to stay out of sight she would need a vehicle and that meant Florida Avenue. He had hit pay dirt on the third lot, a fella he had run "hot" cars for as a teen had sold her a car just a day earlier. He hadn't taken much convincing to give up the McIntyre girl, everyone in this town knew Sokolov's reputation and Jessie's five hundred dollars to squash the registration may as well have been pocket change in the balance.

Terry had been waiting at the condo when Sampson and Borodkin had arrived. Sampson clapped Terry on the back slipping him five crisp hundred-dollar bills as he ushered him out the door. He was already dialing the Spider as the door closed, "Sampson here, I've got a license plate and car description on the girl down here, can you use that?"

The Spider smiles to himself, "sure, we can use the local traffic cams to try to track her, if she shows up on one of those we should be able to tell you where she is or was anyway. They aren't real time but might lead us to where she is staying."

"How long?" Sampson demands.

"Sampson, I don't know... we'll get right on it though," The Spider replies the exasperation showing through. He wasn't a miracle worker, but even Sampson, who understood the tech better than most, seemed to think they could just push a button and get whatever they needed.

"Find her..." says Sampson hanging up. He didn't have her yet but the net was closing, the only question now was how to best take her alive. Sokolov had been adamant and "accidents" weren't tolerated... which probably meant he was going to lose some of his team down here. Hard to stay alive when you can't shoot back he thought to himself, and this clearly wasn't some sixteen-year old school girl that was going to ride in and deliver herself. Alexi's need to personally deal with her was rapidly becoming a pain in his ass, taking her down at a distance would be much cleaner and easier - never-mind safer. But the boss still liked to get his hands dirty. He felt like the men respected him more if he occasionally made a demonstration of the skills that had made him who he was. Sampson couldn't argue with that, but didn't think it necessary anymore, enough people had died at both their hands that no one doubted what would happen if you crossed Alexi or if he simply didn't like you. Never-mind that there wasn't anything particularly intimidating about slowly killing a woman, even one as capable as this one seemed to be. None of that changed anything though, he would find this girl and then Alexi could have his fun.

"Timmy, make sure you get a couple of boys over to each of the girls homes we delivered two weeks ago. It seems this McIntyre knows about them, maybe she'll make a mistake and contact one of them, get the car description out also and do it now, she has a head start on us."

"Yes sir, I also called some guys in from the Miami group, thought we might need a few more bodies."

"Good thinking, now let's find this bitch."

Trailer #3

The best-laid plans and all that, clichés arise not because of a lack of imagination but because repetition begs for definition.

While Lou worked to align his efforts with the FBI, Jack and Jessie were pursuing Sokolov independently. Conversely Sokolov was on the hunt for Jessie even as his instincts started to fire off from the FBI's ramped up effort to bring him down. They were all in a race with no clear finish in sight and no one could afford to lose.

Having lost the staring contest Jessie waits until the little boy closes his door before getting out, she is more than uncomfortable at this point the harried look on the woman's face, the sad eyes of the girl's little brother and the pervading sense of hopelessness surrounding the whole situation, weighs her down.

"Mrs. Chambers?" She asks hesitantly.

The woman gives her a tired look with a grim smile she answers, "honey, haven't been Mrs. Chambers in a long time, spect you'll be askin' bout my Allie." She doesn't wait for Jessie to answer as she pops the trunk and begins to grab a couple of grocery bags. "Well you might as well come in, close that trunk for me dear, it ain't much but it's home..." She exclaims walking up the steps, almost as if to preemptively explain her circumstances. The place is neat but has the syrupy sweet perfume of air freshener barely covering the odor of old cigarettes and deep-fried dinners.

Jessie stands in the center of the living room; the kitchen is off to the left where Allie's mom keeps a constant chatter going while unloading the groceries. "What channel did you say you were from dear?"

"I didn't Mrs. Cham...," Jessie catches herself.

Allie's mom looks up, "That's alright call me Terry, my married name is Johnson now." Standing up the groceries now stowed, "well, if you're not from the TV..." she lets it hang between them.

"Terry my name is Jessie Mc..." she hesitates for a moment, "Jessie McIntosh." She hadn't planned on sharing her real name; this spy shit was going to take some getting used to. "I am doing an article about missing teens and wondered if you would mind sharing your experience. I know I should have called first but I am only in the area for a few days and hoped you wouldn't mind." It sounded forced to her but Terry just nodded, the tears welling up as she bites her lip.

"Sure honey, just let me fix my Jas a quick bite, you come sit down here at the table and we can talk."

Jessie sits at the scarred formica table the chairs a mix match of colors, their metal legs dig into the old carpet catching on the frays from their repeated sliding in and out. She pulls a hand-held recorder from her backpack leaving the top unzipped, not really sure why but feeling more comfortable having quick access to her pistols.

The microwave dings announcing the requisite completion of rotations necessary to generate the mac and cheese that was probably the extent of the young boy's dinner. He sits on the couch, his feet dangling just above the worn carpet as his mom places a TV table in front of him, the noodles still steaming and a napkin wrapped generic cola can. Jessie guesses this is his typical routine, figuring it's unlikely there's a history of happy family meals around the small table. The soft babble coming from the TV will mask their conversation shielding the boy from what has to be a scary subject for one so young.

Terry lights up a cigarette sets a chipped glass ashtray on the table in front of her and asks, "So what you want to know?"

Jessie hesitates, "let's start at the beginning," looking to buy some time while she figures out where to go from here, she actually hadn't expected to get this far. "Tell me about the day Allie disappeared, the reports I read say she left school before her first class, any idea why she would do that?"

Terry gives her a sideways glance, "you're not writin' any article, now are you?"

"Uh... yes, like I said, about missing teens," Jessie works to keep the nerves out of her voice.

"Well honey, that there's a little detail that wasn't released; the sheriff told us they hold stuff back sometimes..." she taps the ash of her cigarette. "How would you know that... maybe you want to tell me why I shouldn't call the police...?" there's an edge to her voice now.

Jessie clicks off the handheld recorder, reaching down she pulls the backpack on to her lap, "No Terry, I'm not writing an article, and I would appreciate it if you wouldn't call the police. But I really do want to hear about your daughter... I am trying to help." While that wasn't strictly true Jessie knew she was on precarious ground here.

Terry sounds skeptical, "I don't know how you could help, 'less there's something you're not..."

She doesn't have a chance to finish, "Mom, mom, there's a man here..." Jason says from the living room. He has the mini-blinds pulled slightly apart and is peering out.

Alarm bells are going off in Jessie's head as Terry gets up and heads over to the front door, "Come on away from there Jas," she says taking the boy by the arm. He is standing next to his mom holding onto her hand as she begins to open the door. Jessie can't react in time as the door begins to open it is simultaneously shredded by the rapid pops of an automatic rifle. Terry Johnson is killed instantly by the second burst, her body jerking upright for a moment before falling back into the trailer's living room. The little boy is screaming now trapped under her and the noisy chaos of combat fills the tiny space. Jessie dives to the floor both pistols out and trained on the door. She knows Terry is gone and can't check on the boy, survival is the first priority, she knows she can't help him if she dies too. It takes a mere instant to process all this as the first man comes through the door his rifle sweeping from right to left. Her first shot catches him in the chest angling up and out his shoulder, she adjusts automatically the second almost simultaneous shot enters under his chin there is no need for a third as he crashes to the floor. The back wall of the trailer explodes as the automatic fire begins again, Jessie rolls to her right toward the front wall. It's a risk as the trailer walls aren't capable of stopping a bullet, but she is counting on human nature. Most folks run in the opposite direction from danger, she is moving toward it hoping to catch the second shooter by surprise. For a moment all goes strangely quiet, even the boy's screams have died to a whimper. The problem for Jessie is she doesn't know how many more there are, but she also can't wait to see either, the trailer is a mousetrap and she is caught inside. She fires three quick shots into the already shredded front door barely hanging from its hinges. The metal erupts screeching as she dives into the living room, guns trained at the doorway. Time slows down for her the second gunmen is on the second step and lets off a volley of shots, they all miss high. Jessie knows from her training that in a combat situation most people using automatic weapons shoot high and to the left. It's a combination of adrenaline and the natural motion of the rifle as it fires and you have to consciously adjust for it, he doesn't and it's a mistake she makes him pay for.

Jessie learned her lesson in Chicago, no assumptions that there are only two this time. She grabs the boy, covered in his mother's blood, and quickly checks him for wounds, his eyes wide with shock he is mumbling something she can't make out. "Just stay behind me…" she admonishes him, he doesn't respond just sits in the middle of the floor not moving, covered in his mother's slowing congealing blood. Jessie works her way down the steps and around the trailer looking for anything that seems out of place, there doesn't appear to be anyone else, but she can hear the sirens growing closer and as her focus expands she notices people coming out of their trailers phones in hand.

"Fuck me dead…" she whispers to herself, there isn't going to be any walking away from this one. She retreats to the Ford stowing her pistols in the backpack, extracting her SAT phone, before locking the trunk. She sits on the trailer steps and manages to fire off a short message to her dad. The first police cruiser pulls up, lights flashing, sirens on, she already has her hands in the air, no sense losing your life to an overzealous cop with an eighth-grade mentality.

A Fly in the Web

The Spider rarely left the command center but even he needed a break and a little solitude to recharge mentally. He had refused Alexi's offer of a condo in the main building, preferring to maintain a simple apartment, more of a loft really, a few buildings over. It was private, close, and a refuge from the daily insanity that had become routine in the Sokolov electronic universe. It was devoid of modern convenience and electronics, not even a television or microwave. He maintained a rare collection of out of print classic books and during these brief but necessary respites, he would brew the dark Russian tea he loved and re-read his favorite passages. Sometimes noshing on dense dark pumpernickel bread slathered with sweet butter, he preferred the simple things in stark contrast to the technology empire he had built for Sokolov.

Of course, the alley was under constant surveillance from inside the command center, but as is usually the case people only see what they expect to see. The Spider doesn't even glance in the direction of the old man huddled next to the dumpster beneath a covering of cardboard boxes balanced to make a haphazard lean to, the stench of urine floats up as he closes the door and hurries past. It isn't that he is insensitive to the plight of the homeless, but there is nothing he can do for the old man, and he is in a hurry. An early dinner before he heads back to personally organize the search Sampson is demanding. He turns in spite of himself as he hears the bang of the dumpster against the wall, the old man is lurching toward him. The Spider turns and makes a dash for the street taking him out of range of the door cameras as the old man catches up seemingly much too quickly.

"Let's not have any more running shall we," Jack whispers in his ear. "You're going to lend an old man a hand and we are going to have a chat," the hard nose of Jack's pistol in his side is more than enough to convince The Spider. He wasn't cut out for street work or even mild violence and the resolve in Jack's voice is clear, better to play this along then die in a dirty alley.

Jack had spent the time after running into Sampson scouting out the alley and gathering the few things he would need to fashion a sufficient disguise. He had learned long ago to keep it simple, the more elaborate the more that could and usually did, go wrong.

The Spider didn't resist as he led Jack up the steps to his third-floor loft, wheezing with exertion upon reaching the top, he fumbles with the keys unable to control the shaking in his hands. Jack says nothing, letting the man's nerves build, preferring to let imagination lay the foundation of what is to come. He doesn't necessarily take pleasure in extracting information from people but he is very good at it. The door is finally open and Jack shoves

The Spider into the spartan apartment, locking the door behind him in one swift move. Jack knows these things tend to go one of two ways, either a fight or complete capitulation, The Spider capitulates offering no resistance when Jack zip ties his arms and legs to the chair at the small table.

Jack sits opposite him, laying his pistols on the table and shrugging off the oversize jacket he had been wearing. "Let's keep this as simple and civil as possible, okay?"

"Why, you are going to kill me anyway..." The Spider sighs with resignation.

"It doesn't have to end that way, it could but it doesn't have to, I need information, my guess is you can give it to me."

The Spider shifts his weight trying to keep the feeling in his arms, "do you know who I work for?"

Jack smiles, "Yes I do..."

"Then you know I am already dead, if I tell you anything he will kill me and if I don't you will kill me..." He looks intently at Jack, "so what kind of choice is that I ask you?" He doesn't wait for the answer, "none, you might as well just do it now and be done with it."

Jack shakes his head, "I had forgotten how melodramatic and fatalistic you Russians are, let's start with an easy question, what's your name, in fact I'll start, you can call me Jack."

"Jack? Is that really your name?"

"Does it really matter?" Jack responds.

"No, I guess it doesn't, I am Alexander Potemkin but everyone calls me 'The Spider'."

"Potemkin? Like the battleship?" Jack asks, ignoring the whole spider thing.

"So, you know your history, yes, named after a great great-great grandfather of mine, or at least that's the story my father always told us."

Jack stands up looking around the small apartment, *not much here* he thinks, moving into the kitchen he fills the small teakettle with water, it's an older one with a spring-loaded cap on the spout, a small hole in the middle lets the steam escape as it heats up, he turns the stove on. Retrieving a half empty bottle of vodka, he returns to the table setting it between them. "Alexander, here is the crux of the issue, Sokolov is trying to hurt someone very important to me... and I simply can't let that happen so...

Potemkin simply nods, "it's the girl, isn't it?" Scooting his chair up and leaning forward as much as his restrained arms allow, "the McIntyre girl, right? I'm right aren't I?" He shakes his head smiling, "you have no idea what you're into here, they already know where she is, Sampson, you know Sampson right? He is already in Tampa..." He pauses for effect, "if you let me go maybe you live, maybe, just maybe, you can disappear."

Jack gives him a big smile, "Alexander my friend, I'm afraid you don't understand. I've been scraping scum like you and your boss off the proverbial shoe of the free world for thirty years..." The teakettle starts to whistle the water heated to a hundred degrees centigrade is boiling and pressure of the building steam escapes through the small hole in the spout, "Believe me, I won't be the one wishing to disappear..." He walks into the kitchen and turns the stove to low, just enough heat to barely keep a low whistle going. "Now where were we, oh yes, you were getting ready to tell me all the things I need to know." Jack glances at his phone, the vibration notifying him of an incoming message, he looks up giving Potemkin a chilling grin.

The bluff played out, Potemkin's voice falters as he strains to look into the kitchen, "We aren't having tea, are we?"

"No, my friend, we aren't..."

The Thing about Jack

Lou had packed up his gear while he and Tim had unsuccessfully tried to talk Albert out of going to New York. Tim was arranging transportation and a Bureau jet for them during which Albert asked some basic question about Paradigm and the work they were doing. Lou's SAT phone started pinging him with a priority message, interrupting the conversation.

"How the hell do you even get a signal in here?" Harrington asks him.

"Well, our systems piggy back on any available network so..."

"Uhh sure, but our networks are all secure and firewalled..." Harrington exclaims.

"Well, for the most part," Lou says with a grin.

"Jesus Christ Lou, thank God you're on our side," Albert says.

Lou reads his message from Jessie and turns to Harrington, "Tim, I'm going to need some help double time on this, my girl was just taken into custody by the Hillsborough County Sheriff's department down in Florida, any chance we can get a couple agents out of your Tampa office to go get her?"

"What did she do?" Tim asks.

"Don't know but if she is surrendering to the cops it must be serious, she didn't have time to include any details."

"Okay let me make some calls..."

"Tim, I got this," Albert chimes in, "the US Attorney down there clerked for me, I'll have her grab a couple of Marshals and take her into Federal custody, nobody argues with the Marshals."

"Thanks Albert, can she call us once she has her?" Lou asks nervously.

"Sure Lou, I'll have her move Jessie to the Federal Court House, we have interview rooms there and the Marshals will make sure she is safe and secure." Albert steps out to make the call to Tampa.

Lou is obviously distracted and is pacing the room, "Lou, let Albert take care of this, he's got good people on it, I'm sure she is fine." It rings hollow but Lou knows Tim is just trying to help. "Listen, let's look at this data again, my big issue isn't where to look or even how to tie this together, this program of yours is like magic... but we have to find a way to make some of it stick to Sokolov... Right now, I have a series of connected dots but no strings back to the center, at the end of the day it's not what I know, it's what I can prove."

Albert steps back into the room, "alright, they're headed to pick her up, Sherry will call as soon as they have her in custody." He sits back down, "Ok, what are we talking about?"

"I was telling Lou that even with all this new data I've got to be able to tie it directly to Sokolov, we need proof we can take to court..." Tim says, looking over at Lou who is still pacing.

Lou pulls out his phone and shoots off a quick message to Jack turning back to the table, "that was a message to Jack Hardy in New York, asked him to call in, maybe he's developed something we can use." Setting the phone on the table, "I needed to tell him about Jessie anyway."

"Can you tell us more about this Hardy fella, Lou?" Tim asks.

"Sure, I guess, like I was telling you he spent thirty plus years in the agency, probably one of the most decorated and accomplished agents they've ever had. You know they can never talk about it and you aren't even allowed to actually receive a commendation, it's in your file and all but there is never any public recognition. It takes a different kind of dedication I guess." Lou pauses for a moment, "anyway Jack's field craft is so good he ended up developing the training program for new recruits, even did some guest training, but you know I've never met anyone as..." Lou pauses again thinking about his good friend and wondering how to describe this man that is so important to him, but without making him seem like a cold calculating individual.

"Go ahead Lou, what were you going to say..." Tim prods him.

Lou hesitates, "well this probably won't sound right, I don't want you to think he is a cold-blooded killer, but I've never met anyone as comfortable as he is extracting information from people."

"You mean torturing people..." Albert blurts out.

"No, not really, it's more psychological than that, although Jack doesn't have a weak stomach when it comes to doing what has to be done... I guess it's just black and white to him, either you are on our side or you're not and if you're not, well, the consequences of your bad decisions are what they are."

Tim lets out a low whistle, "I've always heard about guys like that, never met one, but I guess we all have a role to play."

Albert looks at him like he is crazy, "a role to play, are you serious?"

Lou gives Albert a long look, "look, simple fact is Jack does what needs to be done, I've seen the other side, the side that would give his life for a friend or his country, you can't question the loyalty or patriotism of a man like that, you don't have perspective or standing for that matter." Lou can feel himself heating up again; nobody was going to attack Jack, not while he was around anyway. "Listen, what I mean is I have seen the things he has done, seen the sacrifices he has made, I was there when he did things no one else would that protected our country, protected our people. It might not be comfortable to talk about, hell I couldn't do the things he does, but I understand it and I know the man inside and he is straight up one of the good guys."

"Hey, I'm sorry, I don't know, it's just I guess you hate to think about being in a position where you're forced to basically break the law, I don't think I could handle the moral conflict..." Albert says softly. "But then I look at these animals we are dealing with, they respect nothing, not life, not women or even children and I guess in some ways you have to fight fire with fire, but I just couldn't do it."

"It's alright Albert, I get it, I couldn't do it either, I was agency and would have taken a life if I had to but I guess in a lot of ways, having Jack as a partner protected me from that, and that might be the thing I respect the most about him..." He doesn't get a chance to go further as Albert's phone rings.

In Custody

Jessie didn't move or say anything when the first set of patrol cars had pulled up, sirens blaring and lights flashing, four officers had piled out guns drawn. She had kept her hands held high above her head clearly empty as plenty of people had been killed by nervous locals over the years, vest or no vest. She could see the fear in their eyes and could only imagine what they had been expecting based on the 911 calls from the neighbors. They were yelling at her not to move which she had no intention of doing. The first pair came at her guns drawn almost daring her to, they had come from either side in standard tactical formation, so at least their training seemed to have kicked in she thought to herself. Two other officers were already clearing the trailer making sure there wasn't anyone else inside and she hoped they would be careful with the boy.

The officer on the left, a sergeant roughly pulled her hands behind her back, snapping on the cuffs while Mirandizing her, his partner kept his pistol trained on her the whole time. She hadn't offered any resistance when he had yanked her to her feet and thoroughly patted her down, although he did seem a bit surprised by the vest, but she had remained completely calm offering no explanation but not resisting either. They had taken her SAT phone and car keys, the second officer started searching the Fusion as the sergeant hustled her into the back of his squad car. Three additional cars, a crime scene van, and at least two TV trucks had shown up; the whole thing was threatening to turn into a circus. She kept her head turned into the interior of the car, hoping her dad had received her text message, she didn't want him seeing her picture plastered all over every TV station news feed tonight.

Sergeant Simpkins, the officer that had patted her down and whose car she now occupied was transporting her to the Sheriff's office for questioning. He kept up a steady banter from the front seat, obviously trying to illicit information. She tried to appear indifferent, not so much refusing to answer his questions, simply not responding at all. Jessie had been in enough nerve wracking situations that this was not too difficult for her, however strangely enough this was her first ride of any kind in a police car.

It was going to take a while to sort out exactly what had transpired at trailer #3 in the Strawberry Fields Mobile Home Park, but the locals were sure of one thing, this young woman was clearly in the middle of it. The vest, the backpack with two recently fired pistols and large quantity of cash, combined with three dead bodies all at the trailer of a young woman that had disappeared two weeks ago, this is what careers were made of; so maybe Sergeant Simpkins could be forgiven a bit of excited banter.

It was a short fifteen-minute ride to the Hillsborough County Sheriff's Office located on Faulkner Road as the sergeant pulls up into the sally port, a secure entry portal for transporting prisoners, his arrival draws a crowd. Jessie is processed into the system, the original AFIS (Automated Fingerprint Identification System) for scanning fingerprints had been expanded to include access to both Federal and international databases; her prints are matched in seconds with her military records.

Simpkins lets out a low whistle, *so she was a Major in the Rangers*, he thinks to himself, "I guess that explains the professional level pistol work," he mutters mostly under his breath. He logs her backpack contents and car keys into an evidence locker, signing off on the inventory sheet. He briefly considers what to do with her; best thing would be to just lock her in a holding cell and wait for the Sheriff or detectives to show up. Instead, he decides to bypass the holding cell and the comfortable interview rooms up front opting for the interrogation style ones in the back with their video cameras and two-way glass. Maybe it wouldn't make a difference but he was hoping he could unnerve her a bit and get her talking... although she seemed to be a pretty cool customer so far. Strictly speaking this wasn't in his purview but he had seen the mess at the scene and his curiosity was getting the better of him.

There were plenty of murders in the county, but most were driven by anger, domestic disputes, accidents and gang violence but a true professional style shooting, well those were few and far between.

Sergeant Simpkins enters the room with a bottle of water and hands it to Jessie, "listen, let's talk this through, okay?" he asks. "I need you to help me understand what happened out there."

The Sergeant knows he is indulging himself a bit, clearly this is going to be turned over to Homicide and their detectives, *but what could it hurt to ask some basic questions* he thinks. Not strictly protocol, but she had been Mirandized and it was all on tape anyway.

Jessie looks right at him, "thanks for the water..." is all she says unscrewing the bottle top and taking a long drink.

He doesn't get a chance to ask another question before there is a knock on the door, "sit tight I'll be right back."

That actually elicits a quick smile, "sure, I'll just hang out here, take your time," Jessie says.

Simpkins just nods his head, *I should have just left her in the cell,* he thinks to himself.

Closing the door behind him he looks up, coming face to face with two Federal Marshals and a serious looking woman.

She doesn't hesitate extending her hand, "Sergeant, I'm US Attorney Johannsen, I understand you have a Jessie McIntyre in custody here?"

"Uhh, yes..." he stammers. Regaining his composure, "what can I help you with?"

"Miss McIntyre is an integral part of a Federal investigation, I am here to take her into my custody, can you please have her brought up front for transport. We are going to need all of her inventoried property as well." Starting to turn, "and Sergeant let's get a move on, I want this done now, understand."

"Yes, but I'm going to have to check with Sherriff McKinley, we have three dead victims. I can't just let her walk out of here," Simpkins replies somewhat exasperated.

Johannsen gives him a frown, "Sergeant, you check with whomever you want, but do it quick, I want my prisoner released without delay, is that clear, and when you speak with Sheriff McKinley let him know my office wants complete copies of the crime scene findings including the photographs..."

Simpkins had hesitated for only a second before calling the Sheriff, he wasn't going to argue with the feds, that was above his pay grade, but McKinley had to be told, no way he could let this girl walk out of the jail without the Sheriff saying it was ok.

The Sheriff, a twenty-five-year veteran of the department, Jack Mckinley, was still at the crime scene handling the press and making sure nothing had been contaminated before his techs could process everything. The three bodies had already been bagged and sent to the Medical Examiners more for identification than anything else the cause of death was pretty clear. They hadn't been able to track down Billy Johnson yet so young Jason had been taken into protective custody and was with Child Services and a counselor. The boy was clearly traumatized and hadn't seemed to be in shock.

The last thing McKinley needed now was another complication, but when his phone started ringing and his office ID came up and he figured it was going to be a long night. "Slow down Sergeant, who is there?"

"Sir, the Federal Marshal's just showed up to take custody of our prisoner..."

"Yes sir, the girl from the shooting, her name is Jessie McIntyre, retired Army Major. Sir, she was a Ranger, if you can believe it..." Simpkins start to go on.

"All right, settle down Simpkins, did they bring a transfer writ from the US Attorney?" the sheriff asks.

"Uh, well, no sir, I mean she came herself..."

"Johannsen is there?" McKinley asks in disbelief.

"Yes sir..."

"Jesus Christ on a stick, OK Simpkins listen closely, have Johannsen sign the transfer log and give her whatever she wants. Oh, and let her know we will send over whatever we develop from the crime scene..." He hesitates for a moment, "and sergeant, try not to piss them off, I don't need the headache, ok?"

"Uh, yes sir, are you sure though?" Simpkins asks.

"Dammit sergeant, think about this for just a fucking second, how the hell did they even know about this? And to show up almost immediately, obviously there is more to this than we know and I don't need this department in the middle of some damn war the Feds are conducting so just do what they ask."

"Yes sir, sorry sir, I didn't think of that, I'll take care of it."

"It's fine sergeant, this is a crazy thing for sure, she say anything when you brought her in?"

"No sir, not a word..." The Sheriff clicks off without another word, Simpkins stares at the phone for a moment then gathers Jessie from the interrogation room and heads up front.

Simpkins escorts Jessie to the lobby, hands the backpack to one of the Marshals and asks Johannsen to sign the transfer log, he watches them walk her out to the waiting SUV and wonders if he will ever know what this is all about.

And That Makes Six

Little Timmy and Sampson had just cut into their filets at Charley's Steak House in Tampa, one of the premier spots in town, Tim preferred it to Bern's especially since the relocation to the waterfront made it walking distance from the condo, his phone starts pinging him. He reads the message to himself, knowing Sampson is going to lose it if he hesitates to share the news with the big man. Really no way to avoid it though, "Sampson… two of our guys are down, they ran into McIntyre out at one of the girl's houses we had them checking."

Sampson sets his fork and knife down, "what do you mean down?" he asks quietly.

Even Little Timmy is scared of Sampson, "Uh, they're dead Sampson, she shot them, seems like the girl's mother got caught up in it too, not sure who shot her but she's dead as well."

Sampson doesn't say anything and the seconds seem to stretch in to minutes, "where exactly is the girl right now?"

Timmy misses the threat in Sampson's voice, "she's being processed at the Sheriff's office, they arrested her at the site."

"Are you completely sure that's where she is…" Sampson asks.

"Yeah, I'm sure, we got someone inside that tips us if one of our boys gets picked up or if any of our girls show up… why?"

"Let's go, show me this jail, how far is it from here?"

"Sampson, we can't crash the jail, that's suicide, there's nothing but cops there." Timmy stands up dropping three C notes on the table, "look I'll take you over there, it's only about ten minutes from here... but Sampson, believe me that place is like a fortress."

Sampson has already decided that Little Timmy isn't going to make it much longer working for Sokolov; it's only Sampson's unfamiliarity with the team down here that prevents him from snapping the man's neck at the table. "Let's go, we need her and now we know where she is... how do we talk to our person inside?"

"Well, we use coded text messages, they monitor all the phone and cell traffic in and out of there so we have to keep the messages short."

They pulled out of Charley's and headed down Channelside drive making the right onto Route 60 towards Brandon and the Sheriff's office. Neither noticed the two speeding black SUVs headed in the opposite direction. "Okay, we need to know if she gets bailed out and by who, will our person know?" Sampson asks.

"That shouldn't be a problem, we have a clerk in central processing and another over in the jail that can tell us what cell she is in," Timmy answers him. He parks on the far side of the visitor's lot and keys the message into his cell phone. "Sometimes it takes a bit to get an answer, depends on who's there and what's going on, these guys are pretty careful." His phone starts vibrating almost immediately, "Shit..."

Sampson knows he is already playing catch up and he doesn't have the team he needs to keep up, "what is it?" he asks quietly.

"Feds popped her loose about fifteen minutes ago, she's gone..."

Sampson can feel his hands twitching, he wants to wrap them around this man's neck and squeeze. It's not really Timmy's fault but his nonchalance and 'oh well' attitude is exactly what Alexi had warned him about this morning. *Motherfucker, now he was going to have to call Alexi and tell him the girl was in Federal custody, what a fuckin' mess,* he thinks. Sokolov was going to be beyond pissed, he didn't tolerate fuckups, not even from Sampson, didn't matter whose fault it was. *Shit, shit, shit,* he might have considered making a move at the jail, but taking on the Feds was a different ball game altogether. Never mind not knowing where she was now, he should call Alexi but it wouldn't hurt to check in with The Spider first, maybe he would be able to help, he knew it was a stretch but the thought of calling Alexi made him hesitate?

The phone rings a dozen times before hanging up, there was no voicemail on the Spider's phone, he simply always answered so there had never been a need for it. Sampson tries to ignore the cold ball of nerves forming in his stomach, it is as unfamiliar as it is uncomfortable. He dials up the emergency line to the command center, normally only the Spider would answer this, but tonight it's a voice he doesn't recognize. "Get the Spider, I need to talk to him now..." he demands.

"I'm sorry sir, he's not here... in fact, I was hoping this was him... he left over an hour ago, nobody's seen him since, and he isn't answering his phone," the young man's nervousness is obvious.

"Are you fucking kidding me!" Sampson explodes, "who have you notified?"

"Notified?" the young man seems bewildered, "who would I notify sir? There is no protocol for this, I wouldn't know who or where to call."

"So, you're telling me he's been gone at least an hour and nobody besides yourself knows about it!" If Sampson could reach through the phone this young man would be dead also.

"Uhh, yes sir, I'm sorry sir I didn't know what to do..."

Sampson hangs up without bothering to answer, the last thing he wants is one of Spider's geeks calling Alexi and starting a three-alarm fire over nothing. It's possible the old man is just napping in his apartment, not likely, but with bad news piling up he needed to control the flow of information at this point. "Back to the condo..." he tersely orders Timmy. Sampson dials up the crew in Brighton Beach, "Get a few guys over to The Spiders place, ...yeah the loft on 9th and see if he is there, and be careful..." That done, he turns to Timmy, "Call everyone in, there's no point continuing to look for her, we know where she is, I want all our guys at the warehouse in an hour, clear?"

Timmy just nods, no point in poking the bear, but at this hour it was going to be damn near impossible getting everyone rounded up and in one place that quickly. He was really starting to wonder what all the talk was about, Sampson didn't seem to be such a badass to him, but he sends out a group text nonetheless. They pull into the parking garage under the condo complex, Sampson instructs him to wait in the car, "I've got to grab a few things, see if you can find that pilot, I'm heading back to New York tonight." He doesn't wait for an answer, just slams the door and heads for the elevator. He doesn't see the smirk on Timmy's face, but it doesn't matter, he has already made up his mind about the Tampa crew.

Tampa Federal Courthouse

"Sherry, you got her?" Albert asks without preamble. Lou and Tim watch as Albert nods his head, obviously getting an update, "Okay, keep her there and I'll call you back in ten... and Sherry, make sure she is safe, I don't want her out of the Marshal's sight, am I clear?" He nods again, "Ok, I appreciate it, call you right back." Albert hangs up and turns to Tim and Lou, "Ok, here's the situation..."

Albert explains that when Sherry Johannsen and the Federal Marshals had shown up at the Sheriff's Office Jessie was already in an interrogation room, having been scanned and processed earlier. Needless to say, they weren't too pleased to hear that the feds were flexing their muscle and preparing to take custody of their prisoner. "But Sherry doesn't put up with anyone's shit, she is all business, believe me," Albert says.

"Ok, that's great Albert, but what the hell happened?" Lou asks.

"Well, as far as I can tell she was involved in a shoot-out with two men at a trailer down there in Tampa, they're dead along with another woman, but the details are a bit sketchy." Albert pauses, "she won't talk to anyone, not even Sherry until she speaks to you apparently," he says looking at Lou.

"Ok, how do we do that?" Lou asks.

Tim chimes in, "we can do a video call from here if she is in one of the courthouse conference rooms, we do them all the time."

Albert is already back on his phone, "Ok, give us a few minutes to get linked up, and thanks again Sherry." He turns to Tim, "can you initiate the link from here?"

"Sure, no problem, give me a second to pull it up." He brings the secure conferencing software up on the big screen and selects the Tampa courthouse from the list of linked sites, "which room are they in Albert?" he asks.

"Conference Room #3, it's the fifth one on the list there..."

"Ok, here we go, Lou, you want to move over here so she can see you, ok?" Tim points to the chair next to him, "you too Albert." The screens flashes and the video link comes online.

Jessie is seated at the end of the table, hands cuffed resting on the table in front of her, two Marshals stand behind her and Johannsen is sitting to her left.

"Jesus, why is she cuffed?" Lou asks.

Albert speaks up, "Sherry, can you hear us okay?"

"Yes sir, no problem," she answers.

Albert nods, "good, can we lose the cuffs and we'll try to bring you up to speed from this end, but first Jessie, I am Albert Jimenez, Deputy Attorney General, can you tell us what happened?"

As one of the Marshals removes Jessie's cuffs she looks at her dad, "Dad?" is all she says.

Lou clearly emotional, "it's okay honey, this is Special Agent Harrington and we are going to be working this thing out together from here on out." He pauses for a moment, "are you okay Jess?"

"Yes sir, I'm fine." She is calm and collected and Lou has seen this post action demeanor before in Jack, he puts it aside for now, beginning to understand she may be more like Jack then he had even suspected.

"Ok Jess, I have briefed Tim and Albert on what we've found including the output from NEO, we can go through the detail after, but tell us what happened there."

Jessie walks them through the last two days in Tampa, reciting the details with a clinical detachment learned in the Rangers. She hesitates when she gets to the events of the evening, but plunges on relating the details of the conversation with Terry Johnson and how the two, what were probably Sokolov soldiers, had shown up shooting Terry before she was able to neutralize them. Her replay of the take down of the two and the subsequent trip to the police station was straight forward and matter of fact. Behind her the Marshals are giving each other a 'what the hell' look.

"Ok... well, I'm glad you're okay honey..." Lou doesn't really know what else to say, even he is a bit disconcerted by this unemotional recitation. "I think what really has me perplexed is how these guys even knew you were in Tampa..." he says, trying to move the conversation forward. He turns to Tim, "nobody knew she was headed there, so they are either tracking her somehow or they have penetrated the airlines or TSA, neither of which is a good thing. Have you guys developed any data on their cyber capabilities?"

"Well, we have a pretty good outline of their online presence as far as porn distribution, escort services, things like that, but honestly nothing really concrete." He shakes his head, "fact is, our guys are pretty good, but we haven't been able to crack their systems and anytime we get close they simply disappear and show up under another shadow URL we can't trace back to a firm location. We believe we know who is managing their network, and it's huge by the way, and he is a fucking wizard."

Albert obviously frustrated, "I know you guys all get this technology stuff, but for us simple folk are you saying they might have, what do you call it... hacked into enough systems to have tracked her flights and who knows what else?" Face in his hands, "this is like a bad fucking movie, Jesus..."

Lou can't help but smile, "Yeah, I know Albert, but yes that's what I'm saying, and honestly with the right people and persistence it isn't quite as difficult as it might seem, it's part of what we are combating over at Paradigm all the time..." He turns to Tim, "what's next Tim, can we get Jessie up here?" He looks back at the screen, "Miss Johannsen, I should have said it earlier, but thank you."

She just nods and addresses Albert, "sir, what do you want me to do?"

He looks up, "Sherry, have you guys heard of this group down there, anything at all, even if it's just the locals?"

"Well sir, as you already know we have a pretty significant human trafficking issue here, lots of local prostitution of young women. It seems every other week we see a report of two or three girls held in an apartment or trailer being forced to service hundreds of 'johns' a week. It's pretty rampant down here, and that doesn't even count the 'illegals' MS-13 is bringing up from Mexico and Central America to work agriculture here. If you say this Sokolov is orchestrating it I believe you, but we don't have any specifics in this office."

Albert looks around, "Ok, thanks Sherry, it may be that as this develops we will get your office more involved as things are moving pretty rapidly at this point." He turns to Tim, "Does the FBI have any planes down there?"

"We should, I can check, give me a second."

"Okay Sherry, if we can get a plane rustled up can you have the Marshals escort her up here to DC tonight?"

Lou breaks in, "Why don't we all just meet in New York, we're headed there anyway…"

"Listen up, no plane, but transportation tells me there is a Jet Blue flight direct out of Tampa to JFK leaving at quarter to nine, you should be able to make that." Tim says.

With the travel coordinated and a chorus of "thanks" from the DC group they sign off. Tim has arranged to have a small team of agents meet the plane from Tampa and escort them into the City. They weren't going to take any chances, if Sokolov had penetrated the airlines they would know Jessie was coming, not even the US Marshals and FBI could erase an airline's manifest. Lou tries to reach Jack one more time, but his call continues to go unanswered. He sends one more message: "Jack, call as soon as you can, things have changed" Lou hopes nothing has happened to his old friend.

100° Centigrade

Jack is sitting at the small table, there is almost a sad look in his eyes as he gazes at Potemkin; the kettle continues its mournful whistle in the background. "So, my friend I wish we could avoid all this... are you sure it wouldn't be better to just help me?" Jack asks. "We are both old men, it's been a long time since I have had to make someone talk, you know it's not too late to avoid all this unpleasantness..." he nods towards the kitchen.

Potemkin is on the verge of tears, "Please, don't do this... I can't help you, I just can't... I don't know what you want from me..."

"Alexander, listen to me, are these people really worth the pain and suffering you are going to experience? I promise you in an hour you are going to begging to tell me everything just to make it stop..." Jack shakes his head, "I don't enjoy this my friend, I really don't but what choice are you leaving me?"

"But you can just leave..." Potemkin whispers, "I won't tell anyone I promise..."

Jack raises his voice "Ahhh, you say that now, but it's not true and we both know it, we have come too far to turn back now." Jack leans back in his chair, "did you know that water boils at one hundred degrees centigrade? ...Of course you do, but did you know the steam that forces its way out of your little kettle's spout is even hotter than that?" He leans forward for emphasis, "you see, it's the pressure that does it... makes it even hotter than the water itself... steam that hot will cook the skin right off a person." Jack drops his voice to almost a hiss, "I know what you do, buying and selling these girls like slaves, what you force them to do, did you think there were never going to be any consequences... you will tell me what I want to know."

Potemkin hangs his head, "it's not me, I just run the systems..." He looks up at Jack but finds no compassion there, no pity, nothing but those unflinching eyes.

"The Spider they call you, cause you are at the center of the web, right?" Jack waves his hand... "Don't bother answering, I already know, you manage all of it, the porn sites, the hacking rings, all of it... don't you! You are as guilty as Sokolov himself my friend."

Potemkin doesn't answer, just nods meekly.

"Well Spider, tonight you are going to lose those fingers let's see how you manage a keyboard then... the only real question is whether I let you live or not!" Jack says as he heads back into the kitchen. He turns the heat up pushing the low whistle to a high-pitched keening. With unexpected strength, he pulls the old man still zip tied to his chair into the kitchen where he snips the tie off his right arm. He has Potemkin's right wrist in an iron grip keeping the man from moving.

Potemkin tries to break the grip thrashing his body around, but Jack has him from behind and he can't break free. "Stop moving now! You only make it worse, I'll break your wrists and dislocate your shoulders then you won't be able to move at all."

Potemkin goes limp whimpering in a low mewl. The old man is crying now, "Don't please, please... I'll tell you whatever you want..."

"Oh, I know you will, but now you want mercy, seriously, did you show any of those children mercy, any of those girls... did you? No, I didn't think so..."

Jack learned a long time ago that making the interrogation personal enhanced the impact and convinced the subject of his resolve, if it seemed like a job they tended to resist longer, but unfettered anger tended to increase the fear factor and served to expedite things. There was no real emotion in this for Jack, it was simply something that had to be done, people's lives were in jeopardy and information had the real potential to save them, and in this case, it was someone very important to him. He had never enjoyed this part of the job, and it wasn't something you talked about, even in his ops briefings he tended to downplay this part of things, not everyone understood, especially in the later years of his career. Guantanamo and the Gulf Wars had torn the cover off interrogation tactics and exposed them to the media spotlight and that had really been the end of it. Things had carried on for a while after, but there was no putting the genie back in the bottle. In many respects, it coincided with the overall scaling back of field operatives, the Agency preferring to focus on the electronic surveillance, drones, and cyber-warfare.

Jack's phone begins vibrating again, he ignores it as he re-grips Potemkin's arm, part of him hesitates, he hasn't lost his nerve but *God, if there was some other way to do this...* he thinks. The phone is vibrating again, he is either going to have to answer it now or it will be hours before this is done. Jack pulls another zip tie out and refastens Potemkin to the chair. Jack leaves him parked next to the stove, the kettle whistling in his ear.

Moving back to the small table he pulls the phone out and reads the message from Lou. *What to do* he thinks, if he breaks from the process now he will lose the edge he has built up with Potemkin, the gradual development of stress was an important part of the process, deviation now would allow the man to gather himself and just make things more difficult, on the other hand, what if Lou had developed something that made this all unnecessary. Jack's smile is grim as he thinks to himself, *wasn't so long ago he wouldn't have even considered that as an option, nothing could have made him change his tactics, not even Lou.* He walks over to the window looking down at the empty alley below him, with a deep sigh he dials Lou's number listening as the telltale pings of the encryption system sync up.

Unexpected Partners

Jessie rode in the back of the SUV with Johannsen, two Marshals were up front and another four followed in a second SUV, they weren't taking any chances of something going sideways between downtown and the airport. She was alone with her thoughts replaying the last few hours with an icy detachment. She probably should have anticipated the girl's house being watched, that miss had cost an innocent woman her life tonight, another casualty in an undeclared war. There hadn't been any indication Allie Chambers was a victim of the Sokolov group, but a more experienced operative would have planned for a worst-case scenario. She was learning some lessons the hard way and had just been fortunate the personal cost hadn't exceeded a sore shoulder and a couple of hours in custody. The real question is where was this going, lessons are fine, but acquired knowledge needs to be applied, that was going to require more thought.

Jessie puts it aside as they pull into the Blue concourse at Tampa International, she turns to Johannsen, "I don't know how to thank you properly, but thank you for doing this…"

"I can't say I understand any of this, but some very important people seem to think you're worth it… so be careful young lady," Johannsen responds.

Jessie just nods and gets out, flanked by the six Marshals armed with their automatic rifles and looking extremely serious. They were intent on protecting her, but more than that nobody wanted an incident in a major airport. The group makes its way to the Airside A shuttle the airport police clearing the way ahead of them. She may have been well guarded but there wasn't anything stealthy about this she thought. The group bypasses the normal security line; the two Marshals and Jessie still have to undergo screening before being allowed to board an aircraft. Once complete the TSA agents return the Marshals' handguns and Jessie's backpack to them. Well, back to the Marshals anyway, no one had agreed to give Jessie her guns back yet. They are the last to board and the jet pulls back from gate A15 only seconds after the doors are sealed. It's a two hour and forty-five-minute flight to JFK in New York; Jessie bracketed by the men is asleep as the wheels retract and the lights are dimmed.

In DC Tim, Albert, and Lou are headed to Reagan National where the FBI's Aviation group keeps a few chartered jets available. Lou is in the back seat with Tim when his phone starts to go off. "Oh, thank God..." he murmurs recognizing Jack's number on the screen. "Jack, where are you?"

"Lou, what's changed? I'm in the middle of something here..."

"Listen my friend there is too much to tell, but Jessie was involved in another shooting down in Tampa, she is okay but headed to New York with a couple of Marshals."

"Shit Lou, I'm sorry... she's okay though?"

"She's fine Jack, I'm headed your way with the FBI, I've been meeting with Special Agent Harrington all afternoon, he's heading up the Sokolov case... anyway short story is we are going to work this together..."

"Yeah, I don't know Lou, I'm not sure I'm completely comfortable with that," Jack says looking back into the kitchen at Potemkin. "I'm interviewing one of Sokolov's guys now, probably need a couple of hours, maybe we can meet after..."

Lou doesn't need an explanation to know what that means and he knows there is about zero chance of talking Jack out of whatever he is doing. "Jack, just bring this guy in we can talk to him together."

"Come on Lou, you know that's not how this works..."

"Who is it Jack... who do you have?"

Jack hesitates, they are way off the script at this point, "Alexander Potemkin, also known as The Spider, this guy runs all of Sokolov's cyber networks..." he pauses for a moment, "Lou, he can give us everything we need..."

"I know, I believe you, but listen my friend, bring him in, let these guys make a deal with him... build their case against Sokolov... hell, this is just the break they need."

"What, so that asshole can walk out of a courtroom on some technicality or better yet run back to that rat hole Odessa where he can't be prosecuted? I don't think so Lou, I should have taken the bastard out the first time we had him... no fucking way I'm letting him go this time."

Lou knows he is losing this argument, he doesn't have an answer for Jack and he won't patronize him... "Look, I understand, but at least think it over, I'm going to be in the city at the FBI headquarters in about two hours, sure would make me happy to see you there... and Jack no blaze of glory you promised me..."

Lou hears the call click off, he can only hope he has convinced his friend, but he knows that Jack is not easily dissuaded once he has his mind made up. He turns to Harrington, "who is Alexander Potemkin?"

Harrington doesn't answer directly, "that didn't sound like it went too well..." He hesitates before continuing, "Potemkin is the mastermind behind Sokolov's cyber empire, he controls all the networks, websites, hacking, everything... We can't find him, nobody has even seen this guy in like twenty years, he was one of the architects of WikiLeaks, French police picked him up back then but he disappeared before anyone could put their hands on him, so if your buddy Jack has him... well we need him period, end of story."

"Shit... Tim, you heard the call, I don't know if I was able to get through or not, once Jack sets things in motion it's virtually impossible to move him in another direction. Hell, I'm surprised he even called me."

"Well, at least we know he is in the city somewhere," Tim says, "...he is in the city, right?"

Lou just shrugs, "I think so, he flew into LaGuardia, was going to spend some time in Brighton Beach checking out Sokolov's operation there."

"Well, he doesn't waste any time does he..." Tim asks rhetorically.

"No, he doesn't, Jack's always had a knack for picking the weak spots and manipulating them to his advantage, usually before anyone else even knows what's happening." They have pulled into the charter area of Reagan National, "listen Tim, can you give your guys in New York a heads up on the off-chance Jack does bring him in? I don't want someone to fuck it up and we lose both of them."

"Sure Lou, I've got one of my top guys up there already, I'll let him know," Tim says, picking up his phone and starting to dial.

Jack turns back toward the kitchen still contemplating the call, it wasn't in him to turn away from what he felt he had to do and it wasn't that he didn't trust Lou, but this had always been his role. Lou had never asked him to step back from it before and now not only did he want him to back off but also trust the FBI. He pulls the second chair into the kitchen and sits across from Potemkin, their knees almost touching, the kettle singing between them he leans forward, "Well Alexander, here's the situation…"

Tea Time

Jack swirled the sugar into each steaming cup the crystals disappearing in the hot dark tea dissolving before reaching the bottom. He had moved Potemkin back to the small table and released his left arm from the zip tie that had held it snugly to the chair.

"Drink your tea Alexander… we have a decision to make and not much time to make it I'm afraid." Jack sips the hot tea it's syrupy with sugar in the traditional Russian way as he leans back in the chair. He gives the old man a long look and says, "you know, I had the chance to take Sokolov down back in the early nineties, I think he had just started getting into the arms market. We were watching him load up a freighter in Odessa…" Jack pauses and almost to himself, "I knew he was going to be a problem… I just knew it."

Alexander mumbles something Jack doesn't quite catch. "What was that," he asks, looking up.

Alexander takes a small sip of his tea, "nothing…" he says, but then seems to think better of it. "I wish you had." He hesitates, "maybe things would have been different, I don't know, it's just that…"

"Tell me my friend, what would have been different?" Jack prods him.

Alexander looks up at him tears in his eyes, "Do you remember that ass Assange and WikiLeaks?" Jack nods his head but doesn't interrupt him. "Well, he launched in 2006 but we had been hacking government systems for years before collecting documents and data..."

Jack interjects, "wait a sec, are you telling me that you and Assange were... what partners?"

"No, not really, I had been freelance hacking for years and he paid well... but I wanted out of the shadows and asked him to bring me onboard with Sunshine..."

"Who is Sunshine?" Jack asks.

"Well Sunshine was the non-profit that launched WikiLeaks, anyway... Assange didn't mind using me to hack into these government sites, but he wasn't going to share the spotlight with anyone, especially not a hacker like me. Next thing I know the French police are locking me up and getting ready to extradite me to the US. I was living in Paris at the time, it had to be Assange, no one else could have given them my location."

"Look, where's this going?" Jack asks impatiently. "If this is some kind of misguided delay tactic, I'll just shoot you now and be done with it."

Potemkin takes another sip of the now tepid tea, "okay, okay, short version I did some work for Sokolov back then, nothing big but he must have heard somehow that I was locked up. Anyway, I don't know how he did it, but they released me the

233

next day and I've been working for him ever since." He looks at Jack again, "you have to believe me, I never wanted this but once you owe him the only way out is in a box..."

"There are worse things..." Jack says softly.

"I know I'm a coward but I came to terms with that a long time ago," Potemkin says softly.

"Well then, tonight is your night..." Jack says as he stands up and places his pistol against the back of the old man's head. "I'm leaving here now... it's time for you to decide... are you coming with me or are you drawing your last breath with the weight of your crimes staining your soul?"

"Where are we going?"

"The FBI and your only chance at any kind of redemption... decide quickly, either way you'll be free of this burden tonight."

"Let's go... at least with you I might survive this..." he says without much hope in his voice.

Jack cuts the zip ties releasing him from the chair; there is a loud pounding on the door just as Potemkin stands up. The men exchange a quick look as Jack brings up both his pistols. "Moment of truth for you Alexander..." he whispers. "Now open the door, then drop to the floor, if you don't you die first..."

"Okay," his hands shaking, he begins to unlock the door, "coming just a minute..." he says through the door.

The door pushes in as the last lock that knew where to find Potemkin was a threat. The sharp releases, Potemkin crashes in a heap to the right of the door as Jack's pistols spit in rapid succession. Jack hadn't bothered waiting to see whom it was, anyone scent of gunpowder hung in the air mixing with the coppery smell of fresh blood. Potemkin lay curled in a ball whimpering, Jack ignores him intent on discerning how many bodies lay in the small hallway, knowing that time was rapidly working against him now. "Alexander, up now!" he says harshly, "time to go!"

"Oh my God, oh my God," the old man is whimpering.

"No time for that..." Jack scolds him. He takes Alexander by the arm as they step over the two Sokolov men their suits riddled with holes and seeping dark viscous blood onto the floor and begins to push him toward the stairs. "Is there a back way out of here?" The old man is unresponsive and barely moving.

Jack grabs the front of his shirt and cracks him across the face, the impact snaps Potemkin's head back, but he begins to focus, "yes, yes, back stairs lead to the alley..." he points down the hall in the opposite direction.

"Okay, let's go and be quiet, there's probably another one downstairs and he won't hesitate to kill either one of us, you want to live you do exactly as I say," Potemkin nods a scared look in his eyes. *I should just shoot him and get the fuck out of here,*

Jack thinks to himself. He knows he won't though, Lou wants this guy and if that means taking some risks, well, so be it.

The rush down the stairs seems to take forever, Potemkin whimpering the whole way. They are just entering the alley hidden in the shadows when Jack sees the flare of a match illuminating another one of Sokolov's men leaning against the wall near the street. *Jesus, these guys are fucking* amateurs he thinks. He turns to Potemkin, "you stay here, and if you fucking move I will kill you myself... understand."

"I'm not going anywhere, don't worry," is the nervous response. Jack just gives him a look.

"You better fucking not..." he says and begins to walk down the alley like he's taking a leisurely stroll. "Hey bud, got a light," he calls out to the man. The suppressed shots enter the man's forehead less than an inch apart, dropping him without a sound. Jack doesn't normally like to use a headshot, too many risks, too many chances to miss, but it's the only way to insure there won't be any noise.

"Is he dead?" the voice at his shoulder asks.

Jack jumps almost letting off another round, "Jesus Christ, you just about got yourself killed, yes, he is dead and so are we if we don't get the fuck out of here."

The two men shuffle off looking like two old drunks helping each other home, it's only a few blocks down to the Brighton Beach train station at 7th. It's just past eight thirty when they climb the steps to the platform and catch the Q Train. It will take a little more than an hour with sixteen stops before they reach Canal Street in Manhattan. From there it's just five blocks to Federal Plaza and the FBI offices. They are sitting in the last car in the last seat, Jack has Potemkin wedged between him and the window, even so he feels exposed and knows that a shootout on the subway will probably end badly for everyone involved. He was going to have to trust to luck, not something he was comfortable with, *this had better be worth it Lou*, he thinks to himself as the click clack of the rails seem to be counting down to some impending show-down.

Closing Up Shop

"Alexi, I know, Jesus, what do you want, I missed her by no more than a few minutes... how the fuck do I know how she knew about the girl?" Sampson takes a deep breath; Alexi is raging on the other end of the phone. "Alexi, we have another problem, the Spider isn't answering his phone and the kids in the center haven't seen him in more than an hour..." The cursing comes through the phone, "I already handled it, we've got three of our guys headed to his place right now, they're supposed to call as soon as they have him."

Sokolov takes a deep breath and tries to calm himself, Sampson is his most trusted man, "I told you this was going to happen, didn't I? Don't bother answering that, okay, okay, what's our next move? Can we still get the girl?"

Sampson knows the truth of it but can't go there right now, "maybe... depends on where the Feds have her and what they are doing with her, I don't know, but it won't be easy."

"I don't give a damn about easy, I want her, she is going to pray for me to kill her..."

"Alexi, we have to clean this mess up, we'll get the girl but like you said we're too exposed," Sampson waits for a response.

Sokolov sighs, "fine, what's next?"

"I want to close up the Tampa operation, Timmy down here is a fucking joke and the rest of these guys are a liability now."

"What are you suggesting? Tampa is a pretty good market for us..." Sokolov asks him.

"Alexi, you said it yourself, we got to think long term, smarter, lose a little now but stay in the game..." Sampson has never gone this far with Sokolov but someone had to tell the man shit was burning down around him.

"What do you want to do?"

"I'm meeting with Timmy and his men in an hour at the warehouse, I'll handle it... then I'm flying back up there, should land sometime around one."

"Make sure you close it all the way down, I don't want it coming back to us, the warehouse is clean?"

"Yeah, leased through three or four blinds, listen, I'll call you when I take off."

Sampson hangs up feeling slightly better about things, he had been worried Alexi wouldn't listen, the man was smart, very smart, but he was also just as stubborn and that could make for a frustrating mix.

Sampson grabs his duffel, checks his holster, opens the weapons closet and picks one of the HK MP11s the last of the famous Heckler and Koch machine pistols and six small explosive charges with built in triggers, the remote goes in his jacket pocket. He loves the MP11, still small enough to be a sub, thirty round magazines, armor piercing and it shoots over nine hundred rounds a minute, what's not to love? He slings it over his shoulder and heads back to the garage.

Sampson throws the duffel in the back seat and gets in turning to Timmy, "let's go... did you reach everyone?"

Timmy eyes the HK and nods, "sure did, should be waiting for us?" He tries to be cool about it but doesn't quite pull it off, "what's with the HK anyway?"

Sampson glances over at the man deciding in that moment to save him for last, "no chances... if McIntyre is with the Feds we don't take any chances..." purposely cryptic, it's enough to shut Timmy up.

They pull into the warehouse lot where half a dozen cars are already parked in front of the double doors. Timmy leads the way in, Sampson trailing a few feet behind him; the men are by the steel cage that had so recently held Allie Chambers, talking.

Looking up one of them yells out to Timmy, "what the fuck Timmy..." he doesn't finish the question as he sees Sampson.

Sampson doesn't hesitate, they are all grouped together, the rapid stutter of the HK echoes through the building as he empties the magazine into the men and slams home a second one continuing to fire with barely a break. Timmy is screaming at him as he reaches for his pistol. Sampson drops the HK and grabs the big man in a headlock, crushing his windpipe and dropping him to the floor. It had taken Sampson less than two minutes to kill the nine men and reduce Timmy to a gurgling mess on the floor. He looks around making sure there wasn't anyone else he had missed, finding nothing he turns back to the men, fishing in their pockets looking for car keys. Finding what he needs he heads back to the double doors pushing them open, he moves the cars inside.

With the cars parked in a circle he heads back to the SUV, grabbing the explosive charges he had taken from the condo as Terry Skinner pulls up on his motorcycle.

"Hey Mr. Sampson, sorry I'm late..." he chirps.

"No worries, you're right on time, give me a hand with these." Sampson hands him three of the charges keeping three and the trigger for himself. He takes the young man by the arm and leads him into the warehouse.

Terry stops when he sees the bodies, "holy fuck sir, what happened?" he asks.

"We are closing up shop," Sampson says without a trace of emotion.

Terry looks towards the double doors measuring his chances.

"Don't even think about it, you'll never make it," Sampson says. He points to the bodies, "help me drag these over to the cars, I want everyone in a vehicle."

Terry just nods, he has lost the ability to speak. They trundle the bodies into the cars, Sampson dragging them by one arm as if they were rag dolls, Terry struggling with the weight isn't much help. They place the charges by the gas tanks of each car and toggle the trigger switches.

"Okay young man this is where we part ways..." Sampson says as he shoots Terry in the chest three times.

The young man collapses against the nearest car, his eyes seem more melancholy then surprised. The big man turns and heads back out to the SUV closing the doors on his way. The trigger has a five-hundred-yard range and he thumbs the switch as he pulls through the gates, far away enough to not be affected but close enough to ensure everything works properly. The warehouse is immediately engulfed in flames as Sampson turns onto the main road and heads back to the jetport, this chapter had closed, they wouldn't be doing business in Tampa again anytime soon.

Battle Plans

It was nine thirty by the time Sampson returned to the condo, showered, wiped down the place and removed all the weapons and ammunition to the SUV. Everything else was placed in the dumpsters at the back of the complex. When he was finished the place was empty and looked as if no one has been there recently. With one more look around he closes up and locks the door, pocketing the keys he heads down to the basement-parking garage. He hadn't figured out what to do with the SUV yet, but they could always fly someone down to drive it up to New York once things calmed down. He parks in the executive lot, stows the duffel of weapons in the cargo area grabs his overnight bag and heads into the lobby, hoping his pilot is waiting and ready to go.

Finally, onboard, it's almost ten thirty when they finally taxi and take off, Sampson dials Alexi on his SAT phone hoping for an update on Potemkin and needing to let Alexi know he is on the way, but there is no answer.

Sokolov was unwilling to leave anything to chance and had gathered a few men and decided to head over to Potemkin's himself, cursing that he had allowed the man his own place to begin with. Alexi may be aging, but his men have a hard time keeping up with him as he breaks into a jog across the courtyard

243

and heads towards 11th Street and the Spiders apartment. He lets out a string of curses in Russian as they get to the building and he sees the body lying in the alley. Looking wildly around he grabs one of his men and directs him to head down toward the train platform on 7th, another he sends in the opposite direction. His directions are clear, follow the man but do not stop him or let yourself be seen, call in if you find anything. Grabbing the remaining two men he heads up the stairs to Potemkin's apartment cursing the whole way. The scene is still fresh, the dead men don't bother Sokolov, death is just a byproduct of his life, but the fact that Potemkin is not there and obviously isn't capable of taking his men out does bother him.

    Sokolov doesn't like mysteries, particularly this one. This couldn't be the girl since Sampson claimed she was in Tampa with the Feds, and no way the FBI sent a hit squad like this, so what did that leave? Another organization moving in on him, not likely, he would have heard something, and although the two men upstairs were pretty messy the man in the alley had been done by a professional, no doubt about it. He instructs the two men with him to search the apartment and take anything that might link Potemkin to Sokolov, and then meet back at the condo complex. He leaves them there and heads back to his office, when his phone starts to ring.

    "What…" he asks tersely.

"I have them sir, just boarded the Q to the City…" the man says tensely, "What should I do?"

"Get on that train, I want to know if they get off…" Sokolov pauses, "them?"

"Yes sir, it's definitely the Spider and another old man, I don't recognize him though…"

"Ok, call me if anything changes…"

He clicks off not waiting for a reply, boarding the elevator he punches the button for his penthouse suite, *what the fuck is going on*, he thinks to himself. Once upstairs, he shoos the girls out of his office and calls in Kirilov, one of the two men always stationed outside his door. "I want everyone available here in fifteen minutes…" he shuts the door before the man can answer. Reaching for his interface he searches for the Q train schedule and routes. Sokolov has never learned to type and doesn't use a keyboard, the Spider had set up a completely voice driven system for him. The route outlined in yellow is clear enough, sure, they could stop anywhere along the way, but with the FBI offices only five blocks from Canal Street Sokolov is pretty sure he knows where they are headed. It doesn't make sense to him, but he trusts his intuition, besides there is no way to cover every station between here and there. He dials his man on the train, "If they get off before Canal in the City you take them both out, but the Spider first… clear?"

"Yes sir," the man answers.

There is a knock on the door as Sokolov hangs up, "come in" he instructs gruffly. "Is this everybody?" he asks.

"Yes sir," Kirilov answers.

Sokolov counts fourteen men, not enough he thinks. "Okay Kirilov I want you to take these five and head over to the command center, nobody in or out is that clear?" he says pointing to the five men in front. He wishes Sampson was here, he needs someone who can really lead these men. He turns to the other man that normally guards his door, "Vasily, right?" he asks.

"Yes sir," the man answers.

"You take these six... come over here, let me show you..." He flips the screen on his desk around and enlarges the map. "Okay, I want you to set up here and here between Leonard and White streets... If the Spider shows up I want you to work toward Canal and kill him and whoever is with him..." He looks around at the men, "any questions?"

"No sir... I'll take care of it." Vasily responds.

"Okay go! You don't have much time..." Sokolov looks at his watch, "he is on the Q train and should be at that station by ten."

"Sir, what do you want me to do?" the last man there asks.

Sokolov looks up, "head over to the Spiders apartment on 11th and see if those guys need any help."

Again, he wishes he had more men, he sinks into his chair and leaning back, he faces the floor to ceiling windows and looks out. The soft lights from the boardwalk cast a soft glow upward, there are a few twinkling lights from the few small boats still in the bay, Alexi lets out a deep sigh wondering how things had started to unravel so quickly. Of course, this particular rhetorical question always has the same answer: things have been unraveling for much longer than realized. The smart move would be to pack it all up, even tonight and head back to Odessa where he owned the city, police, and judges, anyone who could be a threat. On the other hand, he had grown comfortable in the US, everything worked better here, but more than anything, his pride stood in the way, he wasn't about to let some girl and those fools at the FBI win. The old maxim about winning the battle and losing the war was in play, except Alexi was losing both and didn't know it. He lets out another sigh, funny how life is he thinks, as successful as he was, as big as his organization had grown, here he was in the dark looking over the water thinking about what might yet be, and just like at the beginning, he was alone.

Coming In

Tim Harrington had called the New York office while waiting to take off from DC, traffic had held them up and they would be landing in New York a bit later than they had hoped. After consulting with the pilots, Lou and Albert; they had decided to reroute to JFK where they would meet Jessie and the Marshals before heading into New York. If they had a chance to bring in Alexander Potemkin, he didn't want anything going wrong while he was in the air. This would be the biggest bust in a very long time. It wasn't so much that the Bureau's reputation had been tarnished, but ever since the Trump administration and the Comey fiasco the US had been taking the fight overseas and that wasn't how or where the FBI operated, so to be able to bring a major international figure to justice here in the states was a big deal. He had briefed Samuel Jefferson on everything they knew, which was admittedly pretty thin, but he wanted agents posted at all the entrances and it wouldn't hurt to have some out on foot keeping an eye on the surrounding blocks. He wasn't even sure what to look for or even how Jack might show up, but it was the best he could do with virtually no notice. There would be plenty of video surveillance in that area, but response times would not be nearly quick enough if something happened. Video after the fact wasn't going to help anyone, least of all Jack.

Sammie was able to pull together a dozen or so agents, not really enough to canvas the area properly, but they had decided to cover the primary avenues approaching the building and hope for the best. Agent Pleshkowski, the noobie in the group, was sent up to the Canal and Broadway Metro station on the off chance that Jack had taken the subway in, it didn't seem likely with all the rideshare, taxi, and other means of transportation available but it didn't hurt to be thorough. Nevermind that the kid didn't really have the experience to pull street duty and blend in, he was going to stand out, and Sammie hoped it didn't cost him in the end.

They had been on the train a little more than an hour, but it had seemed like three to Jack. Fortunately, they had been mostly alone in the last car, just two old men having drunk to much holding each other up in the hard-plastic seat. Jack had waited till the last possible moment before finally exiting at the Canal Street and Broadway station, it wouldn't take a genius to figure out the Q Train was the quickest way into the City, he was probably being overly cautious but then again that had kept him alive this long.

The Federal Building was five blocks straight down Broadway, not a lot of cover, especially if Potemkin had a change of heart. Jack already knew he would take the man out and disappear, but that wasn't going to help Lou and Jessie and he was pretty sure the FBI would be plenty pissed off as well. Lou had sent him a follow up message to ask for Special Agent Samuel Jefferson if he decided to come in; he hadn't responded and had no intention of contacting the agent before showing up anyway. Last thing he wanted was a bunch of FBI guys broadcasting to anyone watching that here he was - come shoot me.

The two men emerge from the subway station, Broadway and Canal straddle China Town and Little Italy usually making for plenty of traffic and crowded sidewalks, but it's almost ten o'clock and things have slowed down. The sun has long since set turning the city into a collage of shadows and muted colors that inhabit the nooks and crannies of the concrete landscape; the accompanying soundtrack of horns, sirens, and scattered conversations punctuates the evening. Jack looks around before taking Potemkin's arm and guiding him around the corner onto Broadway, they don't rush, he wants to blend in as much as possible, just two old men, nothing to see here – hide in plain sight. Jack doesn't go far, pressing into a doorway just past the Walgreens he pulls Potemkin in even closer with his right hand, his left holds the pistol in his coat's oversized pockets.

"Listen to me Alexander, we've been lucky so far, but its five blocks down from here. There's nothing for it but to go slow and blend... don't give people a reason to see us." He looks at the frightened man, "I'll get us there I promise, but if you fuck this up we are both probably going to die, understand?" Potemkin just nods and Jack thinks again what a cluster fuck this is. He had spotted the young agent as they climbed the steps from the station, he didn't bother pointing it out to Potemkin, the man was barely functioning as it was. The agent looked like a kid just out of school pacing in front of the Bank of America. He might as well have been wearing a sign advertising "FBI Agent". If this was the best the Bureau could do it didn't instill a great deal of confidence.

"Alexander, how many men does Sokolov have here?" Jack asks as they slowly make their way down Broadway trying to keep close to the buildings, skirting the scaffolding and piles of rubbish strewn about by what seemed to be one continuous construction project in the City these days. At least there were only a few stray cabs and just a smattering of people hurrying the other way. Broadway was one way here and the construction was helping keep the traffic down, Jack hoped it would work to his advantage. The few people on the sidewalks seemed to know enough to ignore the street people and were giving them a wide berth.

"I don't know, a couple dozen I guess, I have twenty-two that work for me, but they aren't soldiers...why?" Potemkin responds.

"Because, I want to know what we're up against, a dozen well-armed guys can turn this into a war zone..." He looks over at Potemkin, "and I'd like to survive this if possible."

"Me too..." the old man mutters.

Pleshkowski might be new, but he wasn't dumb, having graduated top of his class at Notre Dame before joining the Bureau, he had seen the two old men exiting the subway, there was something about them that caught his attention. Maybe it was the fella on the outside constantly checking his perimeter, you might not notice if you hadn't been trained but the Bureau was now including some basic field craft classes at the FBI Academy. He radios in that he thinks he has them and they are headed down Broadway toward the Federal Building, he is far enough back so he doesn't think either of them have picked him up yet.

The large industrial dumpsters afforded some measure of cover for Jack; they also unfortunately blocked his view down the street as well. They had just crossed over White Street when the first volley of shots rings out, pinging off the dumpster next to them. Jack immediately yanks Potemkin down and crab walks back behind the cover of the large orange rusting dumpster.

"Are you hit?" he asks the man next to him.

"No, I don't think so..." Potemkin says patting himself all over.

Jack has both his pistols out now, "Stay behind me, they are coming, can't afford to sit still this close to the Feds, they are going to want to get this done quick..." There is no emotion in his voice, it's simply what he would do in their position.

The voice startles him, "you okay sir?" Agent Pleshkowski asks him.

Fuck me; Jack thinks before answering, *this was the second time in one night he had missed someone on his six...* "Yeah we're good, what's your name son?"

"Agent Pleshkowski, but just call me Mike..." he answers.

Jack smiles in the dark, "Alright Mike, I can't see exactly how many, but I counted at least six... they are coming, so better if we split up creating a bit of a crossfire... think you can make it across the street if I provide some cover?"

"Yes sir, just say when..."

Jack has unscrewed the suppressors tucking them in his pocket, he hopes the noise will help provide a distraction, "Go!" he whispers as he unloads both pistols down the street, aiming at another dumpster about four hundred feet further down, *no point taking out any civilians if he doesn't have to*, he thinks. He looks across the street where the young agent has squirreled himself into a doorway, it doesn't afford much cover but will have to do. He can see six men now, he wonders if there may be more further down, they are working their way up the street ducking behind the construction equipment as they come, still at least a hundred yards off, outside the effective range of his pistols, most professionals can take a man down at thirty to forty yards, Jack is comfortable at fifty to sixty but at that range there are lots of variables to consider. He is just going to have wait till they are closer, hopefully the kid is a decent shot.

    Jack steals a quick look behind them, anxious not to be surprised again, looking back down the street the gloom is deepening and he can just make out the men inching forward in the shadows on both sides of the street. Well, these guys are a bit more disciplined he thinks, no telltale cigarettes and they were holding their fire for now. Time slows down, but Jack knows once the shooting starts it will speed up and things will happen very fast. He takes a deep breath, bringing both pistols up, *ok here we go he,* thinks to himself lining his sights up...

Firefight

Agent Pleshkowski actually gets the first round off, he is more exposed than Jack but this gives him a better field of view. He sees the first man crumple and fall before turning and looking further down the street. He has already called into Special Agent Jefferson but this will be over before any of the other agents can get there. Jack has taken a prone position hoping to blend into the dumpster and the street, he knows a lower position is more difficult to hit. The automatic weapons of Sokolov's men, who else would it be, are chattering and he can hear the rounds ricocheting off the dumpster and the concrete facade of the building across the street. He squeezes off four quick rounds taking down another soldier. If they are lucky there are only four more. The others have slowed down and are trying to stay under cover, another short burst of fire and Jack can see the side of the building by the young agent splinter, he focusses on the muzzle flash, emptying the rest of his magazine into the dark area fifty yards down the street. He is greeted with a scream of pain; that will do, he thinks.

He turns to Alexander, "you ok?" he asks, as he slams another magazine home.

The man just nods, hunkered down behind the dumpster, the fear evident in his face. "Don't let them get me Jack…please don't let them," he pleads.

Jack doesn't reply, there's no time as the remaining men make a break for it firing their weapons as they come. Jack can feel the bits of pavement prick his face, as the bullets seem to march across the street towards him. He rolls to his left firing as he comes to stop in the middle of the street, he is exposed but they are close enough now it doesn't matter. He takes the man on the right first he can see the rounds enter the man's chest as he shifts his sights to the middle. He hopes Pleshkowski has the one on the left, no way he can get all three of them before having to reload. The man in the middle is down but still moving as the street goes silent.

"Mike, you okay?" he shouts out.

"Yeah, going to be, got nicked in the arm fucking hurts like hell…" the agent responds.

"Put pressure on it," he yells as he starts to run down the street toward the shooter in the middle of the street, trying to get back up. He doesn't break stride as he empties a full magazine from his second pistol into the man, the eighteen rounds catch him square in the chest and the body jerks like a puppet in some macabre play. Jack checks the other bodies but none have survived, which is just fine with him. He reloads with his last two magazines, hoping he won't need them, he turns and walks back toward the agent, "here, let me help you," he takes the agents tie and wraps it around his upper arm tightly knotting it in place. He is about to make the same mistake for the third time that night when he sees the agent's face twist in a grimace as he brings his pistol up pointing directly behind Jack. Jack doesn't hesitate he turns in one fluid motion bringing both his pistols up and dropping to a knee so he isn't blocking the agent's field of fire.

Neither of them had heard the man approaching, but he has Potemkin from behind and is holding a pistol to his head.

"I'm taking him, neither of you move or he dies..." the young man shouts as he begins to back away, the fear obvious in his voice.

"Go ahead, shoot him..." Jack says in a matter of fact voice, "either way you are going to die on this street, end of the line for you son..." Jack's voice doesn't waver or hesitate as he fires two rounds into the man's head at less than fifteen yards, the man drops immediately draped over Potemkin.

Potemkin is whimpering on the sidewalk, "get him off me, get him off me..."

Jack and Mike rush over and roll the man off Potemkin lifting him to his feet, he is covered in the man's blood and shaking uncontrollably.

"Are you hurt Alexander," Jack asks him, holding the man up.

"I don't think so..." he says continuing to shake, "you could have killed me!" he splutters.

"Not at that range..." Jack says matter of factly.

Mike just shakes his head, smiling in spite of the pain, "damndest shooting I've ever even heard of, never mind actually seen."

They both turn, bringing their pistols up again as footfalls echo behind them. The cavalry has arrived; Special Agent Jefferson and half a dozen others run up, automatic rifles at the ready.

"Mike, you okay..." Jefferson asks.

"Yes sir, caught one in the arm but I'm fine..." he responds a bit more bravely than he actually feels.

"You must be Hardy," Jefferson says, turning to Jack. "And is this Alexander Potemkin?" he asks nodding in the man's direction.

"Yes, and yes," Jack responds holding out his hand, "and you must be Jefferson..."

"Uh, yeah," Jefferson says looking around loosely shaking Jack's hand, "quite a mess you've made here..." He turns to the agent next to him, "I want from here all the way down to Franklin sealed off now, use the locals if you need to and get a crime scene team in here." Turning his attention to the rest of his men, "nobody touches anything, understand... this whole area is an active crime scene." He turns back to Jack, "let's get you two down to headquarters, any chance of you turning over those pistols?"

Jack just looks at him, "nope, think I'll hold onto them for now..." he says with a smile while reloading his two empty magazines. "By the way, you need to get your boy Mike some attention, he did good... and put some cuffs on this piece of shit," he grabs Potemkin by the arm and pulls him in close, "you got lucky Alexander, these fellas are going to treat you much better than I would have..."

In Brighton Beach Alexi looks out over the dark water waiting, the strident ringing breaks the silence, it's Sampson's number and he decides to let it go, not wanting to miss a call that isn't coming.

Reunion

The flight out of DC carrying Lou, Tim and Albert lands at JFK and taxies to the General Aviation terminal at ten minutes to eleven, they had a pretty decent tail wind and had made up some time on the way. Tim had expected Sammie Jefferson to be waiting for them, so when two young agents waved him down the nerves kick up a notch. With Lou and Albert stacked up behind him, "where is Special Agent Jefferson?" he asks without preamble.

"Sir, I'm Agent McPherson and this is Agent Gonzalez, he asked us to meet you."

Before the young man can continue Harrington interrupts him, "that wasn't my question..." he looks at both of them, "where is Jefferson?"

McPherson responds nervously, "sir, there was a shootout in the City a few blocks up from the Federal Building, Special Agent Jefferson is overseeing the crime scene and processing the witnesses."

Lou can't contain himself any longer, "were there any casualties? What happened?"

McPherson doesn't acknowledge the question, "sir, we have a chopper standing by to take you into the City..."

Lou starts to push forward but Tim holds him back by the arm, "Agent McPherson, let's slow it down a second, okay, go see if there is a conference room or lounge or something we can use here, okay?" He turns to Gonzalez, "do you have a vehicle here?"

"Yes sir, parked outside..." he answers.

Tim checks his watch, "alright, give me a quick run-down, how many dead and wounded?"

Gonzalez pauses, "well sir there are six... no seven dead and one wounded," he answers.

"Who are they Gonzalez, who was killed?" Harrington asks heatedly.

"Oh, sorry sir, seven men from what I believe is the Soka... Sokolov gang?" he says hesitantly, "and one of our agents took a round in the upper arm, but they said he will be ok..." Gonzalez is obviously nervous, "Sorry sir, I thought you knew already."

"No harm done young man," Harrington says gently. "Listen, I want you to take your vehicle and head up to Terminal Five, that's where Jet Blue's gates are," he looks at his watch again, "find out what gate the eleven thirty Tampa flight is landing at and get yourself down there. There are two Federal Marshals and a young lady coming in on that plane, I want you to bring them here as soon as they land, got it?"

"Yes sir, got it." Gonzalez answers, relieved to be out of the spotlight, he heads out the double sliding doors at a trot.

Tim turns to Lou and Albert, "ok, we probably have about forty-five minutes or so, let's get briefed in on the details, then when your daughter and the Marshals get here well chopper over to the City... make sense?"

Lou just nods, too relieved about Jack to say anything, Albert pitches in, "let's see if we can find something to eat while we are at it..." Tim and Lou both let out a chuckle. "What!" Albert says, looking back and forth between them, "a man has to eat you know!" Before they can answer Agent McPherson is back, he leads them over to a small lounge off the main lobby.

"We can use this as long as we need, it's usually reserved for pilots, but they said this late nobody should be here," he says.

Tim begins to respond but Albert beats him to it, taking a C-note out of his wallet, "here is a hundred, see if anybody delivers food this late and have something brought in, tell them to keep the change and make it quick." McPherson looks confused, not sure if he should take the money or not.

Tim gives him a smile, "go on McPherson, the man needs to eat, we can wait another few minutes."

Lou walks over to the vending machine and slides his card through the reader, "what are you fellas drinking? Unfortunately, there's no scotch in here..." he says. He punches the button for two colas for himself, "Albert?"

"Diet anything," the man responds.

"I'll take a root beer if they have it," Tim says.

Lou makes two trips bringing the plastic bottles over and setting them on the table. He lets out a long sigh, "I have to tell you when he said seven dead my heart fell, I'd never forgive myself if something had happened to Jack."

Tim gives him a long look, "this is why you need to let us handle this Lou, you guys shouldn't have been anywhere near this thing..."

Albert can see Lou's color rising, "sweet baby Jesus, we are not going here again are we, come on Tim, we wouldn't have shit without this guy, his kid and this Jack fella..." he says, "who I can't wait to meet by the way..."

Tim holds up his hands defensively, "ok, ok, you're right I know, but this is our job..." he trails off.

Lou reaches over touching the other man's arm, "I get it Tim, I really do, but we're a team now and we'll get this thing done."

Tim doesn't have a chance to answer as McPherson bangs through the door, "only Chinese still open that will deliver out here, ordered a couple of Lo Meins, a Kung Pao Chicken, Broccoli and Beef, and half dozen Egg Rolls, hope that will do," he says looking around.

"That should be fine, these other two aren't hungry," Albert says starting to laugh.

Tim has McPherson brief them on the earlier events in the City. He gives them a blow by blow of the shootout, the story and

Jack's reputation was growing with every telling. Pleshkowski hadn't exaggerated per se` but his color commentary of Potemkin being held and Jack's deft demeanor and shooting was already becoming legendary.

"So, Jack and this agent Pleshkowski took on seven of Sokolov's men?" Lou asks just wanting to confirm what he has just heard.

"Yes sir, Mike said, Agent Pleshkowski that is, well he said he's never seen anyone like this Jack guy, stuff of legends is what he is saying."

There is a knock on the door followed by the distinctive smell of Chinese take-out, "thank God! That was quick" Albert says.

McPherson excuses himself, "Sir, I need to give Special Agent Jefferson a call and update him, what should I tell him sir?"

"Let him know we are on the ground and waiting for a few more people flying in from Tampa to join us then we'll chopper over, probably another twenty minutes or so, he can call me if there is anything urgent before then." Tim directs him.

Albert has already inhaled his third egg roll while Lou is using his chopsticks like a pro to dig the shrimp lo mein out of the cardboard container, when Jessie bursts through the door. She wraps her dad up in a hug from behind as he tries to get up without spilling the noodles everywhere.

He gives her a kiss on the forehead holding her tight, "Love you honey, glad you're okay," is all he can get out. Gonzalez and the two Marshals are standing awkwardly just inside the door.

Jessie gives her dad another squeeze, "love you too daddy," then turns toward the door. She introduces the two Marshals Jackson and Cunningham to the room, apparently, they only go by their last names. Jessie shakes both Tim and Albert's hand, "pleasure to meet you both in person, really can't thank you enough for your help," she says. And then spying the food containers, "Hey, is that lo mein?!" she asks?

"Here, help yourself," Albert says morosely, pushing the last container and a set of chopsticks over while the final egg roll disappears in two bites.

Tim turns to Gonzalez, "have them spin the chopper up, we need to get on the road. You and McPherson drive the Marshals over, let me know when you get there."

Jessie scarfs down the chicken lo mein, while Albert meets with the Marshals outside, when he comes back in he hands Jessie her backpack, "don't make me regret this," he quips.

"I won't, and thank you again sir, I appreciate everything you've done for us," she says sincerely.

Albert just nods, he isn't used to effusive thanks from anyone, but especially not an attractive woman as lethal as Jessie. *Just a bit disconcerting,* he thinks to himself.

The pilot waves them out and the four of them head to the waiting chopper for the ten-minute trip, all of them anxious to hear Jack's story in person.

Fight or Flight

Alexi settles into the leather couch occupying the "sitting" area of his office and thumbs on the wall size television. It's just past eleven o'clock and he hasn't heard from any of his men, he doesn't need the news to tell him things are fucked up, but he navigates to one of the local news stations anyway. He grimaces, reading the trailer along the bottom outlining the shooting in lower Manhattan, there is an FBI agent speaking with a pretty young reporter, his picture is in a cutout box in the upper right of the screen. *Fuck*, he thinks turning up the sound in time to catch the FBI agent explaining the criminal enterprise he has spent his life building, he doesn't bother listening to the rest.

"Fucking Tom Casey," he mutters to himself, "I should have killed that son of a bitch myself." As angry as he is Alexi knows it's time to move, standing still isn't an option. The FBI will have all it needs, he has no illusions about Potemkin's ability or even willingness to keep his mouth shut. Only question now is how much time does he have, and where the fuck is Sampson, thinking back to the call earlier he realizes he should have taken it. Nothing to be done about it now, he picks his phone up and dials the command center.

"Get me Kirilov," he demands.

It takes a minute before the man comes on the line, "Kirilov here sir," he answers.

"Tell them I want all operations transferred to the center in Caracas, then shut it all down there, everything wiped clean, you follow?" Alexi says forcefully.

"Yes sir, umm, what do you want me to do with..." Kirilov pauses, he already knows the answer but wants to hear Sokolov say it.

"You know what to do, make sure it's clean then burn the place down, I don't want anyone out alive, period, is that clear enough?"

"Yes sir, got it," the man answers.

"We will regroup in three days at the warehouse in Scranton, you know where that is, right?"

Kirilov knows there won't be any meeting in Scranton but answers, "Yes sir, I'll let you know when it's done here," as the phone clicks off.

Alexi looks around the office, *damn, I'm going to miss the view here*, he thinks to himself as he starts to gather up the few personal items he has carried with him for years. He has no intention of meeting anyone in Scranton, but soldiers need orders and at least the illusion of leadership, by the time they realize he isn't coming he will beyond the reach of the FBI. None of his men know enough to do any real harm to his operation, but the loss of Potemkin was going to be difficult to overcome. It wasn't even the money, he had enough money to last a dozen lifetimes, no it was the fact that he had spent a lifetime building this business, had escaped multiple attempts on his life and taken more lives than he could count; simply put, this was his life.

A knock on the door interrupts him; he grabs his pistol off the desk, contemplation left behind, he walks towards the door. Hesitating for a moment, *well the FBI wouldn't knock*, he concludes as he yanks the door open. He drops the pistol and grabs Vasily as the man falls into the room, seeping blood from half dozen wounds. Alexi drags him over to the couch, Vasily isn't going to last long so he grabs the man's jacket, pulling his face close to his, "is the Spider dead, is he dead!" Alexi demands almost screaming.

Vasily opens his eyes briefly, "everybody's dead," he gurgles and is gone, Alexi lets go of the jacket letting the body fall to the couch.

Alexi picks his pistol up, not bothering to close the door all the way and sits back in his chair, spinning it slowly around the pistol now in his lap, *is it possible they got Potemkin*, he wonders, *that would change everything*. He tries to remember what the FBI agent had been saying to the reporter but he really hadn't been paying close enough attention. *Had he acted too quickly to close things down*, Alexi wasn't one to question himself but this was unchartered territory. He needed information but had no way to obtain it and to make it worse the people he normally would rely on weren't available. The only decision that made any sense was to immediately take one of the jets and head to Odessa where the US authorities couldn't reach him. He continues his slow spin, thinking back over the years, the battles, the deals, the girls... maybe it was time to go home, he thinks. He smiles to himself, remembering those first few deals, the hubris of youth, filling cargo ships in the middle of the night with Soviet era arms, hoping they could get them off before anyone knew the warehouses were empty. God, he missed the excitement, the danger, the raw energy of it all. It was time to go but the thrill of the fight tugged at him.

He stirs as he hears the cacophony of sirens drawing nearer. His penthouse faces the ocean so he is unable to see into the neighborhood, but the proximity is confirmation enough that Kirilov has been a dutiful soldier, with a sigh Alexi dials Sampson's number hoping the connection can be made.

The connection sounds tinny and far away, but Sampson answers, "Yes sir?"

"Closing up shop my old friend, time to head home..." Alexi says a touch melancholy.

"What happened?" is all Sampson can get out.

"Burned it down, burned it all down, Potemkin taken or dead, not sure..." Alexi says softly all the while slowly spinning in his chair.

"Alexi, what the fuck are you talking about, what's going on?" Sampson says pleadingly. Alexi doesn't respond, "Alexi, are you alright?"

"Yes, yes, I'm fine, Sampson, do you remember Vasily?"

"Vasily? Who the fuck... I know a dozen Vasilys, who are you talking about... Alexi, I'm worried about you."

"You know, Vasily stands outside my door all day..." Alexi says letting out a laugh, "well he's on the couch dead..." Sampson doesn't know what to say, "FBI killed him... he made it all the way back here though..."

Sampson takes a deep breath, "listen Alexi, I'll be landing out at Republic in about an hour, find somebody to drive you out there and we'll go home." The phone clicks off without an answer.

Kirilov knows he should just grab one of the SUVs and head out of town, Sokolov had been clear, be in Scranton in three days, but there was no way he was going anywhere near one of Sokolov's operations. He hesitates though, this was an opportunity to good to pass up; he swipes the card key and punches the elevator button for the top floor. One last check on things, he thinks to himself. Not quite sure why he draws his pistol as he gets off the elevator, tonight has been pretty fucked up so far, no point in taking any chances. As he draws close to the office he can see blood on the carpet and the door slightly ajar, he pushes it gently but doesn't enter. He can see Vasily on the couch obviously dead, he thinks Sokolov is dead too seeing the chair slowly spin around.

"Kirilov my boy, what are you doing here?" Alexi asks waving him into the room with his pistol.

Kirilov enters slowly not quite lowering his own gun, "just thought I should give everything one more check sir... are you okay?" he asks.

"Just fine Kirilov, just fine... it's time to go so drive me out to the Island, to the airport."

"Yes sir, the car is downstairs..."

Alexi takes a long slow look around, picks up his other pistol from the desk, shakes his head and motions Kirilov out the door, "let's go then..." he says.

Federal Plaza NYC

The chopper lands on the roof of the Federal Building nine minutes after taking off from JFK and just as Kirilov and Alexi merge into traffic on the Belt Parkway. The blades haven't stopped whirling when the four of them jump down and run heads down for the doors. The pad had only reopened in the past few years after all rooftop helipads had been shut down in New York following 9/11. There had been plenty of terror attacks in the last few decades, but the skies over the US had not been compromised again. The war on terror had escalated in sophistication over the years but no one had forgotten a bright morning in September and that alone may have inoculated America from the naiveté that had created the first tragic opportunity. Whatever the case, the city had been reopened to helicopter traffic allowing the FBI to once again begin using the rooftop helipad.

A quick elevator ride to the twenty-third floor and Harrington leads them past the security checkpoint, having badges issued for all of them. Jessie's backpack sets off a loud series of alarms, but Harrington quickly clears them through. First stop is a large conference room where they find Special Agent Jefferson and half a dozen younger agents in conversation with Jack, still wearing his shoulder rig pistols comfortably tucked in and drinking coffee out of a Styrofoam cup. He is clearly holding court and loving every minute of it.

"Jack!" Lou exclaims, rushing over to clap his friend on the shoulder, "thank God you're okay."

Jack gives him a sheepish grin, "thanks Lou, truth is I had some help from Mike over here," he says, pointing to a young agent with his arm in a sling.

Tim and Albert come over shaking hands all around, "so this is the famous Jack Hardy," Tim says shaking Jack's hand.

"Well, I don't know about famous, us old CIA guys prefer anonymity, honestly," Jack says laughing.

"Well, no chance of that now," Albert chimes in.

Jessie stands behind the men, a small smile on her face, she feels a strong synergy with Jack, she isn't really sure what it is, but they had both been under fire in the last twenty-four hours, maybe that had something to do with it. Jack catches her eye as the conversation with Jefferson and the other agents continues and she can see he feels the same, it isn't false bravado on his part, Jack is just once again showing people what they expect to see – even now, hiding in plain sight. She smiles again realizing the lesson being taught is just for her.

The story is told one more time for the new arrivals and it's obvious that Jack and Mike have been through this a few times at this point, their repartee is smooth and they are obviously comfortable with the tale. Jack skims over most of the details covering Potemkin's apartment, serving up a quick hi-lite reel of the last twenty-four hours. As they finish up he turns to Jessie who has taken a seat next to him at the table and asks, "Are you okay kiddo?"

She hesitates for a moment the whirlwind in Tampa and the quick trip up with the Marshals hadn't really left her any time to just absorb the magnitude of what had happened. "Yeah, I'm okay sir, I made some mistakes down there, probably cost a lady her life," she says softly. She can feel the tears rising but there is no way she is giving in to it here, maybe later.

Jack nods, "it's never easy and sometimes we can't save everyone Jessie, we can talk about it later if you want."

"Yes sir, I'd appreciate that," she answers pulling herself together.

Jack turns to Harrington, "what are you going to do with Potemkin?" looking over at Lou, "that bastard ran their entire cyber outfit, they need to get you to talk to him..."

Harrington breaks in, "we need to get him processed and some charges filed so we can keep him. Jefferson says he isn't talking and wants a lawyer, not much we can do until we can make that happen." He looks around, "it's late, my guess is we aren't going to get anywhere else on this tonight, but damn if this isn't the break we needed. We owe you Jack, not going to be any way to pay that debt, but..."

Jack waves him off, "I didn't do this for anything like that." He looks over at Lou, "this is about family and we haven't solved the Sokolov problem yet so as far as I go this isn't finished... but glad to be able to help you fellas out."

Harrington turns to Lou, "man, you have to let us take this from here..."

Lou doesn't get a chance to respond before Albert breaks in, "look, you two, I'm not listening to this argument again, it's one in the morning, let's regroup in the morning and assess where we are. I'll start getting the paperwork together for charges and you guys can work out what's next." He turns to Jack, "is there anything else we absolutely need to know tonight?"

"I've already briefed Jefferson here in on the location of what I believe is the main cyber center, and this Sampson fella I ran into was coming out of those condos right on Brighton Beach, not much more to tell than that. Potemkin did say Sampson was in Tampa so you may want to have someone down there put the word out to look for him."

Albert turns to Tim, "we good then?"

Tim gives a resigned nod, "yeah, we're good, I've got men heading over to the Brighton now, we'll at least stake both places out and see what we see, maybe we'll get lucky and Sokolov will just turn himself in..."

Jack lets out a laugh, "good fuckin' luck with that... and you need to find this Sampson, he is one mean looking son of a bitch."

Albert takes the lead again, "okay, back here at eight then, where's the closest hotel?"

Lou pipes up, "well I took the liberty of booking Jessie, Jack and myself at the Four Seasons, it's basically around the corner, want me to add a couple more rooms?" Tim and Albert both just look at him, "what?" he asks.

"It's like fucking seven hundred bucks a night, that's what," Albert blurts out once again returning to his roots. "We work for a living so that's a bit out of the budget," he laughs.

Jefferson taps Harrington on the shoulder, "I booked you and Mr. Jimenez at the Marriott a couple blocks down on Broadway, I'm there as well, hope that's okay sir."

Tim smiles, "that's fine, appreciate you taking care of it." He looks around the room, "okay, back here at eight then, anything happens before I've got everyone's number, keep your passes, we'll extend them so you can get back in tomorrow, let's just plan to use this room. Jefferson, sit tight, I need a few minutes..." the meeting effectively ends and everyone begins to file out.

Mike is trailing Jack out the door, "sir, you need me to get someone to take you guys over to the hotel?"

Lou answers for him, "No thanks, I think we are just going to walk, its close."

"Are you sure that's a good idea," the young agent asks.

Jack smiles and gives him a pat on the back, "I think we can handle it son, don't you?"

Mike laughs, "I guess so, now that you mention it, good night sir, see you tomorrow."

"Mike, you did good tonight, training or no training that was tough and you held it together." High praise coming from Jack and the young agent beams and nods his head.

"Thank you sir, goodnight."

They part ways in the lobby and the three of them head out into the cool evening air, Lou with his arms around his two favorite people. *Tomorrow is another day* he thinks, *we'll figure this out*. He wasn't bowing out, no matter what Harrington wanted, no way he was leaving the fate of these two in anyone else's hands.

Sinking Ship

Kirilov had pulled out of the parking garage in a hurry, he looks over at Sokolov, the man is just staring out the window, pistols in his lap.

"Go slow Kirilov," he whispers, "don't want to get stopped, stay calm my boy…"

Kirilov takes a deep breath and slows down, he had been with Sokolov for almost three years, recruited after getting out of the army by Sampson, but tonight might have been the most words he has ever traded with Sokolov. He still isn't sure what had possessed him to head up that elevator again, but he was sure now it had been the right decision. No way Sokolov was going to be in Scranton in three days and after closing down the cyber center, hell closing nothing, he had shot them while they sat at their keyboards, it had been quick and merciless but he was all in now. Merging onto the Belt Parkway he brings the SUV up to speed, blending into traffic and hoping the forty-five-minute drive goes quickly. Kirilov has no idea whether anyone is pursuing them, but after seeing Vasily on the couch he was pretty sure whatever had gone down in the City didn't turn out as planned. He didn't mind playing the part of loyal soldier but he had no desire to end his evening dead in a gunfight, especially not for a man who had obviously planned on leaving him and a whole lot of others hanging. He would play his part for now, waiting to see where this would all lead, he suspected they were headed back to Ukraine, not much else made sense at this point. He pulls into the private hanger at Republic, the dashboard clock reads 12:41AM. To the Northwest across the East River the meeting on the twenty-third floor is wrapping up, in Brighton six agents and a dozen of New York's finest are scrambling to cover Sokolov's condo unit and Potemkin's apartment as well as figure out if the two-alarm fire on Twelfth Street is somehow related.

Kirilov and Alexi are standing by the SUV as Sampson's jet lands a few minutes later. Sampson disembarks and wraps Alexi in a brief bear hug while Kirilov stands by watching, pistol at the ready. Sampson pulls the crew aside directing them to get refueled and supplied, they will be leaving for Odessa in twenty minutes. He instructs Kirilov to stand guard while he and Alexi get in the SUV.

"Alexi, tell me everything, what happened?" the big man asks. Sokolov doesn't respond right away sitting in the front seat with a faraway look.

"You know Sampson, it's time to go home, don't you think?" he says turning to the big man. "We've been together a long time old friend, I'm afraid this is all coming to an end…" he trails off waving his hand out the window.

Sampson doesn't say anything, the men sit in silence, watching the crew refuel the jet, Kirilov still as a statue illuminated in the SUV's headlights. He finally turns, "tell me Alexi, what happened, who did this to us?"

Alexi just smiles, "we did this to us Sampson... they have Potemkin or maybe he's dead, I don't really know, Kirilov there," he motions with his hand, "shut down the computer center, they're all dead." He doesn't say anything else for a moment, "Wasn't the Feds though, whoever did this..." he leaves the thought unfinished.

Sampson looks out at the plane thinking, *couldn't be the girl, she was in Tampa with the Marshals, and no way any of the New York families would have the balls to hit them, none of this made any fucking sense.* He turns back to Alexi, "tell me what happened to Potemkin."

Alexi tells him about going to the apartment finding his three men shot, professional style. "We caught up with them taking the train into the City. That's where Vasily and the others set up the ambush," he tells the big man.

Sampson nods, "okay, that all makes sense I guess," he says. "But how did you know he was going to the Feds?"

Alexi looks over with a small smile, "feeling mostly, but the train they were on lets off four or five blocks up from the Feds, just seemed to make sense, and we couldn't cover every station so rolled the dice..." He pauses, "and I was right, sent six guys with Vasily and the one following on the train, should have been enough," he says, mostly to himself.

"Alexi, something I don't get," Sampson asks, "you keep saying them, who was with him?"

"Some old man, never did find out who he was... caught sight of them getting on the train together."

Sampson says to himself, "fuck me..." turning to Alexi, "an old man? Like a grandfather?"

"Yes, I guess, why?" Alexi asks.

"Motherfucker!" Sampson exclaims, "I ran into an old man sitting on the benches out front of the condo, hadn't seen him before, but there was something about him... he stopped me for a light."

"You think this is the guy, he was what, watching us?" Alexi asks.

"I don't know, but... like I said there was something about him, didn't make sense at the time, but now there's an old man with Potemkin?"

Kirilov knocks on the window and almost gets shot for his trouble, "time to go, he says," he mimes pointing to the pilot giving them thumbs up.

The men head for the stairway, Alexi turns to Kirilov, "come on, you're with us now." The three of them board and the jet taxis and takes off heading East into the coming sunrise. Sokolov is leaving behind a significant portion of his operation and the source of much of his revenue, he knows there is no way to maintain his stranglehold in the States without actually being on the ground there. It won't take long before the Italians and the Latin gangs are divvying up his turf and going back to war with each other. It had taken years to build and now in a matter of a few weeks it was in shambles. Sampson is making calls ahead to Odessa in the back and Kirilov is already gently snoring in one of the plush leather chairs. Sokolov thinks to himself as gazes out the window into the dark, *better to regroup than drown on a sinking ship.*

Almost Doesn't Count

It had taken too long to mobilize the agents to Brighton Beach to have had any chance of capturing or even seeing Sokolov or any of his men. The chaos created by the shootout and bringing Potemkin in had delayed their response and they were paying the price.

Engine Companies 245 and 246 along with their attached Ladders, 161 and 169 had responded to the fire Kirilov had set. They were struggling to bring it under control and keep the rest of the block from going up in flames, it would be morning before investigators would discover the gruesome remains of more than twenty people incinerated in the original fire. It would take another day and a half before they were able to confirm they had been executed prior to the fire, but at one in the morning the fire was barely under control and the Battalion Commander wasn't letting anyone near it, not even the FBI.

The agents regrouped and split up, taking half a dozen police officers with each team, they headed to Potemkin's apartment and the condo. The apartment had been ransacked and the three bodies had been left where they were, it was going to be a long night for the crime scene folks. Leaving two NYC cops to keep the place locked down and another two at each end of the alley the lead agent called into Jefferson for further instructions.

Three blocks away the other group had decided to have the NYC cops keep an eye on the front and back entrances of the condo. The story was they were helping the Fire Department in case further evacuations were needed, this seemed plausible enough. The three agents started in the parking garage, finding nothing they headed into the lobby, which was understandably empty at this time of night. A partial bloody handprint on the elevator was enough to warrant a further investigation however. Once inside the car it was obvious someone had headed up to the top floor, but without a card key they were stuck. It took another forty-five minutes and two calls to Jefferson to get someone down there with enough juice to override the security system and let them up to Sokolov's penthouse. In the meantime, Jefferson and Harrington had grabbed a car and headed in that direction as well.

Harrington had found his three agents, two local cops and the building superintendent arguing in the lobby. The super had provided a card key to the elevator, but had refused to open any of the suites on the top floor without a warrant authorizing it. They had threatened to lock him up for obstruction but he was clearly more concerned with repercussions from Sokolov than the FBI. The agents wanted to just breach the doors but the local cops seemed hesitant without the proper paperwork. Even the obvious blood on the floor and the door to Sokolov's office hadn't been enough to move the superintendent.

Harrington pulls him aside out of earshot of the others, "listen we really need to get in these rooms, I can get the warrant but we really don't need it with the blood. That's enough cause for us to believe a crime has been committed, so let's do this the easy way, okay." He looks at the man seeing the fear in his eyes, "we can protect you, you don't even have to go up with us."

The super just says, "you can't protect me, you have no idea what you're dealing with..." he hands Harrington the card key and walks out of the front doors.

Harrington motions to the two cops, "you guys make sure he gets home okay and post someone outside his house till I tell you it's okay." The cops nod and hustle out the front door to catch up with super, both seemed more than happy to leave the condo. Harrington looks at Jefferson and the other three, "okay fellas, you ready? Pistols out, no telling what the hell is up there, so let's go find out."

About halfway up Harrington thinks, *should have taken two elevators, if anyone is waiting this will be like shooting fish in a barrel, too late now, going to have to take our chances.* The elevator doors slide open onto a short hall that creates a T with a second hall. There is a large double door at the end, Tim waves his men out and they begin to creep down the hall hugging the wall. When they get to the double doors to Sokolov's office they can see there are three more doors further down each side of the hallway. The double doors are slightly cracked, and Tim holds up his hand, he motions for two of the agents to stay put and watch the hallway. He pushes the door open rapidly and is followed into the room by Jefferson and the third agent.

Nothing, Tim looks around at the plush office sees Vasily on the couch looking very dead. He walks over and checks for a pulse, more habit than anything else. "Don't touch anything, Jefferson, call it in and get a Crime Scene Team in here, looks like we missed him."

Jefferson nods as he points to a door at the other end of the office just past the couch. "Need to clear this floor first sir, may still be someone here..." Harrington nods back and heads to the door. "I'll take this one sir," Jefferson says, stepping in front of him. He gently turns the knob and pushes the door inward, following with his pistol up and ready. Harrington is right behind, Jefferson stops abruptly and Harrington bumps into him.

"What is it Sammie?" Harrington asks.

"Uh sir, well, uh, see for yourself sir," he says embarrassedly stepping aside.

Tim steps past him into the room finding three very beautiful, and very naked young women sitting on the biggest bed he has ever seen. They are terrified or may be conditioned to not care, but they don't even attempt to cover themselves as the three men enter the room. Tim decides to go formal in his approach, "FBI, is there anyone else in the room?" Tim realizes how ridiculous this sounds as he lowers his badge and looks around, the girls don't move or say a word. He relaxes and says, "ladies, what are your names," and pausing for a moment to look at Sammie who is still dumbfounded, "can you put some clothes on please?"

The girl on the left, a beautiful blond with high cheekbones and piercing blue eyes, who could easily have been a model in any major media campaign, starts speaking in what Tim thinks might be Russian, but he really has no idea. The third agent sticks his head in door, "sir, she's asking where Sokolov is..."

"You speak, whatever that is," Harrington says.

"Yes sir, its Russian, want me to translate?" he asks.

"Yes, tell them to get some clothes on, we are taking them in for questioning, we need their names and ID if they have it, and make sure they know we aren't going to hurt them, what's your name?"

The young agent responds, "Harris sir, my mother was Russian," he turns and rattles off in Russian as the girls get up and begin pulling clothes out of a large dresser on the far side of the room.

"Sir..." Jefferson says, "let's be careful there aren't any weapons in here..." He turns to the agent who is still speaking in Russian to the girls, "go search that dresser, I don't want one of them popping up with a pistol... Hate to have to explain how you got shot while staring at a pair of tits."

Harrington just shakes his head, "Okay, check it out and hold them here, see if they have any ID or if you can get them to talk to you about where they are from or if they know anything, we've got to clear the rest of this floor, come on Sammie."

Sammie turns to follow him out the door and back into the office, "Jesus sir, ever run into anything like that before?"

"Nope, can't say that I have," Harrington responds, "let's get the rest of this place checked out but my guess is we missed this guy. Call it in now and get Sokolov and this Sampson guy on all the watch lists, if they try to flee, maybe we can pick them up." He knows he is missing something obvious, but the lack of sleep combined with the speed things are moving puts it just out of reach. They clear the rest of the floor, there are two more bedrooms which are empty, another two are offices but don't look used, and the last room is a full armory. The agents realize how lucky they have been that no one was here, they would have been significantly outgunned. They return to Sokolov's office and collect Agent Harris and the girls before heading back downstairs.

Harrington eyes closed on the ride down in the elevator, is trying to clear his head when it clicks, there had been one of those to scale model jets on one of the shelves in Sokolov's office. *FUCK ME* he thinks; *how could he have forgotten Sokolov's fleet of private jets*. He quickly dials his phone, "Lou? Sorry man, hope I didn't wake you, did your program identify what airport Sokolov was flying in and out of up here?" He listens for a moment, "got it thanks Lou, I'll bring you up to speed in the morning," he says and hangs up. "Jefferson, get someone over to Republic and see if they can get a list of private jets with tail numbers that have left out of there since say 11PM, then let's get it out on the wire, I want to know where each one is and when they land. Maybe we can still get this guy!" He turns to Harris, "I'll ride back into the City with you, we need to have the NYC police hold these three until we can question them, and I need to get at least a couple of hours sleep. You too Sammie, get someone on it and then call it a night, I've got a feeling we are going to busy tomorrow." *I can't believe we almost had him*, he thinks to himself.

Out of Reach

Ukraine was part of the loosely affiliated but still formidable Russian Alliance, not quite the Soviet Union, it had developed toward the end of Trump administration fulfilling the expansionistic plans of Vladimir Putin and his personal answer to the European Union. Member nations were considered independent even holding elections but shared a consolidated military, currency, and foreign policy. The end result was a weak version of the Soviet Union, where capitalism, organized crime, and corruption ruled the day they did however have a rather formidable nuclear arsenal, and much to the chagrin of the United States and the FBI in particular, absolutely no extradition agreements.

It's a few minutes before seven when Jessie meets her dad and Jack in the lobby, none of them had much sleep the night before but the Four Seasons pampered you to the point where even with just a few hours' sleep you felt amazingly refreshed. They had decided to hit a small breakfast place a block over from the FBI building to have coffee and discuss the day before meeting with Harrington and Jimenez. Lou was worried about the FBI cutting them loose and out of anything further, it wasn't so much that he wanted to continue pursuing Sokolov but rather that he didn't want to be out of the information loop and not see the next attack coming.

They discussed it back and forth over coffee and beignets and decided they would move forward with or without the FBI's blessing. Lou told them about the late-night call from Harrington asking about Sokolov's jets, he didn't think that was a good sign. Jack had made some calls and shared that the Agency had agreed to reinstate him on a temporary basis giving him at least some coverage for his actions. Lou had just gripped his old friend's hand telling him that he hadn't needed to do that, but Jack had just smiled and told him that no sacrifice was too much at this point.

They headed over to the Federal Building once again causing a ruckus at the security screening, passes or no passes, the agents weren't real keen on letting two civilians into the building armed to the teeth. Jefferson finally came down and personally escorted them through. On the elevator ride to the twenty-third floor he quipped, "we are going to have do something about you two..." Jack and Jessie just smiled at him, neither had any intention of giving up their guns.

When they finally made it to the conference room they found Harrington conferring with half a dozen agents and looking as if he hadn't slept at all, Albert was scouring email on his laptop and snarfing down a sesame bagel with smear, with another one waiting in the wings. Tim looks up hearing them enter, "Lou, going to need your help again, it looks like," he says without preamble.

"Sure Tim, anything you need," Lou responds magnanimously. He doesn't really feel it, but a deal is a deal and Tim had held his part up so far. He heads over to that side of the table while Jessie and Jack take a couple of chairs and talk in hushed tones.

Tim quickly brings Lou up to speed on the events from the previous evening, well, morning, he corrects himself. He shows Lou a list of plane registration numbers. "Okay, so these are the flights out of Republic last night from eleven on, we have been able to track all but these last three..." Tim explains.

Lou takes the list and looks at it, glancing up at Tim he asks, "so, umm, what do you want me to do?"

"I want you to plug these into your magic box and find the bastards for me..." Tim says matter of factly.

Lou looks at him for a moment, "you're serious? Tim, you know that's not really how the program works right?"

"Lou, I don't want to know how it works, I don't even want to know how you get the information, but I know you were able to track one of Sokolov's jets by its tail number in the Saudi's system... so do whatever it is you guys do at Paradigm and find this bastard for me."

"All right, I'll do what I can, no promises though, he might not have even been logged wherever he is," Lou explains.

"Just do the best you can, we don't have much else to go on at this point," Tim says exasperatedly. "I'm just getting ready to give the morning brief and figure out what our next move is, why don't you guys sit in and see if anything strikes a chord with you."

"Sure Tim, let me scan and send this," Lou says as he initiates the scan with his phone.

Another dozen agents have filed in and taken seats at the table. Harrington brings everyone up to speed on the events of the past twelve or so hours, including an update from the fire scene that had just come in, setting the casualty count at twenty-three, all of them believed to be Sokolov's people.

"Jesus, that bastard," Albert says softly.

Tim continues ignoring the interruption explaining that they believed Potemkin could be the key they had been waiting for, but he had clammed up tight and wasn't saying a word except 'lawyer' anytime someone spoke to him.

"Let me have a couple of hours with him..." Jack interjects, "might have something to say then."

"Mr. Hardy, we all appreciate you getting him here, but well, I don't even know how to respond to that," Tim says rather forcefully.

Jack just shrugs his shoulders, "just trying to help."

Tim just looks at him before moving on while some of the younger agents are working hard to suppress a grin, Jack's reputation had spread quickly on the lips of Mike Pleshkowski. Harrington goes on to explain that the three young women, he was calling it a rescue at this point, were providing a great deal of information. Two of them were seventeen and had been kidnapped in the Ukraine and the other was eighteen and had been taken in Spain, unfortunately their stories were all too commonplace. The FBI was in the process of trying to reunite them with their families he explained. They would have to testify in the US if specific charges were ever brought against Sokolov in their cases, which right now didn't look very likely.

Tim points to Lou in the back and introduces him to those that haven't met him yet, Lou McIntyre and his staff at Paradigm are working to track three private jets out of Republic last night, we believe there is a good chance Sokolov and maybe his second in command Sampson were on one of them he explains. "Lou have your guys had any hits yet?" he asks.

Lou looks at his phone, "well, on that last one we have hits in Denmark, Germany and Poland all within about thirty minutes and that was about an hour ago, if I was a betting man I would say that's him and he is headed home."

"Shit, if he lands in the Ukraine no way the Russians are going to let us at him," Tim exclaims. He looks around, "any ideas?" he asks.

Albert looks around waiting for someone to speak up, "listen Tim let's start putting our case together, there is plenty of evidence from the condo and the girls. We also need to touch base with Tampa, we know Sampson was down there so we probably have work to do there as well. I'll personally talk to whatever lawyer this Potemkin comes up with and make them the sweetest deal in history if he'll cooperate, maybe this bastard is out of reach, but that doesn't mean we can't be ready when we do put hands on him."

Tim nods, "you're right Albert..." he issues marching orders to his agents, asking Jefferson to coordinate their efforts and make sure to interface with the local crime scene techs to integrate their findings as well. After everyone leaves he and Albert move down to the end of the table where Jessie, Jack and Lou remain.

"Okay, what are we going to do with these three?" Tim asks Albert.

Albert turns to Jack, "true you've been reinstated by the Agency?"

"Temporarily anyway," Jack answers.

"Ok, well you're probably covered then, not that anyone here would dare bring you up on charges after last night, that just leaves Jessie here," Albert says nodding her way.

"Now wait a minute..." Lou starts to object.

"Hold up Lou, don't fly off the handle, I'm not suggesting anything, the folks in Tampa are plenty pissed, but I think we can handle that... I say we let it lie and if some locals want to file charges we deal with it then..." he looks around, "what do you guys think?"

Jessie lays a hand on her Dad's arm, "Mr. Jimenez, that's fine, I don't mind answering anyone's questions if I need to, I feel like everything I did was justified, so you just let me know what you need and I'll be there."

Albert looks around, "we good then... Lou?"

"Ok I guess, but you guys better step up if she needs you," he says grudgingly.

Tim stands up, "Ok then, Lou, let me know if anything comes in and I'll keep you in the loop best I can, I've got to get to work on this though so if you'll excuse me..." he shakes hands all around and heads for the door.

Albert stands up doing the same, "don't worry, I have you guys covered," he says. They all agree to keep in touch, Albert walks them down to the elevators and they exchange goodbyes again. Out on the sidewalk the three look at each other, "now what, Jessie asks?" a bit deflated.

"Let's go somewhere we can talk, Alexi might be out of the FBI's reach, but that doesn't mean he's out of ours," Jack says.

"Oh Jesus, here we go!" Lou says as they head down the block back toward the Four Seasons, Jessie just smiles.

An Interesting Offer

They are holed up in Lou's suite at the Four Seasons room service having just delivered two pots of coffee, a tray of cut fruit, and a platter of sliced lox, bagels, and cream cheese at Jessie's insistence. She is slathering up a bagel and layering on the lox when she sees the two men looking at her, "what? You two aren't hungry?" she asks.

They just smile and shake their heads, "it's pretty amazing, that's all," Jack says laughing.

They have been reviewing all the data on Sokolov as well as the little that Potemkin had shared with Jack prior to the shootout. Jack explains that his reinstatement was solely for the purpose of working on Sokolov, the CIA is interested in taking him down, not so much for the trafficking but because he is a major supplier of weapons and explosives to Jihadist cells everywhere. Lou wants a bit more detail, Jack explains that the Agency is short on field agents, especially experienced ones, and he knows Sokolov and his outfit better than anyone at this point, it made sense for everyone. Lou presses him though about what exactly the agency wants from him. Jack finally throws his hands up says, "come on Lou, don't play Boy Scout with me, you know damn well what they want, they want him gone..." He stands up and walks over to the window, "look, this is my last job," he pauses and looks back at them, "no matter what happens," he says softly.

The silence between them is expanding when Jessie turns to Jack, "well, I'm going with you," Jack shakes his head no, "who else is going to push your wheelchair?" she says before either of them can protest.

Lou walks over to her, taking her in a big hug, his chin resting on her head, "I can't let you do that honey, you have no idea…"

He doesn't get a chance to finish as Jessie pushes away, "Dad I love you, but I am not six years old, I've killed six men in the last week and I spent ten years in the toughest and best trained Army in the world, believe me, I can do this…" She looks up at him, "In fact, I think this is exactly what I'm supposed to be doing…" she says having a moment of realization.

"Honey," Lou chokes up fighting back tears, "I just can't, I can't lose you too…" he finally splutters out the tears coming on their own now.

"Daddy, it's okay," she says, wrapping him back up in both arms, Jack stands by the window realizing how much he cares for these two. Jessie looks over at him, "besides Dad, I'm going to have the best teacher there is, aren't I Jack?"

"Lou, I had nothing to do with this, but I promise you on my life I won't let anything happen to her," Jack answers walking back over.

Lou shakes his head, holding Jessie at arm's length and looking at her, "I know Jack, this has been coming for a while now, I tried to ignore it and pretend it wasn't." He hugs her again, "honey you have always blazed your own trail, and done what you thought was right, damn the consequences and I have always loved you for it…" he can't find any other words.

"I know Daddy, I got that from you…" she says.

"Jack, I think she needs to be in the Agency if this is going to work, she has no coverage if she is freelancing out there, beside you guys are going to need all the logistical support you can get."

"Of course Lou, let me make a couple of calls, I don't think it will be a problem, might need to fly down to DC to get her sworn in and set up." Jack says, picking up his phone.

Jessie didn't consider it a sacrifice, maybe if she had thought it through, but the pragmatic problem-solving side of her personality saw an opportunity to permanently solve the Sokolov issue, if that required a certain commitment on her part, well so be it, nothing came for free. She had spent more than half her life either training to, or solving her country's problems, wasn't this just an extension of that? And fuck those Special Forces guys, she was going Agency where they didn't seem to have any hang-ups about women.

Jack interrupts her inner dialogue, "Ok you're in, apparently they have been following this thing pretty closely so you are a known entity down there, going to have to go to DC though and sooner the better. We have a green light on Sokolov, but you will have to go through the normal training protocols when we are done..." he looks around realizing he has been gushing a bit, dialing it back he asks, "Jessie are you sure you want to do this? It's a big commitment."

"I'm sure Jack, in fact I think I've been waiting for this, I just didn't know it," she says.

"Ok," he replies, "how many languages can you speak?"

"Well, I speak Spanish like a native, both European and Mexican dialects, my Arabic is pretty good, Italian not bad, and enough Russian to probably get by travelling. Oh, I also was taking some Japanese through Thompson but probably only a handful of phrases on that, why?" she asks.

"Well, like I said, the Agency has a full training regimen they are going to want to put you through, but if you can handle basic language skills, and I know you can shoot, then we can probably bypass all of that for now..." Jack answers.

They spend another hour working through the details of how to get to DC, Lou still has the suite at the DoubleTree so they decide to base out of there. Of course, it's not quite so simple, Lou makes one more attempt to dissuade Jessie from going through with it, but it's half-hearted, he can tell her minds made up. Jack wisely stays out of the discussion, knowing how Lou feels, but he also knows Jessie is made for the job.

Jessie leaves the two men making flight reservations, Lou is going to head back to Boulder the day after, she needs to pick up some clothes and a few supplies. It seems like a month ago, but all her belongings are still in a retro hotel on the Gulf coast of Florida. She heads up Broadway, no real destination in mind, figuring to see what strikes her on the way. She takes a deep breath, drinking in the spring air, the bustle of the city, the raw energy with all its cacophony of noises and smells and she finds herself smiling. The City has no memory, no fears, it exists in the purity of the moment, each breath unscripted and without any preconceived outcomes, it is the essence of freedom. She hasn't felt like this since graduating the Academy and she knows in her heart its more than the relief of making it through the past forty-eight hours, it's the recognition of what's next in her life and the knowledge that she has finally found what she is meant to do.

She wanders as far as Central Park, deciding to camp out on a bench and people-watch for a while, there is still a spring chill in the air, but the sun is out and plenty of people are in the park. She has an old habit of making up stories for the lives flowing past her and a park is almost as good as an airport for people watching. The stories are of course just a distraction from any real introspection that might creep in; she can't avoid it though and finds her self-reviewing the events of the past weeks which of course naturally opens up the doors to everything else. She doesn't often indulge herself like this, but if ever there was a turning point in her life this was it. The unanswered questions are always the same, she often wonders if things would have been different if her mother had lived. That wasn't really fair to her dad she knew, but she had grown up in a man's world and her dad's unwillingness, well that wasn't really it, more like inability to even consider another relationship had probably had a more profound effect on her own willingness to have one than she cared to admit. Her dad had and did love her in every way a parent could love a child, but his adult relationship was his work, his company, his Bronco. In many ways, her commitment to country and career mimicked him. It didn't bother her and she didn't feel unfilled and maybe that was what tickled her conscience the most, if she had been honest the relationship with Tom would have disintegrated at some point like all the others, she was simply unwilling to elevate her relationships above herself and career. This was a running conversation with herself that seemed to pop up whenever it was time to make a major decision, where most would have left these episodes of introspection with doubts Jessie only felt resolve and a reaffirmation of what she had already decided.

    She leaves the park surer than ever of her decision. Heading down Madison Avenue she window shops through the high-end designer stores, they don't hold any attraction for her, it's all beautiful but not who she is. Backtracking she picks up a few essentials at Victoria's Secret before heading over to Paragon

Sports for some new running shoes, a couple of basic outfits and two sets of workout clothes. With three bags in each hand and her backpack slung over her still sore shoulder she heads back to the Four Seasons and one man she loves more than anything in the world, and another she is yearning to learn from.

Odessa

Sokolov's jet touches down at a small airfield just North of Odessa, the runway is almost too short for the corporate jet, but they are guaranteed no attention. It was eleven thirty on the East coast of the US, however, Odessa is seven hours ahead and twilight was already setting in, Sokolov, Sampson and Kirilov disembarked to ten heavily armed men and three blacked out SUVs. Sampson had been busy making sure no one had a chance to take a shot at them, it was an unlikely scenario but after the past few days he wasn't taking any chances. It takes the caravan a little more than forty minutes to navigate through Odessa to Sokolov's gated compound on Morska Street, not far from the Black Sea Yacht Club.

Kirilov joins the other Sokolov soldiers in the guesthouse, a modest four bedroom home adjacent to the main house and attached to the outside wall next to the main gates. From this vantage point Sokolov's soldiers had a full view of the grounds, as well as the main entrance to the compound. The perimeter of the compound was wired with motion sensors and a wireless video system, these were supplemented by a heat detection system that would pick up any signature larger than a cat. All systems were monitored in the guesthouse with a secondary viewing station in the main house where two soldiers were permanently stationed. It was as secure as a place could be made while still maintaining some semblance of normalcy within the confines of the city itself. Sampson added a roving patrol of four men around the grounds before joining Alexi in the main house.

    Sampson found Alexi in the living room sipping bourbon, a habit he had picked up in the States, looking out over the patio and pool through the open glass doors lining the wall, in the kitchen the cook and housekeeper is busily humming to herself as she prepares an evening meal for the two men, she has been with Alexi since he was a young man and with the exception of Sampson is probably the only person he trusts implicitly. It was peaceful and if you weren't aware of the chaos of the past twenty-four hours you would have thought two old friends were catching up on the day's events before sharing dinner. Sampson sits in the love seat opposite Alexi, bourbon in hand, neither says anything, it's a brief moment of decompression. There will be time tomorrow or even the day after to assess the repercussions of the past week and make decisions on what comes next. For now, the two men enjoy the comfort of not having to speak, soaking up the silence.

    "Sampson, do you remember when we were just getting started? Filling those damn containers in the middle of the night…" Alexi trails off.

    Sampson doesn't answer right away, "yes, I remember Alexi, those were simpler times," he says after a moment. He looks over, Alexi has his eyes closed a small smile on his face as he leans back on the couch, "those were tough days my friend," Sampson continues.

Opening his eyes and looking over, "sure they were, never knew who was gunning for us, did we?" He doesn't wait for an answer, "at least, you could see it coming though..."

Sampson just nods, this nostalgic melancholy Alexi isn't something he is used to or comfortable with. Maybe the old man was losing his grip on things. The big man thinks about what that means, not just for him but for everything. There weren't any retirement parties for old gangsters, nobody just faded away, and they didn't peacefully hand the business over to the next man in line. Sampson wasn't even sure who that would be in this case anyway. He was the closest to Alexi, but that didn't mean the old man was sharing the keys to the kingdom with him, and although Alexi had fucked his way around the world he didn't have an heir following behind him.

"Sampson, Sampson..."

"What... sorry was just thinking about how tough it was before you took me in..." Sampson says, hoping he sounds convincing.

"Been together a long time, haven't we?" Alexi answers.

The big man leans forward, setting his glass on the coffee table in front of him, "Alexi, you can't be talking like this, not in front of the men, I understand, I do, but it's not healthy..." he trails off wondering if he has gone too far.

Alexi nods his head, "you think I'm getting soft Sampson? Maybe the old man can't handle it anymore? That what you're thinking maybe?" he asks, staring at Sampson.

Sampson smiles and leans back in the chair taking a sip of his bourbon, "Ah now, there's the Alexi I remember from the old days!"

Alexi continues to stare at him; "any time you want to make your move..." he says softly the steel in his voice clear.

Sampson stares back, "Alexi, I have always been loyal, that isn't going to change..."

"Make sure it doesn't..." is the barely veiled threat.

The smells from the kitchen along with the clink of dishes being laid out signals the meal, the two men move to the table, Alexi's last word still a tangible separation between them. "Sampson, let it go my old friend, I am tired, I mean nothing by it..."

"Of course Alexi, as you wish..." he responds possibly a bit too formally.

The men sit as the babushka serves them varenyky the Ukrainian version of pierogis, lamb roast, baked fish and sauerkraut and peas. They silently fill and refill their plates, Brighton Beach may have had all the comfort foods of home, but being home seemed to make all the difference.

Alexi wipes his mouth on the linen napkin next to him and looks up at Sampson, "tomorrow we cut our US operations off, let our clients there know they need to source elsewhere, we shore up our European connections making sure we fulfill all orders, and we refocus our efforts on weapons in the Middle East and Africa… I don't want this mess to spill over to the rest of our operations." He takes another varenyky, dipping it in sour cream before stuffing it whole in his mouth, "also let's see what we can salvage of the online stuff, find whoever our best person is for now to manage it while we find another spider…" He looks up at Sampson, "and you find me a way to get my hands on that little bitch…"

Sampson nods, he isn't going to argue with Alexi, not tonight, but he doesn't see a way to make that happen especially not from here. The two men finish the meal in silence and Sampson takes his leave. He checks in on the men leaving specific instructions to call him if anything even seems suspicious. Normally he would take one of the SUVs but he keeps a suite at the La Gioconda Hotel a brief ten-minute walk from the compound, he needs time to think as he heads out into the dark.

Alexi finishes his glass of bourbon before heading upstairs, this one's name is Svetlana, not that he asks or cares, she is only there to serve one purpose and tonight she will bear the burdens of the past few day's frustrations.

Langley

Lou, Jessie and Jack had flown out of New York late in the afternoon landing in DC in time to catch dinner at Rasika's on D Street, one of the city's best Indian restaurants and a personal favorite of Lou's. They talked late into the evening rehashing the shooting in Tampa and New York, there was no new ground to cover but the pace of events had been overwhelming and each of them was still trying to catalogue their thoughts and emotions. Jack was most comfortable or at least knew how to put the best face on it, but even he had to admit this was the first time he had been in a shootout like this. He hadn't related the two times he had been surprised from behind, but the thought he might be slipping weighed heavily on him. Jessie, for her part, was coming to grips with the death of Terry Johnson in Tampa, neither man had any comfort to offer, casualties were part of the game, there wasn't anything you could do about it. Lou was heading back to Paradigm in the morning, Albert had managed to get Potemkin's lawyer to encourage his client to work with the FBI, at least start providing a list of names of the girls in Tom Casey's files. The Paradigm team was going to be working to identify potential leads on the victims, the FBI was hoping they could at least locate, if not rescue some of them. They had finally called it a night when the restaurant had emptied of patrons leaving them and the stacked chairs and staff the only ones in the building.

Lou caught the eight-thirty flight back to Denver the next morning, the goodbyes in the lobby were tearful but he had put aside his worries, kissing Jessie on the forehead and telling her how proud he was; her bone crushing hug was the only thanks he needed or wanted. She and Jack headed out to Langley, the CIA headquarters, she had paperwork to sign and they had an operation to plan.

Not everyone was onboard with bringing Jessie directly into the National Clandestine Service (NCS), never mind the Special Activities Division (SAD), these were coveted slots and required significant training and had very specific background skill requirements. SAD was responsible for covert and special activities including the paramilitary component of the CIA so for an outsider to walk in and fill an operational slot simply did not happen and wasn't going to sit well with everybody. Jack had covered this ground before they arrived not wanting Jessie to have a distinctly negative experience from the start, but there was no hiding all of it. For her part, she took it in her stride, crashing the party so to speak had been her style since joining the Rangers, a few sideways glances and some muttering weren't going to deter her here. The Deputy Director, Vance Simpson a long-time operative himself and friend of Jack's had already cleared the appointment with the NCS Director; Jessie would be working directly for him on what they were calling for now "special projects".

The three of them were meeting in Simpson's office reviewing all the data they had on Sokolov with two Staff Ops officers, a counter terrorism specialist and a Ukrainian specialist. Simpson wanted to make sure everyone, particularly Jack and Jessie understood that at its heart this was a locate-and-track mission, the ultimate goal was a snatch and grab of Sokolov by a SAD team that would be waiting just offshore. They wanted Sokolov alive if possible, the Jihadist movement was picking up again and the hope was that he could provide enough data to begin rolling them up before they were at full strength. It wasn't their job to identify the US policy decisions that were causing this resurgence, but they were definitely expected to proactively work to suppress it. Simpson had been a senior field officer during the Trump and then Dixon administrations and seen first-hand the horror visited on Europe and then the US mainland, no one wanted a return to those days.

Jack insisted they keep the plan simple, this was Jessie's first operation and as skilled as she was a complicated operation didn't make sense. They would fly commercial into Kiev and rent a vehicle before heading to Odessa. The cover was simple. Jessie, a Canadian middle school teacher, was traveling back to Ukraine with her father, a return to the homeland to visit the place of his childhood and reconnect with long lost relatives. Their only goal to locate Sokolov, identify any patterns of behavior, local travel habits and accumulate as much data on his physical operations as possible. They would relay these through a long placed Ukrainian operative to the SAD team that would be in place ten days from now. Not a great deal of time, but they all believed it was better to act while Sokolov's operations were in disarray than to give him time to rebuild and find his footing. As the meeting broke up Simpson pulls Jack aside for a quick word.

"Jack, if this goes even a little sideways I want you to pull back and get the hell out of there, okay?" he says.

Jack nods, "I understand sir..." he answers.

"I'm serious Jack, I don't want to risk her out of the gate, I've been waiting for an asset like this and I don't want to lose her on the first operation because we pushed too fast... we clear?"

"With all due respect sir, I would never risk an operation if I didn't think we could succeed, but there isn't any way I will put Jessie in harm's way... you can count on that," Jack says forcefully.

Simpson pats him on the shoulder, "Jack, I know that, but you and I both know you will be in harm's way, it's the nature of what we do, just be careful and don't push a bad position, this guy simply isn't worth the trade, ok?"

"I got it sir, loud and clear... let me get her downstairs and outfitted, you can count on us."

"Good, go on now, safe travels Jack."

313

Jack leads Jessie down the hallway to the elevator banks. Once inside she asks, "What was that all about?"

"The usual, be careful, don't kill anyone you don't have to and remember to duck…" Jack says with a smile.

"Bullshit," Jessie responds, "keep your secrets old man, that's fine…"

Jack turns to her, "Jessie, they just want to make sure we do this right and you are safe as possible…"

"I can take care of myself…" she says.

"Listen young lady, that can get you killed… this is a different game out here, no support, no extraction, no room for mistakes so make sure you pay attention," Jack admonishes her, "I know you can do this, I know what you are capable of, but there literally are no rules for the other side so any assumptions you have about that you need to leave here, as brutal as you can imagine, well it's probably worse."

"You trying to scare me?"

"Nope, I'm trying to save you…" Jack says.

They exit on the first level and Jack leads her into the Logistics Division. Here they are outfitted with new identities, clothes, passports, currency, credit cards issued on Swiss banks, everything but weapons, which they will pick up once they land. The goal is to erase any evidence down to the clothing brands they wear, that they have an affiliation with the United States, and no one does this better than the CIA, plausible deniability.

They are also issued plane tickets first stop is Toronto with a two-day layover, then a Lufthansa flight with a layover in Frankfurt before going on to Kiev, and then the drive to Odessa and the start of Jessie's new life.

Rebuilding an Empire

The interesting thing about criminal organizations is they are structured like multi-national corporations, but employ a military style chain of command and decision matrix. Sokolov's empire consisted of a number of different product lines, distribution channels, sales groups, and fulfillment centers no different than any large corporation. However, there was no board of directors, no discretionary decision making, there was only Sokolov the CEO, President, General, Supreme Leader, take your pick, the title didn't matter, it was both a strength and a weakness.

On the plus side Sampson is able to shut down their US operations with half a dozen phone calls. The hard assets property, cars, boats, condos would remain dormant, owned by a series of shell corporations until Sokolov decided he needed them again or they were seized by the FBI either way there was none of the red tape a normal corporation would have faced. This wasn't exactly Sampson's strong suite, but he was getting the hang of it, and no one had argued the point – even on the management side of the organization his reputation preceded him.

They were working from the compound and while Sampson was shutting things down, Sokolov was already shoring up their existing contacts and reaching out to his longtime customers reassuring them that this was just a temporary shift, that US operations had become cost prohibitive and he was moving everything back to Ukraine. If you didn't know better you would have hung up believing this was Sokolov's idea and that any FBI noise was just coincidental. It didn't hurt that he was offering some excellent deals and discounts for those that remained loyal customers. Of course, he didn't say so, but most everyone knew that if you sought out another supplier, you were probably due for a significant if not fatal accident in the near future. Sokolov didn't tolerate competition very well and that included customers who thought it was a good idea to seek alternative sources.

The two men broke for a lunch of leftover lamb sandwiches, potato salad, and mineral water. Sokolov seems like his old self to Sampson, maybe it had just been the strain of the past few days, either way Sampson was glad to have Alexi back.

"Any problems shutting things down," Alexi asks between mouthfuls.

"Not to speak of, we have a couple of unfulfilled orders for the Chicago families, but I told Atlanta to send them what they needed before shutting down. We already had it set up so no reason not to," Sampson answers.

Nodding his head, "good, good, so what do you think of this side of the business?"

It's a loaded question and Sampson hesitates before answering, "well, it's different, definitely not what I am used to, but I can do whatever you need Alexi..."

"I know you can Sampson, nobody knows our operation better than you do, it's time I started bringing you into more of it... I want you to pick your replacement on the security side... it's your call, but look at young Kirilov, he did a good job in New York." It's not exactly a suggestion even if Alexi couched it that way.

"I will, he is already taking control of the unit here at the compound..." Sampson says with grudging respect. He wasn't entirely comfortable ceding control of the security side of the house to someone new, protecting Alexi had always been his responsibility.

"Well, think about it, he shut Spider's operation down including all those tech people, that took some balls and he had enough smarts to make sure I was okay before leaving..." Alexi says with just a hint of sarcasm.

Sampson doesn't miss the dig, fact is that was his job and the kid had been the one to get Alexi to safety before the Feds had showed up. "I'll talk to him, see how fast we can bring him along, start giving him some bigger things to work on..." Sampson concedes the point, Alexi would have his way cause he always had his way.

As lunch is finished Sampson asks, "What's next for me, anyone else you want me to call or take care of?"

Alexi pauses, "Yes, call that fuckin' prince in Riyadh and tell him we aren't supplying any more girls, he needs to find someone else... and you tell him I said don't fuck with us, not everything in the desert stays buried unless he wants that body showing up again... can you handle that?"

Sampson smiles, "with pleasure... you want me to send him some of the pics?" The Spider had managed to set up a network of hacked laptops, security cams, even cell and SAT phones, that had allowed them to capture pictures on all of their high-profile clients, pictures nobody wanted to see the light of day, something the Interior Minister of France had found out the hard way.

Alexi pauses for a moment, "no, hold onto the pics... which reminds me, any leads on a replacement for Potemkin?"

"No, but I have the kid running the Caracas data center reaching out to a few people for us..." Sampson responds thinking to himself, *I really am getting the hang of this*.

"Ok, we need to plug that hole quick though," Alexi says, heading off to his office.

Sampson spends the afternoon tracking the prince down, the man was obnoxious, spluttering and threatening right up until Sampson mentioned arranging a special delivery involving the body of Allie Chambers and the Crown Prince, he took the

319

silence on the end of the line as a sign of acquiescence. There wouldn't be any issue out of Riyadh, he was sure of that. His call to Caracas woke up the young tech scrambling to hold everything together, once he cut through the whining, the young man calmed down. Sampson wanted to call potential replacements for Potemkin; the young man tried explaining that this wasn't possible, the people they wanted don't do phones. An exasperated Sampson tells him to use whatever means necessary then, money is no issue, he explains whatever we need to pay, just make it happen. By late afternoon he is rethinking this whole operations idea as a frustrating pain in the ass. He walks over to the guesthouse to get some fresh air and look for Kirilov, he finds him in the kitchen with two of the others grabbing a cup of coffee. Kirilov offers him a cup and nods to the other two, who excuse themselves.

Sampson can see the man has already begun to assert himself, "let's get some dinner tonight," he says without preamble. "Need to talk through some things with you, why don't you stop by La Gioconda around eight."

"I'll be there," Kirilov answers, "and sir, thank you…" he adds.

"Sampson doesn't react, "you can thank Sokolov," his meaning is clear he is not yet as impressed as Alexi is.

Kirilov to his credit doesn't react either and with a nod answers, "I'll see you tonight then," he isn't sold on Sampson either.

Sampson heads back to the main house, he isn't the least bit happy about Kirilov, the man lacks respect, he thinks to himself, nobody had challenged him in a long time and it didn't sit well with him. He knocks on Alexi's office door, opening it without waiting for an answer, Alexi looks up and waves him over as he hangs up the phone. "I'm headed out, just wanted to update you, the prince is all taken care of; he is a supreme prick by the way..."

Alexi laughs, "yeah, well maybe we fuck him just because we can then..."

Sampson smiles, "well, anytime you want to I'm all in on that, also meeting with Kirilov tonight for dinner."

Alexi looks up, "you don't like him, do you?"

Sampson sighs, "he lacks respect..."

Alexi laughs again, "so did you in case you've forgotten, I like him so make it work."

Sampson gets up and heads for the door, "I'll make it work, but we need to go slow with him..." a last-ditch effort to reign Alexi in.

Alexi just waves him off, "and Sampson, have them send another girl over tonight..."

Sampson nods as he closes the door. *Well, apparently the boss is back to normal,* he thinks to himself.

In the Field

Jessie and Jack spend the two days in Toronto studying their new identities and reviewing the maps they have of Kiev and Odessa. There are also a series of satellite photos of the Sokolov compound and surrounding neighborhoods that the SAD team was using for its planning. Jack and Jessie were tasked with gathering as much real-time information as possible, including information on the number of people Sokolov had at the compound, vehicles used, traffic patterns, anything that might be useful to the extraction team. It meant hiding in plain sight Jack had told her, the only way to determine much of this was to see it first hand, that meant being exposed and in harm's way. There just wasn't time to train Jessie as extensively as he would have liked, the biggest lesson he told her was to pick up on patterns and always listen to your gut, if something doesn't seem right it probably isn't, he repeated at least once an hour. The biggest adjustment for her though was the oft-repeated anthem that weapons were an absolute last resort and probably meant the operation had been blown, this seemed counter-intuitive to her, but she guessed it made sense. Covert in the Rangers had meant sneaking up on the enemy before unleashing hell fire, here it meant never getting caught and being gone before anyone even knew what happened, not quite the same thing; she was going to have to adjust.

Jessie slept most of the way from Toronto to Frankfurt trying to overcome some of the exhaustion that had been piling up from the past week. Her nerves started to kick in on the short flight from Frankfurt to Kiev, Jack pretended not to notice, knowing it was something she was just going to have work through, no point in patronizing her with empty platitudes.

They picked up a small navy-blue Skoda sedan at the airport rental counter and headed into Kiev, Jack had been to the city a number of times and navigated quickly to a small shop on the outskirts of the industrial section. Jessie couldn't help but smile when he asked for Salazar Hernandez, there was no exchange of funds, the old man just led them into the back where a locked storage container required a thumb print and six-digit code. Salazar, or whatever his real name was, had already retreated to the front of the shop when Jack opened the locker. To say it was a small arsenal would be a gross understatement, in the end they both left with a pair of Czech made suppressed 9MM pistols, two extra magazines apiece, the equivalent of one hundred thousand US dollars in local currency, a pair of field glasses, two SAT phones, and twenty-five feet of rope. As they are finishing up Jessie grabs a Kizylar tactical knife and sheath and two concussion grenades. Jack looks at her, "what part of covert didn't you get?"

"What?" she answers, "hey, I'm a Ranger, give me a knife and a grenade I'm halfway to happy!"

Jack just shakes his head, "let's go before you find something even noisier..."

They leave out the back door and loading everything into the Skoda head out to E95 and the drive to Odessa. Jack estimates about six or so hours depending on the traffic, it's a straight shot from Kiev. E95 is a major four lane highway but some parts are in such a state of disrepair the going can be slow, never mind the tandem tractor trailers that barrel through seemingly immune to the dangers. The highway bisects central Ukraine running through miles and miles of sparsely populated farm-land. Jack is sleeping while Jessie drives, alone with her thoughts, the cool air coming in the window heavy with the scent of wet earth and diesel fumes from the passing trucks. She's trying not to feel like the whole thing was a bit of a letdown, she had expected to hunt Sokolov, find him, and eliminate the threat. She understood, but switching gears was proving difficult, this wasn't about Tom Casey, or even her anymore, there was a bigger national security aspect to it she would have to absorb. Even in the Rangers there were always clearly defined objectives to focus on, they never deployed just to see what might happen. She wasn't disappointed so much as struggling with how to define success for herself, the operation was one thing, but she had always been driven to achieve specific goals that were tangible; things would be different now. She smiles to herself, Jack would tell her if you manage to stay alive you achieved your goal, he had a simple way of explaining things that was elemental if nothing else. She understood now why her dad and Jack were such good friends, they fit together perfectly.

"What ya thinking about?" Jack asks casually

"Everything and nothing, why?" she answers.

"Christ, just like your father," he says laughing.

It was early evening when they arrived in Odessa, they were booked in adjoining rooms at the Hotel Otrada on Zatyshna Street, only a little more than a block from the Sokolov compound, it wasn't by accident since you could see over the compound walls from the roof of the hotel.

"Let's get settled in and some dinner then we can walk the neighborhood a bit," Jack says.

"Is that safe?" Jessie asks without really thinking about it.

Jack gives her his trademark look, "no it isn't, I'll see you downstairs in thirty minutes and wear dark clothes," he says shutting his door.

Jessie retreats to her room next door thinking, *well that was fucking stupid, is it safe... what the fuck.* She wishes she could call her dad she knows what he would say though, "you shouldn't make commitments you're not ready to keep," it was a favorite anthem of his. She sits on the bed thinking about what has to be accomplished, her training starts to reassert itself, *come on McIntyre* she chides herself, *this is a mission like any other identify the objectives and develop a plan to achieve them, and stop the whining.* Pep talk over she starts to think more clearly about what needs to be done, she realizes the difficulty isn't going to be collecting the data, but the two of them hiding in plain sight a block from one of the world's most ruthless crime lords.

They met in La Terrazza, the bar and grill on the first floor, grabbing a table off to the side where they could talk freely without having to worry about the crowd at the bar overhearing them. Jessie explained she had been thinking it over and thought their biggest challenge was not being noticed. The cover story was fine, but it was unlikely that any of Sokolov's people would take the time to ask those types of questions. Two people filling their general descriptions seen together so shortly after the New York episode, well it was bound to trigger a warning.

Jack leans back in his chair, it was something he had been thinking about as well, but without a resolution, "what do you have in mind?"

"We have to split up," she answers. "It's the only way, you know that," she continues before he can object.

Jack doesn't argue with her, "ok, but you have to do exactly what I tell you, clear?" Jessie just nods with a smile and though there is still plenty of training ahead her transition is complete.

Countdown

The problem isn't being recognized on the street, it isn't about field craft, it isn't even about them being together. No, the problem is Kirilov is sitting at the far end of the bar having a vodka before heading over to Gioconda to have dinner with Sampson. All the training and preparation in the world can't make up for a few seconds of bad luck, the wall at Langley is covered with the stars of Officers that turned right instead of left or were in the wrong place at the right time, there was no predicting the little things that could end up getting you killed.

Kirilov had no doubt who they were, he found it curious and disconcerting that they had managed to follow so soon after Sokolov had fled Brighton Beach though. He was a circumspect man however and was content to watch them from across the room, he couldn't hear of course, but the import of their conversation was obvious just by watching their body language. Kirilov had spent ten years in the elite Spetsnaz – Russian Special Forces before becoming a GRU officer; a dedicated Russian he had left the GRU during the last round of political purges opting to serve his own purposes instead. He had purposely concealed his true identity and background from Sampson and Sokolov, better to be perceived as a simple soldier than a threat. He pays his tab and heads out, content to let this sit for now, maybe these two could be used to his advantage, he would have to think about it.

Jack and Jessie don't see the well-dressed man leave through the back of the restaurant, he fit in perfectly and might not have set any alarms off anyway, but the dance had just become much more complicated and they were no longer in control of the playlist.

The sun has set and a chill is in the spring air as they exit the hotel lobby and turn left heading up the tree lined avenue, the leaves are just starting to bud and there are small patches of daffodils starting to poke through the flower beds, it would only be a few more weeks before everything was in full bloom. It only takes them ten minutes to circle the short block before they are on Morska and approaching the gated compound that is Sokolov's domain, there are a scattering of people on the streets walking back from the beach clubs and restaurants in the area, Jack and Jessie fall in acting casually. The walls are nearly fifteen feet high and the double gate across the main drive is easily a dozen, the thick iron bars strong enough to withstand the impact of a normal car. The street itself is narrow and small and also acts as a natural barrier. They can see the video surveillance and motion triggered LED spots from the street, there wasn't any real attempt to disguise them. None of it was unexpected, but reinforced what they already knew; it wasn't going to be easy.

They head back to the hotel to compare notes and determine next steps.

Kirilov walked the eight hundred meters to Gioconda arriving exactly eleven minutes late, enough time for it not to be an accident and just another obvious tweak of Sampson's ego. He was playing a dangerous game with the big man, but turning predators on each other was never an undertaking for the faint hearted. Sampson had given himself away earlier mentioning Sokolov as the source of Kirilov's opportunity. He had planned on letting things develop slowly playing it patiently, but with the arrival of the two American's it was time to accelerate things. He needed to sow seeds of distrust between Sokolov and Sampson, he knew the big man would never betray Sokolov, but if he could separate them Sokolov would be vulnerable. He would need to maneuver the Americans to take care of Sampson and if they died in the process, all the better, then he would deal with Sokolov himself. The age-old adage of to the victor goes the spoils was now in play.

Kirilov works his way through the tables to the back of the dining room where Sampson is clearly annoyed at being kept waiting. He unceremoniously takes a seat across from the big man waving for the waiter.

"You're late..." Sampson growls.

Kirilov doesn't answer but turns to the waiter, "mineral water," turning back to Sampson, "sorry, had a few things to take care of," his tone implies that he isn't sorry at all. Kirilov doesn't offer any further explanation just waits for Sampson to respond. *This is going to be easier than I thought*, he thinks.

Sampson glares across the table, but doesn't rise to the bait, he might not have Kirilov's training but he knows when he is being played. "Alexi wants you more involved on security..." Sampson uses Sokolov's common name to purposely hi-lite their relationship.

Kirilov doesn't react, "would I be working directly for you?" he asks.

"For now, anyway," Sampson responds leaning back in his chair, giving Kirilov a long look. "This is a chance for you to show us what you can do, I suggest you don't waste it."

Kirilov smiles, "I have no intention of wasting it, when do I start?"

Sampson grunts, "just slow down, I'll have to talk it over with Alexi, I'm going to have you start by going out to our other operations and meeting the people we have."

Kirilov nods, not giving anything away, "of course, that makes perfect sense," he responds thinking, *and it lets him get me out of the way for a while.*

The two men order the seafood pasta special, eating while Sampson questions Kirilov about his background. Kirilov spins a tale about growing up in Vladivostok before joining the army at eighteen and serving for twenty years before being pushed out. None of it is true of course as he is actually forty-two, having spent ten years in the Spetsnaz and another ten in the GRU after graduating from Moscow State University at the tender age of twenty-one.

For his part Sampson had loosened up and spent a good deal of time bragging about the old days in Odessa with Alexi. It was late in the evening when Kirilov took his leave, debating whether to make the walk through the alley bordering Zdorovya Park, it was dark and not well lit and a known haven for petty criminals. Figuring he could use the exercise after all that pasta he heads down the alley, the broken concrete crunches underfoot as he plays back the evening with Sampson.

"Ahh, young Kirilov..." the heavily accented voice says in Russian out of the dark.

Kirilov stops dead in his tracks trying to slow his breathing and listening intently for anything that will betray the location of the voice. He slowly starts to slip his pistol free.

"You won't be needing that my young friend," the voice says from somewhere to his left. Jack lights up a cigarette, giving his position away and leaving the next move up to Kirilov as he steps out of the trees and into the center of the alley facing the man. He offers him a cigarette and holds the lighter out; Kirilov nods, taking one and leaning forward lighting the cigarette with a deep breath.

"You're the American?" it's more of a statement than a question. "Are you in need of directions or possibly information on a good restaurant?" Kirilov asks mockingly.

Jack smiles "we want the same thing, the only question you need to ask yourself is whether you want to walk away from this at the end."

It's Kirilov's turn to laugh, "Old man, I could kill you here and leave you for the birds to feast on..." he stops short, feeling the cold steel of a suppressor pressing against the back of his neck.

"I don't think so..." Jessie says quietly reaching inside his jacket and removing the pistol he had been reaching for earlier.

Fucking girl he thinks, *I forgot the fucking girl...*

The Enemy of my Enemy...

Jack and Jessie may have missed Kirilov in the bar, but the compromised security system monitored by the young analyst back at Langley didn't. They had tasked a satellite to this operation and had picked him up coming out of the bar and heading down the alley to the hotel. Langley had long ago hacked the rosters of the GRU and the current generation of facial recognition technology was built into the monitoring tools used to process video data from any source in the world; they had pegged Kirilov before he had finished his first vodka.

The coded message with Kirilov's dossier had been waiting for them along with satellite video upon their return to the hotel. It had been Jessie's idea to stake out the alley in hopes that he would return the same way. She had convinced Jack that if Kirilov was as professional as Jack claimed most GRU agents were, then just maybe they could work a deal. Jack had smiled, it wasn't called a deal at the Agency but she was right, and since Kirilov had obviously seen them there wasn't much to be lost at this point.

They had almost decided to call it a night when they had heard the crunch of footsteps in the dark. Jack had the most dangerous part, he had insisted. Jessie had quietly slipped out of her shoes trusting that her stocking feet wouldn't make any noise as she stealthily approached from behind. It was like night ops in the Rangers, except there was no backup and your government would act like they didn't know you if something went wrong. She had stood off to the side, pistol trained on Kirilov, while Jack worked through the details of their hastily prepared plan. Kirilov for his part had quickly seen the wisdom in cooperation, besides, he figured it didn't really change his end game.

Jack flicks his cigarette away and motions Jessie over, "alright we have an agreement," he turns to Kirilov, extending his hand, "day after tomorrow comrade."

Kirilov takes the proffered hand, "day after tomorrow... don't be late, I won't wait."

"Agreed," Jack says, he turns to Jessie, "give him his pistol back."

She hesitates for a moment looking Kirilov in the eye, "here," she hands him the pistol never lowering her own, "we'll be there, don't fuck it up or I will find you..." she adds.

Kirilov turns to Jack, "typical soldier..."

Jack nods, "yes, but an excellent marksman..."

Kirilov chuckles to himself as he walks away in the dark.

"Can we trust him?" Jessie asks, "never mind, stupid fucking question, I've got to stop doing that..."

"It's okay," Jack responds, "we all ask, you just learn not to do it out loud," he says, smiling in the dark. They make their way back to the hotel and camp out in Jack's room.

"It's not really about trust," Jack explains, "our objectives are aligned, so as long as that remains true we can trust Kirilov will act accordingly." He pauses, "so it's not exactly trust, you see the difference?"

She yawns, "sure do, now I'm catching some shut eye, see you in the morning." She opens the door between their rooms, "and Jack, thank you."

He is sitting on the bed, "for what?"

"For believing in me, for teaching me, I'm sure there's more..."

"Good night Jess," he says at a loss for words.

Kirilov makes his way into the kitchen of the guesthouse and pours a cup of coffee before sitting down at the kitchen table. The evening certainly hadn't turned out the way he had anticipated, and he was going to have to move much quicker than he had planned. For Kirilov everything depended on being able to fill the gap left when Sokolov couldn't deliver. He had no delusions of grandeur, he simply wanted to usurp the arms business, going after the whole thing was unmanageable and Kirilov was well aware of his own limitations. He hadn't let on but Jack Hardy was a legend even within the GRU circles, Kirilov had no doubt he would deliver, he smiled again thinking about the girl. She was brash, no doubt about it, still she had gotten the drop on him and that wasn't an easy thing to do.

Like all successful operations this was going to depend on timing, simplicity, and precise execution of all the moving parts and not a small amount of good luck. The fact was you couldn't accurately predict what a human being would do from one second to the next. Sure, there were patterns and behavioral analysis and all the other psychoanalytical models every intelligence agency in the world developed, but the simple fact was in the moment every human reaction was unique and unscripted.

Kirilov for his part was simply the delivery man, when in Odessa Sokolov followed a fairly static routine, it was born of arrogance, complacency and the belief that of anywhere in the world, here he was safe.

On Thursday's, Misha's cafe, a small four table hole in the wall with an open kitchen served fresh made kovbasa sandwiches with caramelized onions. Kovbasa is an un-smoked Ukrainian sausage made with a combination of pork, beef and spices, Misha had long since passed away but his son Petro still bakes it with onions as his father had taught him, creating a marriage of flavors that is irresistible. Sokolov never misses a Thursday when he is in Odessa and has been coming to Misha's since he was a boy. These days he pulls up in the alley behind the open kitchen and Petro himself will run out a box of sandwiches wrapped in foil, he never asks for payment, but Alexi has never forgotten Misha slipping him a box of food on days he was hungry and too poor to pay for it. As a young boy, he would hang out in the alley and Misha would give him odd jobs to do, sending him home with enough to feed him and his mother.

Alexi always trades a crisp hundred-dollar bill for the box; American money was still the underground currency in Eastern Europe, especially since the switch to the Russian Ruble had decimated the exchange rates. It was Kirilov's job to drive Sampson and Sokolov. Thursday around seven they would stop at Misha's before heading over to the Yacht Club where Sokolov and his local cronies would indulge their taste for cards, young girls, and American liquor.

Jack writes up the op notes, keying in on the scheduled trip to Misha's for the next evening. He and Jessie wouldn't be directly involved but would be having an early dinner inside the café, available as backup if anything went wrong and would be the final call on whether to abort or not. The SAD team would be using non-lethal force, mainly tranq darts that would render the average man unconscious in less than six seconds and keep him that way for approximately twelve hours, the neurotoxin had no lasting effect other than a significant hangover. Rumor was the formula had actually been built on the chemical makeup of saliva found in the skin of a rare South American frog. Nobody was quite sure who the brave or crazy individual was that had licked the first frog though.

The SAD team would render the occupants unconscious and commandeer the vehicle using it to transport Sokolov to a minor dock off the main harbor where they had a small motorboat waiting to take him offshore to a trawler, that was actually a CIA listening platform. Jack and Jessie didn't need to know how the planned on moving him from there, nor were they told how the team would get to Misha's; compartmentalization was an Agency specialty.

Kovbasa

At ten minutes past six Kirilov gets the call to bring the SUV up to the main house, he double checks his watch, *fucking early* he thinks. Nothing to be done about it though, he hopes the Americans are ready, if not he has his own plans in place.

Sampson takes the front seat while Sokolov sits in the back, both are dressed in suits. "Where to boss?" Kirilov asks, he already knows but sticks to the script.

Alexi pats him on the shoulder and before Sampson can respond, "I'm going to take you to the best cook in town my young friend! You've never tasted kovbasa like this."

Sampson just scowls, his ill humor is back, "take a left out of here I'll tell you where to go."

Alexi has perched in the center of the rear seats like a teenager cruising with his buddies, one hand on each front seat. "Sampson, he's one of my boys now, we have to show him around, first kovbasa and then the club."

Sampson doesn't respond, "can't wait sir, tell me more about this kovbasa, in Russia my grandmother called it kolbasa and my dad would smoke it before frying it for us," Kirilov explains.

"Take a right here," Sampson growls.

Kirilov turns right onto the street Misha's is on, Alexi points to the alley just beyond the cafe, "turn in here Kirilov and you will learn about real sausage tonight..."

The two shots are deafening in the cab of the SUV as Sampson's brains splatter against the glass and his body starts to sag against the seatbelt. Kirilov doesn't hesitate, jamming on the brakes and throwing Alexi forward he brings the gun up and smashes it into the man's forehead. Alexi slumps to the floorboard, the gash over his eye bleeding profusely. Kirilov pulls forward another fifty yards and puts the truck in park behind the cafe, Alexi is starting to moan in the back as Sampson's blood begins to pool in the front passenger well. Opening the back door, he takes Alexi's pistols from him and smashes him on the side of the head again, Alexi is out. Tossing the pistols over the seat into the back he shuts the door and heads for the kitchen. He strolls casually into the front of the cafe spotting Jack and Jessie, "all yours..." he says, motioning out back with his thumb, he doesn't slow down as he heads out the front door straightening his jacket and fixing his tie.

Jack and Jessie look at each other for just a moment before bolting for the kitchen, the SAD team isn't supposed to show until seven and things are way ahead of schedule at this point. Petro is shouting at them, but they ignore him as they head for the alley and the SUV.

"Fuck me," Jack exclaims seeing the bloody mess on the front window, "around the other side Jess, careful now, I'll cover the alley," they both have their weapons out.

Jessie checks the driver's side and slowly opens the back door, "clear Jack, Sokolov is down though bleeding pretty bad," she checks for a pulse, "he is still alive though." She looks across to the front seat, "Sampson is gone, Jesus Christ, head shot at less than a yard... what a fucking mess," she exclaims.

Jack keys the SAT phone, "abort, abort, repeat abort!" he heads back to Jessie, "listen we have to go now!"

"What about Sokolov?" she asks, "We can't leave the son of a bitch here," she says.

"Look, it's over Jess, time to go, it didn't work out okay..." he is almost pleading now.

"Fuck that," she opens the back door again, two quick spits and it's over, "I'm not running from this asshole the rest of my life Jack, now it's over, let's go." She starts to jog down the alley looking over her shoulder, "move it old man, time to hustle," she says in her command voice. Jack takes another look around and follows her lead.

They had parked the car one block up from the far end of the alley, it was already packed and ready to go. The plan had been to retrace their steps to Kiev and fly out under the same identifications, that wasn't going to work now. "Jessie, we need to head down M15 to the South, we can work our way through the big national park down there, I think it's Dniester park, anyway there is a crossing into Moldova there that's only manned by the park police, odds are they won't be paying as much attention."

Jessie just nods, concentrating on the road in front of her, "whatever you say Jack, why Moldova?" she asks.

"Safe house in Tiraspol about two hours from here, I know people that can set us up with new papers and we can figure it out from there, besides Moldavians have no love for the Ukrainian government so they aren't likely to be too cooperative, especially over a dead mob boss," Jack explains.

It takes two days to and most of their cash to secure new passports and a pair of tickets out of Chisinau to Frankfurt, where they can catch Lufthansa back to the states. They elected to stay with Canadian passports since they already had something to work with. Jack darkens his hair taking all the grey out, it makes him look ten years younger, while Jessie adds some simple highlights to hers. "Subtle changes are enough," Jack cautions, "this isn't the movies," he says. With new photos and the chips imbedded in their passports reprogrammed they are ready to go.

Jack has ignored repeated requests from Langley for details on what went wrong, the truth is he hasn't decided how to frame what happened. Once they land in DC though it will be too late, they need to work this out on the flight from Frankfurt. It isn't so much that he disagrees with what Jessie has done, just that he has been in long enough to know it won't fly and will need to be handled in a way that doesn't raise more questions. The simplest answer is probably best he concludes, Kirilov killed them both, it was over before he and Jessie even got there. It was sure to raise at least an eyebrow, but if they were steadfast in their story there really was no way to dispute it. It helped that they had already identified Kirilov as ex-GRU, he was more than capable of handling the two men in close quarters, of course his motivation wasn't quite as clear.

The flight out of Moldova was delayed close to three hours, not unusual, the small country's infrastructure was in a permanent state of disarray and every industry depending on it seemed to absorb its own share of the chaos. Fortunately, their connecting flight in Germany was much later that afternoon.

Jessie is pretending to be absorbed in the airline's magazine in an effort to control her nerves, the longer they are on the ground the more exposed she feels. This part of the job was definitely going to take getting used to. The constant state of feeling like you were being watched was disconcerting, she was going to have to ask Jack about it. He leans over, "relax Jess, we are okay, you make it worse when you appear nervous."

"Easy for you to say," she murmurs back at him.

"Don't worry, they will teach you how to handle all of this, you'll be fine," he responds, leaning back and taking out his own magazine. "We need to talk about what happened back there, got to be on the same page by the time we get home."

The hum of the engines increases and the plane begins to lurch forward, "Ok, but I did the right thing..." she answers.

They begin to accelerate down the runway and gently glide upward, "it's not about right or wrong Jess, you need to stop thinking in absolutes, most of what we do is various shades of gray. What's more important is you and I have to be in sync on this."

"It's hard, I've spent my life dealing with absolutes, this is a big switch," she looks over at him, "I can do it though."

"I know you can, otherwise I wouldn't have recommended you," he says.

"I thought you didn't have anything to do with it," she asks perplexed.

"Oh, did I say that?" he says with a smile.

They had been met at Dulles in DC by two senior CIA officers and escorted directly to Langley to meet with Vance Simpson, the Deputy Director wanted a full briefing before they met with the post operations team to conduct a mission post mortem. It had taken three days to fully debrief, almost as long at the operation itself. In the end, everyone conceded that there really had been no way to predict the actions of Kirilov and although his motives weren't clear the end result was still a positive from the Agency's perspective.

Tim Harrington and his team over at the Bureau were unhappy about not getting Sokolov, but Potemkin was now singing like Pavarotti and they had enough hard evidence to round up scores of Sokolov's men and his customers as well. The FBI would also be busy attempting to locate and reunite with their families the thousands of young women who had gone missing over the past decade and a half.

Jack and Jessie had met individually with Albert Jimenez, there were no charges filed in New York on Jack, but Jessie was still facing potential charges in Tampa. Albert assured her that now that she was with the Agency everything would be taken care of and not to worry. She wasn't, but it was nice to hear him say it. It had been a week since their last meeting when Jack had called and asked if she was ready to really begin training, Jessie had never been so sure of anything.

Epilogue

It had been six months since Jessie had flown into Dulles, completing her first operation for the CIA. She had spent the summer training at The Farm, the secret CIA facility at Camp Peary just outside of Williamsburg, Virginia. Her cover identity had her living in Georgetown, the affluent neighborhood in DC, as a visiting professor at the nearby university.

Jessie crossed over Thirty-Third Street and slowed to a fast walk, the leaves were starting to move past pretty and you could feel the chill of winter on the way. She had covered the ten-mile run in just a few seconds under an hour, her personal best. Taking the steps of her town home two at a time she unslings the backpack she wears everywhere and extracts a bottle of water and her keys. Closing the door quietly behind her she pulls out the Kimber 9MM, she still carries it with her everywhere, she can sense that someone other than her has been here recently. Silently she clears the front sitting room and inches down the hall towards the kitchen where she can hear the murmur of voices.

"Jessie, about time you got home!" her father yells out, "put that thing away before you shoot one of us!"

She smiles as she turns the corner to find Jack and her dad wearing aprons and fixing breakfast. "You know you two are a mess!" she says smiling.

Jack walks over and gives her a big hug, "a little bird told me you might be traveling soon, figured we would come see you before you left," he says.

Her dad hands her an overly cream cheesed bagel, "here you go baby girl, go get washed up and then bring us old spies up to date on everything."

If you enjoyed this book please consider leaving a positive review on Amazon – Thanks, JC

Acknowledgments

This book is dedicated to my wife and kids for their unfailing support. Many thanks to the family and friends that have provided encouragement, feedback, suggestions, and have been steadfast supporters through this process.

A special thanks to: James Coyle for his editing, Master Patrol Officer Tommy Morris, Plant City Police Department, Retired for his help in explaining the ins and outs of the arrest process, jurisdiction, and basic jail layout, additional thanks to Colonel Randy Williams, US Army, Retired for his insight on the military, the Army Rangers, and the rigors these brave soldiers face in both training and combat. Any errors or exaggerations are solely a reflection of my inability to listen and in no way reflect on the expertise of these fine men. Special thanks to Ms. Krysteena Runas for always getting my "vision" and making perfect covers!

Statistics & Information

Human trafficking is a growing international issue. The Polaris Project is a Non-Profit US based organization providing hotline services to victims and education to the public. The following statistics are gathered from their website: www.polarisproject.org

Although slavery is commonly thought to be a thing of the past, human traffickers generate hundreds of billions of dollars in profits by trapping millions of people in horrific situations around the world, including here in the U.S. Traffickers use violence, threats, deception, debt bondage, and other manipulative tactics to force people to engage in commercial sex or to provide labor or services against their will. While more research is needed on the scope of human trafficking, below are a few key statistics:

- The International Labour Organization estimates that there are 20.9 million victims of human trafficking globally.
    - 68% of them are trapped in forced labor.
    - 26% of them are children.
    - 55% are women and girls.
- The International Labor Organization estimates that forced labor and human trafficking is a $150 billion industry worldwide.
- The U.S. Department of Labor has identified 139 goods from 75 countries made by forced and child labor.
- In 2016, an estimated 1 out of 6 endangered runaways reported to the National Center for Missing and Exploited Children were likely child sex trafficking victims.
    - Of those, 86% were in the care of social services or foster care when they ran.
- There is no official estimate of the total number of human trafficking victims in the U.S. Polaris estimates that the total number of victims nationally reaches into the hundreds of thousands when estimates of both adults and minors and sex trafficking and labor trafficking are aggregated.

BLUE CAMPAIGN
One Voice. One Mission. End Human Trafficking.®

Everyone has a role to play in combating human trafficking. Recognizing the signs of human trafficking is the first step to identifying a victim. Our resources [https://www.dhs.gov/blue-campaign/share-resources] page has materials for a more in-depth human trafficking education and a catalog of materials that can be distributed and displayed in your community.

Do not at any time attempt to confront a suspected trafficker directly or alert a victim to your suspicions. Your safety as well as the victim's safety is paramount. Instead, please contact local law enforcement directly or call the tip lines indicated on this page:

- **Call 1-866-DHS-2-ICE (1-866-347-2423)** to report suspicious criminal activity to the U.S. Immigration and Customs Enforcement (ICE) Homeland Security Investigations (HSI) Tip Line 24 hours a day, 7 days a week, every day of the year. The Tip Line is accessible **outside the United States** by calling **802-872-6199**.
- **Submit a tip at www.ice.gov/tips**. Highly trained specialists take reports from both the public and law enforcement agencies on more than 400 laws enforced by ICE HSI, including those related to human trafficking.
- **To get help from the National Human Trafficking Hotline (NHTH), call 1-888-373-7888 or text HELP or INFO to BeFree (233733).** The NHTH can help connect victims with service providers in the area and provides training, technical assistance, and other resources. The NHTH is a national, toll-free hotline available to answer calls from anywhere in the country, 24 hours a day, 7 days a week, every day of the year. The NHTH is not a law enforcement or immigration authority and is operated by a nongovernmental organization funded by the Federal government.

By identifying victims and reporting tips, you are doing your part to help law enforcement rescue victims, and you might save a life. Law enforcement can connect victims to services such as medical and mental health care, shelter, job training, and legal assistance that restore their freedom and dignity. The presence or absence of any of the indicators is not necessarily proof of human trafficking. It is up to law enforcement to investigate suspected cases of human trafficking.

Made in the USA
Columbia, SC
23 October 2023